3 4143 10081 5024

D0188325

Mary Jane Staples was born, bred and educated in Walworth, and is the author of many bestselling novels including the ever-popular cockney sagas featuring the Adams family.

www.transworldbooks.co.uk

and published by Corgi Books

NURSE ANNA'S WAR

Mary Jane Staples

WARRINGTON BOROUGH COUNCIL	
34143100815024	
Bertrams	15/09/2011
AF	£17.99
WAR	

BANTAM PRESS

LONDON · TORONTO · SYDNEY · AUCKLAND · JOHANNESBURG

TRANSWORLD PUBLISHERS
61–63 Uxbridge Road, London W5 5SA
A Random House Group Company
www.transworldbooks.co.uk

First published in Great Britain in
1982 by Hamlyn Paperbacks
under the name Robert Tyler Stevens
Corgi edition published 2011

Copyright © Robert Tyler Stevens 1982

Mary Jane Staples has asserted her right under
the Copyright, Designs and Patents Act 1988 to be
identified as the author of this work.

This book is a work of fiction and, except in the case
of historical fact, any resemblance to actual persons,
living or dead, is purely coincidental.

A CIP catalogue record for this book
is available from the British Library.

ISBN 9780593065198

This book is sold subject to the condition that it shall not, by way of
trade or otherwise, be lent, resold, hired out, or otherwise circulated
without the publisher's prior consent in any form of binding or cover
other than that in which it is published and without a similar condition,
including this condition, being imposed on the subsequent purchaser.

Addresses for Random House Group Ltd companies outside the UK
can be found at: www.randomhouse.co.uk
The Random House Group Ltd Reg. No. 954009

The Random House Group Limited supports The Forest Stewardship
Council (FSC®), the leading international forest certification
organization. Our books carrying the FSC label are printed
on FSC® certified paper. FSC is the only forest certification scheme
endorsed by the leading environmental organizations, including
Greenpeace. Our paper procurement policy can be found
at www.randomhouse.co.uk/environment.

Typeset in New Baskerville by
Kestrel Data, Exeter, Devon.
Printed in the UK by
Clays Ltd, Bungay, Suffolk.

2 4 6 8 10 9 7 5 3 1

NURSE ANNA'S WAR

BRUSSELS, dawn, 12th October 1915

At the place of execution, a rifle range outside the city, a German company of 250 men awaited the arrival of the condemned. Immediately the cars pulled up, Miss Cavell and Philippe Baucq obeyed the request to step down. They had time for a last glance and a last smile at each other, Baucq with his head high, she in spiritual peace. The sentences were read to them in German and French. Pastor le Seur spoke the Grace of the Anglican Church to her. She touched his hand. He caught her final quiet words.

'. . . and I believe my soul is safe and am glad to die for my country.'

She was tied lightly to a pole, as was Baucq. She was still calm, still composed, but as a German soldier blindfolded her, he saw her clear grey eyes fill with tears. They seemed like the tears of a woman to whom life had given so much and to whom death was a bitter-sweet sadness.

Edith Cavell, and her loyal associate, Philippe Baucq, died instantly under the dawn volley of shots.

Chapter One

Belgium, 1915

The greater part of the country was under German occupation. Not an easy cross for the Belgians to bear, but they bore it.

In the light of a grey evening, a girl was running over farmland some twelve kilometres from Brussels. Panting, she climbed a gate, her skirt and petticoat flying as she leapt into a field lying fallow. She hared across it in the direction of huddled farm buildings. She had long since lost her hat, and her fair hair, loose and disordered, flew bright and wild about her head. Her black handbag swung from its long strap. The ground beneath her feet was still hard from winter. Rough and uneven, it made her flight hazardous. But supple with youth and driven by fear, she made light of it. There was a deep ditch on the far side of the field. She saw it, and she saw too the rutted causeway that led over it to the farmhouse and outbuildings. She checked her stride, hesitating. The Boche were not far behind her. They would search the farm buildings. She hurried up to the ditch to see what shelter it might provide. She caught her foot on a hump and stumbled. As she teetered on the edge, a figure rose up amid the leaves and debris, an arm reached and a hand pulled at her. She gasped and tumbled down on top of a man.

'Join me, mam'selle, if trouble is on your heels.'

Startled and fearful, she saw an unshaven chin, a dirty face, a glimmer of bright teeth and blue eyes. The eyes were alert and encouraging. Around the mouth, however, were pinched lines of pain.

'Oh, m'sieu—'

'Mam'selle, be so kind as to lie beside me and not on top.'

She blushed as she scrambled about and squeezed herself deep into the ditch beside him. She saw then that he held his left arm stiffly across his chest. He turned on to his side, facing her. It was a confusing moment. She was fraught with desperation, and he, surely, was hardly in the ditch from choice. His eyes peered at her through clinging bits of disintegrated leaves. She felt apprehensive of the unknown quality he represented.

'M'sieu—'

'The Boche, I saw them in the distance,' he said. 'Are they after you?'

'Yes,' she gasped.

'Ah.' A little smile creased his pinched mouth. 'Then we're both in the same boat. Or the same ditch, shall we say?' He spoke in a cautious but quite cheerful whisper. She wondered if the pursuing German soldiers had seen her climb the gate. She prayed not. But even if they had momentarily lost sight of her, they would be sure to spot the farm buildings and cross the field to investigate. 'Mam'selle,' whispered the encouraging voice, 'we must dig ourselves deeper. The farm is no good. The family are afraid, and who can blame them?'

Belgians who assisted the enemies of the occupying power were liable to be shot. She knew that as well as this man obviously did.

'Dig deeper, m'sieu?' she whispered, very conscious of how close she was to him, and also that as they were as far down in the cold, hard ditch as any two people could get, they could not very well sink farther.

'Yes. We're very visible. Push your legs into the culvert.'

Their feet were at the entrance to the arched drain that ran under the earth causeway leading to the farmhouse. Although the ditch was fairly dry, the culvert was full of damp grass, leaves and mud. Sure that she could hear the Germans now, she pushed urgently with her feet, her body squirming. Beside her, the man thrust his legs in. She blushed again, for her skirt and petticoat refused to enter with her limbs. Her legs wriggled in deeply, up to her thighs. Her clothes stayed outside. She crimsoned.

'Oh—'

'Endure it, mam'selle. Have no fears in pursuit of victory.' His whispering voice was almost tender in his understanding of her confusion.

'Victory?' she breathed, extreme embarrassment struggling with practical necessity.

'We shall outdo them,' he said. His sound arm moved. He put a finger to his lips, and clutched handfuls of ditch debris and scattered it over the visible parts of their bodies. Showers of twigs, crumbling leaves, bits of grass, clotted lumps of earth and dried mud showered down on them. Under their messy camouflage the grey light darkened, and they lay very still.

She heard the Germans. The trouble with the Germans was that they were resolute, thorough and very correct. When ordered to hunt down an offender, they conducted themselves tirelessly. They would call a halt at nightfall, the correct thing to do in most circumstances, but they would resume the chase at daybreak. That too was correct.

There were two of them. The sound of purposeful, booted feet came to her ears. Little thumping echoes disturbed the ground. The men were hurrying over the fallow field,

12

making for the farm entrance. They would cross the ground above the culvert. If they stopped to look around, to glance along the ditch, or directly down into it—

They did stop. She held her breath, knowing they were above her. Beside her, the stranger lay as quiet and as still as a buried fox. She was sure heads were bent above them, eyes peering down at the heap of litter which covered them. The moment was so frightening that icy cold ran eerily down her back and shivers funnelled the length of her spine. Her heart pounded, her eyes stared into the other eyes beneath the ditch litter. Incredibly, they smiled for her in that cold, gloomy little cavern. She had never been so close to a man. She saw his mouth again, tight with pain, though the eyes were bright with encouragement. Amid her freezing fear was a sense of distress because she was helplessly squeezed against his injured arm.

The Germans were talking to each other. The sound of their voices was petrifyingly close. She waited for the harsh command to get up, or for the prod of a rifle barrel.

'*Komm,*' said one man sharply then, and she heard again the muffled little thumps of booted feet as the Germans strode over the causeway towards the farmhouse. In her concern for her companion, she moved as much as she could, squeezing herself back against the wall of the ditch to lessen the pressure on his arm. His smile was a flicker of appreciation. He said not a word; neither did she. The culvert felt messily and coldly damp, and she shuddered at the thought of frogs lurking there. Her legs felt naked; his felt warm. Her stockings were uncovered, and not only her stockings. Shy, confused blood flushed her again. From a distance came the sound of the Boche beating on the farmhouse door.

The man spoke then, in the most cautious of whispers. 'We must wait, my child.'

'Yes, m'sieu, I know,' she breathed.

'Brave girl.'

The evening was so cold. The ditch felt like frosty January, not April. But they gave each other some warmth, even though she transmitted hers in embarrassment. He, aware she was sensitive with innocence, carefully and gently brought her face into his shoulder. There she hid her blushes.

Voices reached them again. The Germans were talking to the farmer.

'M'sieu—'

'Don't worry.' Her companion's murmur was reassuring. 'Our situation is more desperate than improper. We lie together only as comrades, and if we lie quietly enough for long enough, we shall cheat the Kaiser's bloodhounds.'

She felt a melting gratitude for his understanding and for the comfort of his presence.

14

Was he a vagrant, or even a wandering thief? It did not matter. And no, he was not a vagrant, surely, for his French was very correct, without the Belgian brogue to it. If he was a Frenchman, that would explain why he did not want the Boche to catch him.

Her face was tucked in the hollow of her companion's shoulder, her hair festooned with leaves and twigs, her ears strained for sounds. It was silent out there now. What was happening? Had the Germans gone into the farmhouse to search? It was impossible to tell. The silence was ominous, not comforting. Next to her the man swore softly. At least, she suspected it was swearing. Then he said muffledly, 'Damn it.'

She stiffened. He had spoken in English.

She whispered in the same language, 'M'sieu, you're English?'

'Yes. I'm damning my arm. It's broken, I think.'

'Oh, my grandmother is—' She stilled her impulsive whisper and froze. The German voices could be heard again. She heard a Belgian voice too. The Germans seemed to be trying to find words in French, for the Belgian – presumably the farmer – obviously spoke no German. After a minute, silence fell abruptly again. She remembered the man had said the family at the farm were afraid to help. Had the farmer tried to tell the Germans he had had a suspicious caller?

15

A door banged open. The sound sent a quiver through her. She was sure the outbuildings were about to be searched. That meant they were sure she was somewhere around. She prayed. She lay very still, and so did her companion. Each communicated warmth and hope to the other, though the cold crept insidiously around her buried legs and she shivered.

'Bear it a little longer.' His whisper was warm too.

She was in fear only of the Boche now, not him. Theirs was the comradeship of the hunted. But the coldness of the clammy culvert brought cramp. Her legs strained and her toes curled in. Waiting became a pain that made her grit her teeth. But at last she heard the Germans again. They were retracing their footsteps, returning to the causeway. They tramped solidly over it, then to her horror turned and stopped beside the ditch. She stiffened from head to toe. The Englishman's hand squeezed her shoulder. *Courage, mam'selle,* his touch said. But their covering was so meagre, merely a layer of nature's wintry discards. Their salvation was dependent on lying in utter stillness. Her heart jumped as she heard the Germans move. They marched quickly along the edge of the ditch, making their way towards fields. It took them on a parallel course to the way they had come. And that might mean they felt they had missed her, that she had found a hiding place somewhere. She shivered again, in relief.

But her companion would not let her move yet. He suspected they were both in a life-or-death situation, and it plagued him that a girl so young should be in such straits. His hand stayed warningly on her shoulder. They heard the Germans shout. It was acknowledged by distant comrades. The Boche were thick on the ground today. For ten more minutes he kept her in the ditch with him, still and silent. Then he cautiously lifted his head. The debris fell aside and he raised himself higher to take a quick look. The fields were empty. He made a bolder survey, and gave a murmur of relief.

'All clear, mam'selle,' he said, bringing his feet clear of the culvert. Stiffly, she eased her limbs free. She took a hasty look at her stockings before covering her legs. She shuddered at their state. He was sitting on the edge of the ditch, and he reached with his right hand and helped her to her feet. They looked at each other. They were both indescribably dirty. Although, under the circumstances, that was hardly important, she wished she could have looked more presentable.

'Oh, m'sieu,' she said breathlessly, 'my condition is deplorable, I know, but I am so grateful to you.'

'Mam'selle, your company was a pleasure. Two together are always better at this sort of game

than one. Sit a moment. They've gone, I think.'
He smiled out of his dirt and she sat beside
him. She was in a dark grey costume and a light
grey blouse. Her companion's garments were
altogether disreputable; his brown peaked cap
was limp with age, his rusty-looking overcoat
was ragged, and the cuffs of his trousers were
muddy. With his right hand he folded back the
skirt of his coat, fished into a trouser pocket
and brought out a large handkerchief. He
inspected it dubiously, for it was in sad need of
laundering. 'Forgive its condition, mam'selle,'
he said, 'and permit me to be of service, for I
can't have it said that I make young ladies look
grubby and then do nothing about it.'

He was so cheerful, despite his injured arm.
Carefully he cleaned her face, and she emerged
for him. Her features had the fine, soft clarity
of unlined and unspoiled youth. Her skin was
smooth and delicate, her mouth wide and pink,
her oval contours promising to give her the
beauty of a woman in years to come. Her hazel
eyes were shy under his regard.

But with quite old-fashioned gravity she said,
'Thank you, m'sieu.'

He smiled at her. They had a moment or
two for dawdling. The fields were devoid of all
movement, the farmhouse keeping its peace
and the evening casting a welcome quiet.

'A privilege, mam'selle,' he said. They were
conversing in English, which she spoke as

naturally as she spoke French. 'Before, you were a little – er – dirty. Now you're pretty. I think the least I can do in return is to get cleaned up myself.' He scrubbed his face, and his handkerchief grew soiled. As he came out from under his coating of mud and bits, she was curious to see what he looked like. His eyes and mouth impressed her, his eyes very blue and cheerful, his mouth firm and determined. The bridge of his nose was slightly dented, as if at some time it had suffered a break. He was, she thought, a very adult man, adult in a way that was as much to do with his attitude as his age, which she guessed was about thirty. He seemed a man capable of commanding others. Certainly, even though he was in need of a shave, he was not the worst person in the world to have shared a ditch with. Aware of her concentrated regard, he said lightly, 'I still look a sight, mam'selle?'

'M'sieu, even if you did I should not dream of saying so. To be quite truthful, you are much improved.'

He laughed. They shared a feeling that for the moment the Boche could be discounted, that a laugh or two would not bring them back. He stood up, winced a little and said, 'Hell.'

'M'sieu?' she said, not in disapproval but concern.

'Pardon my language,' he said. 'We must go in a moment. It's quiet now, but the Boche have been all over the place today, and they might reappear while it's still light. But, first, what is your name?'

She hesitated. She supposed it was right that they should introduce themselves. She must hope that her growing faith in him was not misplaced.

'I am Louise Victoria Bouchet,' she said.

'That, mam'selle, if I may say so, is a delicious name. I'm Major Ned Scott of the Norfolk Regiment. British Army.'

A major? A *commandant*?

'M'sieu?' she said disbelievingly.

'I agree,' he said, 'I'm not at my best. It's a long story. And I suppose no one would think a British officer stupid enough to break his arm at a time most inconvenient for him. Now, how old are you?'

She might have said she was eighteen. She was only three months short of it. Not given to prevarication, however, she said, 'Seventeen.'

His blue eyes regarded her almost affectionately.

'Mam'selle, you're a very brave seventeen. You must have your own story to tell. But not now. I hoped to reach Brussels this evening. The Boche, however, have been active around here for hours.' He peered into the distance. There was no sign of the Germans. 'This isn't the first ditch I've been in. D'you see that wood?' He pointed. She saw a wood lying a little distance beyond the gate she had climbed. 'Well, in there is an old hut. I left it earlier today, but had to go to ground when I realized the area was swarming with Germans.'

'They were looking for me, m'sieu,' said Louise. 'I've been running all ways all day.'

'Tell me about it later,' he said.

She rose to her feet and said, 'M'sieu, your arm . . . ?'

'I'll have to take it with me. Can't leave it here, you know. I broke it a couple of hours ago when I jumped a wall and fell awkwardly. Come on, before the Boche decide to return.'

'I am ready, m'sieu,' she said. Whether what he had told her was true or not, whether he was a British officer or an impostor, she did not know, but she went unquestioningly with him, for in reaching out to Louise Victoria, seventeen and alone, he had turned a desperate girl into a trusting one.

Eight months ago, Kaiser Wilhelm of Germany had demanded unhindered passage for his troops through Belgium in order to attack France. King Albert of the Belgians went to Parliament House to address the crowded Chamber of Deputies. He made a speech of dignity and courage. He finished by declaring that a people who defended their freedom could never die. And so the Belgians defied Kaiser Wilhelm. Their small army stood at Liège, for days resisting the might of General von Kluck and the German 1st Army of over 300,000 men and denying them a rapid advance into France to capture the Channel ports. This delay cost the Germans dear, for it gave the French and British time to bring their armies into position and it saved the Channel ports. Belgium was inevitably overrun in the end, but its army escaped. Under the command of King Albert it engaged in a fighting retreat and successfully joined the French and British divisions. The Germans, subsequently defeated by the combined Allied forces at the Marne, never regained the initiative. Naturally, they blamed the Belgians and were still angry with them.

Occupied Belgium suffered an administration addicted to the stern doctrines of Prussianism – the keystone of German unity and German greatness. What it meant to the Belgians, besides loss of liberty, was restraint, and deprivation. They had to take care how they behaved, for failure to comply with any edict published by the Military Government risked the severest penalties. Food was scarce, unemployment rife, fuel hard to come by. Hope of an Allied victory was the flame that warmed the Belgian spirit, even if it could not ease hunger or stop the cold April wind from biting.

But neither Louise nor the major felt the cold too much as they began to move across the field.

Their adrenalin was in full flow. A sense of vulnerability still lurked, and they ran. They climbed the gate, the major muttering under his breath because of his arm, and dashed towards the wood. They saw no one in the grey light of cheerless evening. The Germans were either widely scattered or on their way back to their command post. The wood loomed up. It was a deceptive-looking haven, they knew that. Woods were always a magnet to the hunted, but also the favourite beating places of the hunters. However, this wood was the only haven at the moment. They had to climb another gate, for it was part of an estate, and then made their final dash, Major Scott with his left arm held against his chest and Louise Victoria with her skirt hitched. They reached the trees undetected. They listened; there was only quietness. Stiff leaves scattered with brittle rustles beneath their feet as they entered the wood and evergreens enclosed them. She followed him as he went his known way, and saw the hut he had spoken of – an old timber building with a rickety slate roof. Breathless, she went into it with him.

'M'sieu,' she whispered, 'do you think – that is, the Boche, won't they search this wood, looking for such a hiding place as this?'

'They were here earlier, mam'selle, and made a thorough search. Those I glimpsed in chase of you were additional hounds. Don't worry, we should be safe here for a while, I think. And they'll give up when it's dark. What d'you say to a fire? It would keep us warm. That's something, isn't it?'

The idea of a small, crackling blaze was bliss to her. Although the hut was far cosier than the ditch, there were draughty gaps where boards were cracked or broken. The major, using his right foot, attacked a cracked one. It splintered under the blow of his boot. He bent and wrenched the pieces from their nailed moorings, using his right hand.

'M'sieu,' she said, 'please let me help.'

'All right, chicken,' he said cheerfully, 'I'll boot the boards and you pull them clear.'

He kicked in several boards and stood back, watching her as she pulled the shattered wood free and built up a pile of it. Her bright hair flowed like a darkly golden river. Her expression was serious. She made a young and very sweet comrade.

'There, m'sieu,' she said, looking up from the pile.

'Well done, Louise Victoria.'

'Shall I get some twigs?' she asked.

'I shouldn't. They'll all be pretty damp and fill the place with smoke. But it was a good thought.'

She saw a small heap of ashes in the middle of the stone floor.

'Your previous fire, m'sieu?' she asked.

'Quite so.' He was still making light of things,

though she was sure he must be in pain. She faced up to him.

'Before we do anything else, m'sieu,' she said, 'your arm must be seen to.'

'Yes, when we can find a doctor who'll set it.'

'I mean, we must do what we can now. If I can provide a bandage and sling, there's wood we can use for splints, isn't there?'

'My dear child—'

'Won't splints and a sling help, m'sieu?' She was earnestly insistent.

'Yes,' he said.

'Then please turn your back,' she said. He did so. Louise Victoria drew up her skirt and petticoat. Her slim legs were encased in grey silk stockings. She shuddered again at the dirt encrusting them and quickly brushed much of it off. She gathered her petticoat, made a tear in the hem with her teeth, and ripped off a wide circle of the soft white cotton.

'What are you doing?' The major asked the question from the door, where he stood listening. The wood was quiet, but two people on the run from the Germans could not take things for granted.

'See, m'sieu?' she said. He turned round. She had broken the circle of cotton and showed him the long length of the piece.

'That's torn it,' he smiled.

'M'sieu?'

'Oh, just a saying. In your case it means a

25

ruined petticoat. Thank you, young lady. D'you think you could now help me off with this old coat?'

She was as careful as she could be. The right sleeve was no problem. The left sleeve was another matter. She drew it downwards very slowly, but he still bit his teeth hard together. It made her clench her own teeth in tense sympathy. Gently, she persevered, and the coat came off. He wore an old blue woollen jersey underneath. Its left sleeve seemed very tight over his forearm, and she knew the injury was badly swollen.

'Oh, m'sieu, it must be so painful,' she said in distress.

He touched it gingerly, then said, 'No splints at this stage, Louise Victoria. But a sling would be some help, tied around the wrist. Will you do it, comrade?'

The swelling was at its worst near the elbow. The wrist was only slightly puffy, and he was able to let her wind the improvised bandage around it. Again she took great care, then brought the two ends of the material up around his neck and tied them to make the sling. He let the arm rest. The sling reduced the tension and eased the painful ache.

'Thank you, that's very good,' he said, and smiled at her.

'Is it just a little better like that?' She was still very concerned.

'Much. Now, can you help me back into the coat? The patient, if possible, must be kept warm.'

'M'sieu, I don't know how you can stay so cheerful,' she said.

'Well, you're as good a reason as any other I can think of,' he said. He slipped his right arm into the overcoat. She drew the shabby garment over his shoulders and his injured arm. She carefully buttoned it up. The left sleeve hung loose. She tucked it into the pocket. 'Thank you, my young mam'selle,' he said, 'that's very comfortable. Now, the fire.'

'It will be all right to light one? We shan't be discovered?'

'I hope not,' he said, 'we've some trout to cook. So let's risk it.'

'Trout?' The thought of satisfying her hunger created a wetness in her mouth. 'Trout?'

'Caught yesterday, with the help of a boy. The sun came out; so did the trout in some Belgian landowner's private stream. I ate two of them earlier. There are two left. Will you dine with me, Louise Victoria?'

'M'sieu, you are being very good to me,' she said.

'My feeling is that we're being good to each other. Are you hungry?'

'Famished,' said Louise frankly.

'In that case,' he said, 'enter the left-hand pocket of my coat.'

She slipped a hand into the sagging old pocket and located a bulky parcel wrapped in newspapers – copies of *La Libre Belgique*, the underground newspaper which was published monthly in Brussels, despite persistent efforts by the Germans to suppress it. Mysteriously, it appeared every month on the table of General von Bissing, the Military Governor of occupied Belgium, much to his cold rage and much, of course, to the warm delight of the Belgians.

Louise unwound the papers and the glistening trout appeared. They were plump and weighty. Louise's mouth watered again.

'Oh, m'sieu, a feast,' she said happily.

'My friends call me Scottie. You can call me Uncle Scottie.' He took the newspapers from her as she carefully placed the fish on a piece of board from the pile. 'A pity to consign such valiant symbols of Belgian resistance to the flames, but we too are resistant, aren't we, my child?'

'I am, m'sieu, very much,' she said.

He smiled, stooped, and placed the newspapers in a loosely crumpled ball on the ashes.

'Mam'selle, some of the smaller chips of wood, if you please.'

She selected small bits and pieces, and built them up around the paper. Her every action had the quicksilver fluency of a girl whose natural physical grace went hand in hand with her vitality.

'That is satisfactory?' she said, looking up, and he saw her pleasure at being of help.

'That's excellent. Do you have a match?'

'Oh, alas, m'sieu.'

He laughed. It was a warm chuckle. Her little expression of regret had been very Belgian, very continental.

'Dig into my left pocket again,' he said.

She did so and found a box of matches.

'M'sieu, you have everything,' she said with the admiration of the young for the experienced.

'Not quite,' he smiled. 'Louise Victoria, light the fire. The honour is yours. All is quiet.'

She stooped and struck a match. She was very sweet, he thought, and very valiant. The paper flared. A portion of it was damp from contact with the fish, but most of it was dry. The flame was magical in its promise of warmth and cheer. The wooden chips began to burn. Her face took on a glow as she knelt to encourage the little blaze, her hazel eyes reflecting its light, and the light danced. He watched her with interest. She was a mere girl, but the Germans, conceding nothing in wartime to tender youth, had set her running for her very life.

'Oh, how good,' she said as *La Libre Belgique* provided the combustible foundation of fire and warmth. The chips, of dry seasoned boarding, flared.

'Larger pieces now, mam'selle,' he said, very

29

willing to watch her feed the fire because she intrigued him so much.

His cheerful voice was a comfort to her, though she knew their situation was still desperate. She selected pieces from the pile of wood and built the fire up until it was crackling as merrily as summer crickets. It did not make a paradise of the bare hut, but it did create pleasure and a sense of warm comradeship.

'How are we to cook the trout, m'sieu?' she asked.

'By roasting them. Now's the time for wet twigs,' He went out of the hut and scavenged around in the gloom of a fast-failing evening. He returned with some stout twigs. They sat on their haunches before the fire, each with a speared trout dangling from a twig, and over the flames they began to cook the fish. It was not precisely how the chef of a Brussels restaurant would have gone about it, said the major, but the redoubtable Scouts of Baden-Powell, given the same circumstances, could not have done better. Louise said she thought they were managing very well. She kept the fire fed with earnest conscientiousness.

'Tell me,' he said, 'how is it you speak such good English?'

'Because my mother used it so much. It was her own mother's language.' A little sadness showed. 'I miss her dreadfully, m'sieu.'

'Your mother is dead?' he said gently.

'My father too, m'sieu, whom I also loved. He was an officer in the Belgium army and was killed at Liège.'

Major Scott was silent for a moment. The steaming trout began to smoke. Through the little haze he saw loneliness in the girl's eyes, and memories that brought a hint of tears.

'My sweet young mam'selle, I'm sorry, I'm very sorry,' he said, 'but we'll forget melancholy for a moment. You're a brave daughter of Belgium, and of your parents, and you and I together have outdone the dreaded Boche. Now we have a fire and we're roasting trout.'

'Oh, mine is burning,' she said, lifting her speared fish clear of the flames. Its tail was curling and crackling.

Toast it, Louise Victoria, don't cremate it,' he said, and smiled at her wrinkling nose. She carefully repositioned her trout. It was a matter requiring patience, toasting and roasting the fish over the fire, when she and he were both so hungry. But they persevered, and eventually he said, 'Done, I think, comrade.'

'Yes?' she said.

'We'll see,' he said. They placed the hot, smoking fish on a slat of wood. He took a penknife from his right pocket and handed it to her. She pulled out a blade, and as neatly as she could she slit the trout. She opened them up. Pinkly-white flesh steamed. 'By the beard of old Job,' said the major, 'done to a turn, I'll wager.'

She used the knife to lift the bones and they ate ravenously, dismembering the fish with knife and fingers.

'Oh, m'sieu, it's good, isn't it?' she said with relish, and he felt a pang because she was so young and alone.

'Well, I think it's very good, by Jove I do,' he said. When they had finished he wiped his hand on his coat tail. To her he offered his grubby handkerchief. 'It's the best I've got at the moment.'

Louise used the handkerchief, wiping her sticky fingers with it.

'It's in dreadful need of a wash, m'sieu,' she said.

'I know, but things have been a bit tricky—'

'Even under the most trying circumstances, m'sieu, a handkerchief should be washed. There is always water somewhere.'

'Really?' said the major.

Louise, a strict adherent of personal hygiene and immaculate handkerchiefs, suddenly realized she had let fastidiousness run away with her head. She blushed crimson.

'Oh, m'sieu, I do beg your pardon, that was dreadful of me—' She stopped as he rushed a finger to her lips. He was listening with ears straining, his eyes more alert than ever. She listened too, her heart beating fast. It came, a sound they both heard clearly. There was someone in the wood; feet were disturbing the leaves. They were up in a flash. She dived for her handbag, which carried all that was precious to a girl, though a man might have thrown more than half the contents away. He took her hand and they were out of the hut as quickly and as silently as they could manage. The darkness smacked into their faces. But he had been in this place before and knew something of its geography. He turned left, away from the approaching sound, and took her without hesitation around the hut to the rear. There he calmly sat down, pulling her to sit beside him. She wondered and worried for a second or two before realizing they were, of course, much quieter just sitting than creeping or scurrying about.

A man, a lamp swinging in his hand, approached the hut with a firm, authoritative tread. An angry voice shouted through the open door, 'Come out of there! Do you hear me? Come out!'

Chapter Two

The major pressed Louise's face into his shoulder. It gave her a warm feeling of being shielded and protected, but her heartbeats still behaved erratically in her fear for both of them. The newcomer was not a German; his voice was unmistakably Belgian. But he sounded menacing. He was one of the estate gamekeepers, perhaps. It would not be wise, unless he discovered them, to ask him for help. He might give it. Many Belgians would, but it put such people at terrible risk. It was better, if possible, to know something of the character and sympathies of people before declaring oneself to be wanted by the Boche.

She heard the man enter the hut.

'Where are you, eh? Come out. What, gone, have you? And left your fire? You scoundrels.'

The major, his right arm around Louise, kept her close to him. They sat within the deep bulky blackness cast by the hut. It minimized their visibility. Stillness and silence were again their enforced lot. Little wings of nervousness fluttered around her heart. The man had spotted the fire, no doubt, through the gaps in the boards.

'Show yourself, whoever you are.' The voice, raised, came from outside the hut again. 'You're up to no good, you miscreants. I'll get the dogs on you, whether there's one or a dozen of you. Coming here, breaking the place up, making fires, chopping up trees – you'll bring your beds next. I'll catch you, damned if I won't.'

The man began to move on. Louise and the major listened to the slow, ponderous tramp of feet and the angry grumbling as the threats continued. They glimpsed the lamp, a moving light that grew smaller and fainter. It vanished among trees, but for a while they could still hear him. Then silence descended. Perhaps a man like that, a conscientious estate employee, kept a regular lookout for people who stole into the wood at night to cut down branches and chop them up for their fire grates. That was how it was now in Belgium; quite good and honest people were reduced to making desperate little sorties into wooded areas, using axes, saws and knives to win for themselves enough timber and kindling to keep a fire going for a day or two.

'M'sieu?' whispered Louise.

'Well, we've lost our little fire, but that's all,' murmured the major.

'No, it's still alight,' she said. She could see the glow through a crack in the rear boards.

'I mean we can't return to it,' said the major in a cautious whisper. 'He's left it burning, d'you see? And wandered off. That, young lady, is a manoeuvre designed to draw us back to our fire, I'll wager on it. Then he'll come back too, growling for our blood. Otherwise he'd have stamped the fire put. You heard him growling? A bear of a man, Louise Victoria, and ready to eat us both. You first, as you'd be tenderer. But we'll not fall into that trap, eh?'

'No, m'sieu,' said Louise, a smile in her voice. 'We will go, yes?'

'Much the best thing, I'd say, wouldn't you?' he said, and she thought how easy it was to like him.

'M'sieu, you spoke of wishing to reach Brussels,' she said, keeping her voice as low as his.

'I've no idea how to get there in the dark,' he said. He got to his feet. She rose with him, moving in her supple way.

'In Brussels, you can find a doctor or a hospital,' she said. 'I know the way, even in the dark, and I should be very happy, m'sieu, to be your guide. You would not mind if I came with you?'

'Mind? I'm not going to manage it without you.'

'It's twelve kilometres,' said Louise, 'and if

we go the quietest ways we can get there by ten o'clock. And I'm sure we shall be able to find a kind, discreet and capable doctor, who will be able to set your arm himself, which would be better, yes? Better, I mean, because you're a British officer.'

'Young lady, you're heaven-sent. But is Brussels your own destination?'

Louise's destination had been anywhere that was safe. Brussels was now her preference, though she did not know how safe it would prove.

'Yes, m'sieu, Brussels is where I wish to go.'

'Twelve kilometres, you say?'

'It may be a little more,' she said, 'but it is also quite likely to be a little less.'

The major smiled. 'Lead on, then,' he said, 'and we'll take it more or less as it comes.'

'I must tell you, m'sieu,' she said as they made cautious tracks away from the hut, 'that you'll find many German soldiers in Brussels.'

'Well,' he said, and Louise smiled. The English were always saying 'well' or 'really'. 'Well, let's cheer ourselves up with the fact that to one German, two comrades are a crowd, and to a thousand Germans they're insignificant.'

She smiled again. They left the wood, making their way with a quiet care that was now instinctive to them. The April evening had become black night, but they grew cats' eyes and saw the gate they had to climb. They negotiated it silently, the major making a more awkward business of it than the quicksilvery girl. She turned, leading the way. He came up beside her, and they walked through the darkness, over fields until they reached a narrow road, where they turned east towards Brussels. Far to the south sounds like muted thunder rumbled. The guns of war were seldom quiet in Flanders, and when the wind was in the right direction they could be heard in Brussels itself.

They walked briskly, the major's left arm resting in its sling beneath his overcoat. Belgium seemed locked in darkness and, the guns apart, in silence. But not all the units of the occupying power were stationed in Brussels, and the travellers knew it was possible to bump into the Boche in the quietest places, and by night as well as by day. The clouds had gone and the stars were out. The night, though, cold, promised to be fine.

'Shall we talk, Louise Victoria?' said the major. 'I think we might, without waking up too many Germans, and if you'd care to tell me your story and why you're running from the Kaiser's bloodhounds, I'd like to hear it all. Are you out of school yet?'

'Out of school? M'sieu, of course.' Louise was a little indignant; although it had only been six months or so since she finished at a young ladies' academy in Brussels.

'Well, then, how did you come to end up in a ditch with me?'

Talking, with voices kept low, was going to make the journey more agreeable, and Louise found herself very willing to tell her story. She lived with her aunt, her father's sister, just outside the ancient little town of Dendermonde in East Flanders. Her mother had died a year ago, and her father, a Belgian officer of the reserve, had been called up at the beginning of the war four months later. He was killed during the German attack on Liège.

As a young man, he had accepted an offer to study for two years in St Petersburg, where he met an entrancing young Russian lady whose mother was English and whose father was one of the Tsar's ministers. This happened six months before his time in St Petersburg was up, but during those last months he fell incurably in love. The young lady was not merely entrancing, she was divinely lovely, deliciously witty and utterly adorable. Naturally, with such assets and such qualities as these, she was being courted with dramatic Russian ardour by some of the handsomest men in St Petersburg. Although he was by no means a retiring young man – in fact, he was commendably dashing – the dazzling splendour of the competition made him unusually diffident, and he advanced his cause with such a lack of self-confidence that he knew himself to be in constant retreat.

'Are these your words, Louise Victoria?' asked the amused major.

Louise assured him that almost every word originated from her father, who often told this story of his courtship. When he was at last due to return home to Brussels, he realized he had spent six months getting precisely nowhere. This, he confessed, was due to the sense of inferiority that ravishing beauty and Russian competition fostered in him. Therefore he was determined, before it was too late, to be entirely bold, and to advance either to ecstatic victory or honourable retreat. He composed himself for defeat, since he thought little of his chances.

On the night before he left St Petersburg, he called on his heart's desire with the firm intention of proposing. Her parents' house was full of people. Uniforms quite brilliant were everywhere, and great handsome Russian moustaches seemed an intimidating luxuriance, especially as he was clean-shaven himself. He went forward with his head high, however, to greet his lady fair, and was smitten by disaster. He tripped over the edge of the carpet and fell flat on his face. There was the most spellbinding roar of Russian silence—

'A spellbinding roar of Russian silence?' queried the fascinated major.

'That is what my father called it,' smiled Louise, swinging along by the side of her newly found comrade in the darkness. She went on to say that the silence was followed by an ear-splitting gale of Russian laughter, and a score of hands pulled her father to his feet like a popping cork. And all in front of the eyes of the young lady of his heart. He gathered himself together as manfully as he could, bowed to her and, making the best of the farce, announced that if she would permit it, he would turn his arrival into immediate departure and go straightaway to the optician's, for he had no doubt he was in serious need of spectacles. She laughed. She thought that splendidly delicious and loved him for it. But he thought she only laughed, as might any girl, at a clown. He accepted defeat. He did not mention he was departing for Brussels in the morning. He did find time to call on his way to the station, however, and to leave her a note. She was out and her mother took it. In it he declared himself devoted to her and wished her lifelong joy and happiness.

Much to his astonishment, when he reached his home in Brussels, a telegram from her was waiting for him. There were just six words.

IS THAT WHAT DEVOTION
MEANS – GOODBYE?

He sent a telegram in immediate reply, proposing to her. Back came a second telegram from the lady of his heart.

'M'sieu,' said Louise, 'do you know what

was in it? Just one word: YES. But in English, Russian and French, and written fifty times. Mama often said that as Papa's advances were always retreats, she was not going to be less than positive herself. So she said yes fifty times. In a telegram, and in English, Russian and French. Did you ever hear of anything more romantically extravagant? You see, she was as much in love with him as he was with her. Mama was nineteen then, Papa twenty-three, and they were married six months later, in St Petersburg.'

Louise was born the following year. She was also given the name Victoria, after her English grandmother. She was part-Russian, part-English and part-Belgian. Mostly she was Belgian, of which she was proud. She was the only child, but a very happy one. She found that Mama really was adorable. She was also more English than Russian in many ways. She was not dark, she was fair. She did not have a Russian temperament, she was always calm and serene. She was never known to lose her head in a crisis, and no matter that Papa said it could not be managed, they went to St Petersburg every year and always managed it very well. Mama's English mother was fair too, and a most gracious lady, although sometimes she was more imperious than even the Tsarina could possibly be. That probably came from being English—

'Ah, we're a haughty lot,' said the major.

'Oh, m'sieu, I am deplorably tactless.'

'You're delicious,' said the major, 'please carry on.'

Mama had English relations through her mother, of course. They lived in Somerset, so sometimes Mama and Papa went there too. Somerset, said Louise, had something of Mama about it, because it was calm and peaceful and serene, and the English cousins were always glad to see Mama and Papa and herself. Life simply whirled by. The summers were full of colour, activity and high spirits, of friendships and visits, of being out in the fields or by the sea, of seeing the golden wheat standing high in Somerset and the flax standing lush in Flanders. Easter was nearly always spent in St Petersburg, where the religious rites were enthralling and very moving.

At home, Papa was sometimes inclined to have little moments of excitement. He was very extrovert and energetic, so that just getting ready for a walk could assume all the urgency required to mount a desperately needed cavalry charge. Mama would just smile and say, 'Henri, *mon chéri*, listen, the roof is falling in.' And everyone, even Papa, would stand very still and listen. Nothing would happen, of course, except that Papa would suddenly laugh and say, 'Your mama, Louise, is telling me I'm getting excited about something of no importance at all. But it may rain and no one has thought of an umbrella – where's the umbrella?' Mama would laugh, but somehow they would all leave the house together, which Papa would say was due to his genius for organization and Mama would say was in the nature of a miracle. No one was to know that one day a forgotten umbrella would bring tragedy.

Papa's sister, Aunt Tilli, who lived near Dendermonde, often came to visit. She was an attractive and cultured woman, but a dreadful perfectionist. Everything and everyone always had to be just so. Nothing outside Belgium was ever just so. She did not like the French, thought little of the English, and considered the Russians to be near to barbaric. She graciously conceded that Mama was an exception, and because of Mama's connections she prefaced any criticism of England or Russia by saying, 'You'll forgive me, but I must be frank, Katrina.' That was Mama's name, Katrina. Aunt Tilli, in being frank, was invariably tactless, but Mama took it all with a sweet smile, and the only time she ever struck back was when she said, 'Tilli, I'm sure that on the day you arrive in heaven, God will see to it that the angels have brushed their wings and the place is tidied up. So you may go your way in peace and without worry.'

Despite being a good-looking woman, Aunt Tilli remained unmarried. Papa shook his head about her, for admirers came and went with shameful regularity. People said each gentleman was wise enough to admit he was unable to fit the role of perfection Aunt Tilli would expect of a husband. It made her develop a very poor opinion of men, although that was only consistent with her general opinion of almost everyone.

Life went on, winters were cosy and spring always meant a blossoming of outdoor pursuits. And then Mama, suffering from a heavy cold, visited a friend. She took her umbrella with her, in case it was needed, for it was April and the weather was variable, sunshine alternating with showers. It was fine when Mama left her friend's house to walk home. She loved walking. She forgot her umbrella, simply because the sunshine was so bright, the sky so clear. She was caught in a sudden storm of rain that was cold and wintry. It soaked her in minutes. Pneumonia rushed on her like a raging tempest, and she was dead within days. They were so grief-stricken that they scarcely knew how to comfort each other. Louise thought Papa missed Mama so much that, when he fell at Liège, death would have had few fears for him. He was probably very happy to join Mama, and he—

'Louise Victoria, however much he loved your mama and however much he missed her, do you think he did not suffer a last moment of anguish in his thoughts of you?' The major's interruption was gentle, his voice warm. 'I'll wager he fought a good fight, a fight to survive, for he still had you and would have wanted to live for you. So would any father of so brave a daughter.'

'Yes? Well, he is with Mama now. Perhaps that is not too sad, m'sieu, for they belong together.' Her voice was husky and she became silent for a while. The major thought it was because of tears. He did not intrude on her little moment of sadness, and when she continued with her story she was in quiet control of herself again.

Suddenly alone and heartbroken after all the years of love, after all those swift summers and cosy winters, Louise was invited to live with Aunt Tilli. Her St Petersburg grandparents – Petrograd, she had to call it now – also offered her a place with them, and so did her English relations. She loved her maternal grandparents and was fond of her English cousins. But her heart belonged to Belgium, more especially now it was at war with Germany. So she went to live with Aunt Tilli at Dendermonde.

Aunt Tilli proved sympathetic and kind to begin with, but it was not long before, out of habit, she let sympathy turn into criticism of the causes which had orphaned her niece. Incredibly, and much to Louise's hurt, she declared it was Mama's weak Russian blood which had led her to contract pneumonia. The blood of all Russians was tainted by their excesses, she said. And she blamed England and France bitterly for Papa's death. They had not come to Belgium's aid quickly enough, although by treaty they had been honour bound to do so. They were still indifferent and incompetent allies, with no idea at all of how to fight the Germans, and Belgium was likely to remain under the heel of the Boche for ever.

Meanwhile, she asked what Louise was intending to do. Louise would have liked to do something to help Belgium, and said so. Aunt Tilli said, nonsense. Louise, biding her time, opted to study music, as Papa had, and Aunt Tilli engaged a retired orchestra leader as a tutor for her.

There were numerous warnings posted up around Dendermonde concerning fugitive Allied soldiers. Belgian, French and British soldiers on the run must, when discovered, be given up to the German authorities or their whereabouts reported. Any Belgian civilians found harbouring them or assisting them in any way would be summarily tried, and were liable to be shot. There had been a very menacing warning promulgated in September 1914, by the German Commander in the Mons district, to the effect that citizens were forbidden on pain of death to give any help whatever to Allied soldiers. Further, any such soldiers who did not give themselves up within ten days would be shot when captured. International law gave an occupying power the right to take quite extreme measures for the safety of her forces, and death penalties for people who disobeyed decrees were perfectly legal.

A week ago, said Louise, she was walking home from Dendermonde when she met two men. One was a French soldier, the other an English one. They had been on the run from the Germans for weeks in their attempt to reach the Dutch border. She talked to them, and met them again later, when it was dark. She brought the men unobserved to the house and hid them in the cellar. She did not have her aunt's critical outlook, nor did she share her opinions of the French and British. She knew what Mama would have done, and what Mama would have done, she did: she gave shelter to the soldiers. They were both exhausted and starving. She smuggled food and drink down to them, plundered from the meagre stocks in the kitchen. The two men asked if they could stay just a few days, when they would then feel strong enough to renew their attempt to reach Holland.

'How could I have said no, m'sieu? They were our allies, and one was English. Mama had English blood and I have it too. Could I have disgraced myself and Mama by refusing to help them? They had been fighting the Boche, and if Belgians turn their back on soldiers who have fought their enemies, then our King would tell us we don't deserve freedom. What would Papa have thought if I'd gone to the German authorities and betrayed those soldiers?'

'Don't be in doubt, Louise Victoria,' said the major. 'Your father will always rest easily in the knowledge that you'd never betray anyone.'

Louise said not a word to Aunt Tilli. Aunt Tilli, in her disillusionment with the Allies, had already made it clear that Belgians who assisted any French or British soldiers deserved all they got for their pains. She was, in any case, certain the Allies were fighting for a cause already lost.

The two soldiers were there for three days, creeping up from the cellar at night when Louise and her aunt had retired, and going quietly into the garden for fresh air and exercise. Then, on the third night, returning to the cellar through the dark house, one of the men knocked over a potted-plant stand. Aunt Tilli was awake in a flash and hurried into Louise's room. There was someone in the house, she said. Louise suggested it was one of the servants, but Aunt Tilli soon ascertained that the servants were sleeping soundly, their basement rooms farthest from the noise of the crashing pot. She insisted that Louise must go on her bicycle and fetch the police. Louise, who guessed what had happened, said no.

'Then I'll go myself,' said Aunt Tilli. 'You stay here and keep your door locked.'

The game was up. Louise confessed. Aunt Tilli took the news calmly, but her expression was disapproving and severe. She did not go down to the cellar, or to the police; she went back to her bed. In the morning she once again asked Louise to go and report the men to the German authorities in Dendermonde.

Louise refused. 'I can't, Aunt Tilli. They'll be shot.'

'They should have thought of that and given themselves up long ago,' said Aunt Tilli. 'By coming here they've put us in danger, as they must know. Louise, you've been foolish and misguided. Go and report them.'

'No, Aunt Tilli. I'm sorry, but I can't. They've been fighting for Belgium.'

'For themselves, you mean,' said Aunt Tilli pityingly. 'They don't give a rap for Belgium. If you won't go, then I will, although you are responsible. I wanted to give you the chance to correct your error. Since you refuse, I must correct it for you. I'll be as charitable as I can; I'll tell the Germans these men wish to give themselves up. But they haven't been here for three days. They arrived of their own accord this morning. Do you understand that?'

Louise, aghast, said, 'Yes, I understand, but you can't do it. You mustn't. The Germans are still liable to shoot them. That would mean we'd betrayed them.'

'Nonsense,' said Aunt Tilli. There were

no shades of grey in Aunt Tilli's book of life. Everything was set down in clear black and white.

'Aunt Tilli,' said Louise desperately, 'the Germans will ask questions. They'll ask questions of the soldiers and us, and perhaps find out the men have been here three days, after all. So they might shoot us too.'

'Us? Us? It's not I who have done this stupid thing.' Aunt Tilli was coldly angry.

'Then perhaps they'll only shoot me. They hate Belgians as much as they hate our allies. They hate us for having resisted them in the first place. They say we cost them Paris and the Channel ports by holding them up at Liège. Aunt Tilli, Papa died at Liège for Belgium. I am never going to let Papa down, never, never. Nor can you. Papa was your brother. You can't do it, and I won't believe you can.'

'You foolish girl, you're endangering us all. You're endangering yourself, me and the servants. If the Germans find out, if there's an informer around, they'll descend on us and I don't doubt more than one of us will be shot then. Do you want that? Do your two soldiers want it? Go down and see if they do. Go down and tell them to go away, to give themselves up.'

'No,' said Louise, pale but resolute.

'Very well,' said Aunt Tilli, 'you will stay here while I go to the authorities. It won't be necessary, I hope, to lock you in your room?'

Since Aunt Tilli knew her to be a truthful girl, Louise said, 'If I can't stop you doing this, then I can't really be of any further help to the men. I shall say nothing to them, because if I do, if I tell them they're going to have to give themselves up, they'll almost certainly make a run for it and we shall be in serious trouble when the Germans find they're not here. In any case, once you've reported them they're bound to be caught, even if they do run. I've done what I thought was right, and you're going to do what you think is right. I'd rather not speak about it any more. I shall just sit and wait.' She told her first real lie as calmly as she could, looking into her aunt's eyes and hiding her anger and disgust. It was a convincing performance.

Louise watched her as she put on her hat and coat and marched out of the house. She realized Aunt Tilli lacked charity and compassion, that she had little love for people. This was why she had few close friends and no husband.

In alarm now, Louise immediately warned the two fugitives. At once the men decided to bolt, delaying only long enough to thank her and tell her she was brave and precious, and for the French soldier to kiss her gallantly and the English soldier to squeeze her. Then they were away. They were men, she thought, whom the Boche would not find easy to catch.

And now she had herself to think about. When the Germans arrived with Aunt Tilli, they would find the birds flown. She herself would be arrested for helping them, and tried for treason. Under the laws of the occupying power, that was the charge that could be laid against her. That meant either the death penalty or long years of imprisonment, if she was found guilty. Dead or imprisoned, she would be of no further use to her unhappy country. She knew that her parents would not have sat and waited to be arrested. She flung on a hat and jacket, seized her handbag and fled.

She spent two days running and hiding. She secured very little to eat as she worked her way towards Brussels. The Germans, angry and frustrated, scoured the countryside for her and the two soldiers. Their telegraph wires buzzed. On the third day she tried to buy some food in a village. Supplies were so poor that all she could get was half a small loaf of bread. Her description must have been circulated and someone must have informed on her, for after knocking on several doors in her desperation for help and food, she spotted a distant patrol of Germans approaching the village. She ran, but they saw her. She left the road and headed across fields and farmlands. She ran crouching along ditches. She climbed gates. She ran and ran. There came a moment when she knew they were not far behind her. She climbed another gate, but thought she was not going to elude them.

'But then, m'sieu, I found another ditch, and you.'

Major Scott, walking beside her, walking through the darkness towards Brussels with her, thought of the tragedy of her lost parents, her loneliness, her youth, her fears and her courage. He thought of her defiance of the Germans and her defiance of her intimidating aunt. He put his right arm around her shoulders and gave her a squeeze. How else could he communicate that he held her in affection and pride? At seventeen, she had already proved the bright, brave daughter of her parents. Both would have been very proud of her.

'We found each other in that ditch, Louise Victoria, and I shan't easily lose you now, not until such time as I know you are safe. Together we foxed the Boche. A memorable achievement, considering the tenacity of the Boche and what the ditch was like.'

Louise laughed, banishing the sad memories that had inevitably returned as she told him her story. His protective comradeship had drawn it all from her, and in the telling she had eased her heartache. It had almost been a sweetness, talking to him of Mama and Papa, and because of the way he had listened, they had lived again for her. She hoped he understood now

54

something of her mother's enchantment and her father's gaiety, and why she had had to defy her aunt.

She said lightly, 'Oh, it was the ditch which was most memorable, m'sieu.' She supposed she ought to call him Major Scott. 'Please, will you tell me if your arm is troubling you, if it's hurting badly?'

'Well, it's hurting, but not badly.' In fact, it was throbbing like the devil, but in the company of this courageous girl it was not something to cry about. 'What d'you think the Germans did with your aunt?' he asked as they walked the narrow byways, with farms lying black and silent under the night sky.

'Oh, she has a very crisp tongue and a facile command of words and logic,' said Louise. 'She would claim at once that she had done what their decree commanded her to. I think, m'sieu, she will be sitting in her house at this moment, upright in body and clear in conscience, but finding grievous fault in me. I can't go back to her. I could never go back, nor could I ever forgive her. Mama was a better Belgian than Aunt Tilli will ever be. Mama would never have betrayed Allied soldiers to the Boche.'

'It's just possible your aunt may have been thinking of you,' said the major.

'Yes, it's just possible,' said Louise, but with frank scepticism.

They were still walking briskly, threading

their way through the dark, quiet lanes. Louise did not feel too fatigued, considering all she had been up against during the last few days. At night she had had to come to terms with conditions that were outlandish to her, for the best she could find in the way of resting-places were barns. Sleep had been uneasy and fitful. A clean warm bed would be heavenly, she thought. A kind doctor, if she and the major could find one, might perhaps be able to direct them to a place where there would be beds for both of them. Meanwhile, her spirits, so much brighter now that she was no longer alone, kept tiredness at bay. Her companion was a man from her maternal grandmama's country, a man, she felt, whom Papa would have liked.

'M'sieu,' she said, 'would you please tell me why you came to be in that ditch?'

'Well, it may be boring, but it's a way of passing the time,' said the major.

'Oh, you haven't been at all boring yet,' said Louise.

'I hope I can keep it up.'

Chapter Three

Major Scott's story was straightforward. His family home was near Cromer, in Norfolk. His father was a farmer, his mother the natural wife for a farmer. She was a woman of ruddy country health and strength. She was a comforting figure and a practical person. On harvest festival Sundays she thanked God for all his works and wonders, but was not averse to pointing out that the family had had something to do with raising the land's bounty. There were two sons and a daughter, and there was work for all of them on the farm, which had been in the family for a hundred-odd years.

However, said the major, his own inclinations led him off the land into the army, which he joined as a cadet. He was a captain when the Norfolk Regiment embarked to participate in the war, and a major by the time the first battle of Ypres was over. During subsequent fighting around Ypres in March, his company was overrun and he was among a number of prisoners taken. He escaped from the column a couple of hours later, when the British mounted some fierce counter-attacks, taking the German forward and reserve trench position and breaking through at several points. The Germans began to rush up reinforcements, and in the confusion of the moment, the major simply dropped out of the line of prisoners and walked away. As two German soldiers came up at the double, he feigned a limp. When they stopped him, he said he'd been told to report to the nearest German dressing station – where was it? They didn't understand him. He tried French, and one of the Germans pointed and gestured him on. The other, suspicious, went with him. The major halted after a while, bending to groan over his knee. The German peered, and the major kneed him in the stomach, then knocked him out. There was no alternative then but to cut and run.

A Belgian farmer and his family sheltered him for a day and a night. They gave him food and some very old civilian clothes, and directions on how to reach Brussels across country, avoiding roads used by the German army.

He lost his way. He needed a compass, which he did not have. He roamed for days, going to ground whenever he had to. He managed to beg food here and there, and received further directions concerning the best way to get to Brussels, where he hoped to find some kind of escape organization which would help him to get over the border into Holland. He met a cheerful boy who was going fishing. The boy, once he knew he was a British officer on the run, invited him to join him in poaching some trout from a forbidden stretch of water. They took turns to keep watch and cast the line. Since they used poacher's bait and not flies, and since the sun was up, the frisky trout bit. They cooked one each in a little place where the boy lit a fire, and shared out the remainder: four each. They parted very good friends and the major went on his way.

He cooked two of the fish the following day, when he found a quiet wood and a small, unused hut. On leaving the wood, he had to do a quick bolt for new cover, on account of the sudden appearance of foraging German soldiers. He spent the whole afternoon dodging about from one retreat to another, and broke his arm when jumping from a wall. He was eventually forced to double back to the vicinity of the wood, where he lay low for some while in a ditch, nursing his injured arm. From there he spotted a couple of Germans in the near distance and, across the field, a running girl, who leapt over a gate and flew towards the ditch like a gazelle with wings.

'A gazelle? With wings?' Louise laughed.

He liked the sound of her laughter, warm and clear, but he said, 'Softly, young lady. It all seems very quiet, but not every ear may be asleep.'

They were passing the outskirts of a village. Not a light could be seen. The temperature had dropped sharply, and frost was casting its pale glitter. A hundred million pearls of it danced on the steeply shelving roof of a cottage. Somewhere a dog barked.

They left the place behind, the major covering ground with the easy stride of a soldier, Louise with her youthful swing.

'M'sieu,' said the girl, deep in thought, 'I think that, like the two men I hid in my aunt's cellar, you aren't going to be captured too easily by the Boche, either.'

'It all depends on Lady Luck, Louise Victoria, and Lady Luck is notoriously fickle.'

'But you are determined to try to reach Holland?' she asked.

'If I can get some help in Brussels,' he said.

'M'sieu?' She was a little hesitant, a little shy. 'M'sieu, could we go together? If I then got to England, or to St Petersburg, I could perhaps become a nurse and serve in a military hospital. That would be helping the friends of my country wouldn't it, and so help my country too?'

The major did not think he was prepared to involve this sweet girl in any endeavour which might land her in the arms of Germans. A safe refuge in Brussels was preferable for her. If he himself were captured, he would become a prisoner of war. What the Germans might do to her for giving deliberate assistance to Allied soldiers was uncomfortable to contemplate. Years in prison, at least. She was so young, so alone. Prison would surely destroy her.

'Louise Victoria,' he said, 'we'll take one step at a time.'

'Oh, yes, one step at a time would be quite the wisest thing, m'sieu,' she said in some elation, as if the Dutch border were nevertheless already in sight.

'So first let's see what Brussels holds for us, shall we?'

'Yes, m'sieu,' she said, and he thought what an air of refinement and good manners she had; while she thought everything was so very much better than it had been before she met him. She no longer felt desperate or alone. 'If I may say so,' she said shyly, 'I am so glad we found each other.'

'Young mam'selle,' he said, 'you're such a great comfort to a man clumsy enough to break his arm that I've come off the better of the two of us. March on, comrade.'

He gave her so much cheer that Louise said, 'Oh, it's easy to march with you.' The sky was black and limitless, the stars coldly glittering. They had covered several kilometres, and in his company every kilometre had sped beneath her feet. 'We must keep on and reach Brussels, m'sieu, for you must have your arm seen to as quickly as possible.'

'Well, that's a point, isn't it?' he said.

'M'sieu,' she said, 'do you have your own family, a wife and children, perhaps?'

'I'm not married, Louise,' he said, 'but I did discuss it tentatively with a young lady a few years ago. She was a friend of the family, a farmer's daughter. She loved horses, green fields, straight furrows, and even such things as turnips and potatoes. Anything which was to do with the land, in fact, anything which was symbolic of nature's gifts. She made it clear in the most tactful way that it wasn't her greatest ambition to marry into the army. She hinted she would much prefer me to raise horses. Or turnips.'

'Turnips?' Louise laughed softly.

'You have my word on it. She had no real desire, d'you see, to go beyond the bounds of agricultural Norfolk. I, of course, as a regular soldier, was deeply committed to an army career. I decided to give myself a year to see which way my feelings finally pulled me. It was as well I did, for when she wrote to tell me she'd become engaged I felt no inclination to shoot myself. I may have thought myself in love. Obviously, I wasn't. I attended the wedding, where my eye alighted on one of the bridesmaids. A regular charmer. My luck was out, however. She had already fallen for the bride's brother.'

'And the bride, m'sieu,' said the intrigued Louise, 'was it a farmer she married?'

The major laughed. 'No, a chemist. You see what a huge bag of tricks life is? Did you notice the bridge of my nose was a little dented? I used to box a little during my first years in the army. Came up against a fellow in an inter-regimental bout, and couldn't believe my eyes. He was all bones and scrag ends.'

'Scrag ends?'

'Hardly an ounce of flesh on him.' The major sounded amused at his recollections. 'No idea how he made the weight. I tapped him around fairly gently, not wanting to break him in half, and it gave me a chance to show off some fancy footwork. Then, *bang*. I was on the canvas with a bloody nose, and not a chance in hell – pardon me, mam'selle – of beating the count. Bag of tricks, don't you see. I never had much beauty. Even less after that.'

Louise laughed, then clapped a hand over her mouth. 'I'm forgetting to be careful,' she said, 'and we're nearer to Brussels. Brussels, m'sieu, is a city full of dragons' teeth which overnight sprout more Boche.'

'Then we must tread lightly over them, chicken, so keep marching.'

She was still not really fatigued. She was glowing from the long walk. She only hoped the soles of her shoes would last out.

* * *

63

They approached another village. She explained it wasn't possible to go round it, that they must walk through it. They had travelled the quiet byways without a hitch so far, but as they entered the little street a man came riding up behind them on a bicycle. They heard him and felt the light of his lamp on their backs. He passed them, pulled up and dismounted, leaning his cycle against the front of a cottage. Louise, in dismay, saw that he was a German soldier, a sergeant. And he was helmeted, which meant he was on duty, not riding back to his unit after an evening out. They saw the dull glimmer of his helmet and greatcoat buttons. His rifle was slung. He came towards them.

'Your papers,' he said in good French, unslinging his rifle. And as he approached them he put out a hand.

Louise had never seen a man react as fast as Major Scott did then. His sound right arm shot straight out, and the German sergeant literally walked into the blow. A clenched fist, iron-hard, struck him between the eyes. Such was the impact that he dropped, stunned, and his rifle clattered noisily. Before cottage curtains could be drawn aside in enquiry, the major had Louise by the hand and was running with her. She expected him to take the direction in which they'd been heading. But no. He took her back the way they had come. She saw the sense in that quite quickly. The German, the moment he recovered, would be up and after them, and almost certainly he would think they had continued on through the village.

The German sat up after a minute, tried to get to his feet and rolled over again, his brains addled, his nose broken and streaming blood. He staggered to his feet, shook his head, wiped away blood and remounted his cycle. But he did not ride through the village; he too went back the way he had come.

Louise and the major were pounding the verge of the road. They pulled up. Coming towards them, not more than a hundred metres away, were scores of winking bicycle lamps. There were numerous mobile cycle companies in the German Army. Louise and the major made a dash for a gap in a hedge. He pushed her through. The hedge plucked at her and she stumbled on hard, exposed roots, but she kept on her feet and dived for cover in a ploughed field. The major's injured arm was an impediment, and as he plunged through the gap after her, he caught his left foot on the roots and fell. He hit the ground, and his broken arm took the full impact. Louise heard his involuntary hiss of intense pain. He lay there, sick, sweating and dizzy.

The German cycle unit pedalled by and ran into their advance man, the sergeant. The whole unit stopped. The sergeant, his nose still streaming blood, let go with a voice full of fury and pain. Within seconds, the Germans were pedalling fast for the village.

Louise ran to the grounded major. 'M'sieu!' she gasped and dropped to her knees beside him.

He turned over very slowly, his face showing the sweat of pain, his mouth a grimace. 'My God, chicken,' he breathed, 'I've done myself no good at all.'

His teeth grated, biting on sounds which she knew were of intense pain.

'Oh, m'sieu, what can we do?' Louise felt stricken. 'We must find a doctor, quickly. Oh, I'm so sorry – can you get up? See, I'll help you. We'll find someone in the village—'

'Not yet.' He spoke through his teeth. Even in the darkness she could see that his face was white, the perspiration a wetness. 'They'll search the village. Leave it for a moment. Don't worry. Don't worry.'

But she could not help herself. Her tears were running.

The Germans were searching. They rummaged and rampaged through every house, looking for the man who had broken their sergeant's nose. They had been riding on a night exercise to Brussels. The assault on their front man was the most serious of crimes. For breaking his nose, the miscreant would receive a bone-shattering beating before being shot. There had been a girl with him. That should

66

make the pair of them not too difficult to find. So the Germans searched thoroughly.

Louise and the major heard the banging on doors, the shouts, the commands, the anger. They waited. It had been a day of running and waiting, but it was a very painful waiting this time.

'Oh, m'sieu, what can we do?' Louise kept repeating the words in her extreme worry and concern. And the major could only tell her to wait.

The Germans at least did not take long. They had already dispatched a number of men to scour the dark roads and lanes beyond the village. The rest emerged from houses, gardens and other places to reassemble in the street. Mounting their machines, they rode off in several groups to extend the search. None came back, and the village returned to quietness. Louise helped the major to his feet. They knew they could not continue their walk to Brussels for the moment. There was too much risk of meeting cycle troops wheeling about ahead of them.

'M'sieu, the village,' said Louise, 'someone there will help us, someone will find a doctor.'

'Yes, we'll risk it,' said the major heavily.

They entered the dark village. Louise wondered at which cottage to knock, and chose one which gave them easy and discreet access to the back door. It kept them out of immediate sight of any Germans who might return. The major stood aside while Louise advanced and knocked on the door. He was in a well of darkness savage with pain. The original fracture had been so badly exacerbated by his plunging fall on rock-hard ground that the bone felt smashed.

He heard the back door open.

Louise was confronted by a frigid-looking old lady, silver-haired and bony-faced, who leaned on a stick.

'Oh, madame—'

'Who are you? What do you want?' The aged voice was quiet. It was also unreceptive.

'I need a doctor, madame – I have a friend – his arm is badly broken—'

'So, you have a man with you. And you are a young lady.' Which told Louise the old woman knew she and the major were the people the Boche were looking for.

'I am sorry to have troubled you, madame.' Louise, in despair, turned away. The stick moved and touched her gently on the arm. A whisper reached her ears.

'The second house, mam'selle, go there. It is the house of my granddaughter.'

The door closed.

Louise whispered to the major. They re-entered the silent village street and found a little cobbled alley that took them round to the rear of the second house. Again the major stood aside, conscious of the spirit and resolution of a young girl whose brave comradeship now represented his one chance of help and escape.

Lightly, Louise rapped on the back door. The major heard it open, then a woman's voice, and the low murmur of conversation as Louise talked to her. Louise called softly, 'Come, m'sieu,' and they went inside. The woman closed the door quietly and took them into her living room. A single lamp cast its limited light over brown furniture.

The woman saw the sweat on the major's face and the pain in his eyes. She was in her late twenties and dressed in black. She had warm red lips and her brown eyes were large, soft and sympathetic.

'It is right, you are English, m'sieu?' she said, her French soft with the Belgian brogue.

'Yes,' said the major, very pale beneath his tan.

'You and this girl, you are the ones the Boche are looking for?'

'Yes.'

'It's true, madame,' said Louise. 'We don't wish to deceive you. We shall understand if you can't help us.'

The woman looked again at the major. 'I am told by your young friend, m'sieu,' she said, 'that you have managed to break your arm twice today. Please sit down and let us look at it.'

He sat down. The woman unbuttoned his

69

coat and opened it up. Louise bit on a cry. The left sleeve of his jersey was wet with blood. The forearm looked twice the size of the other.

'Oh,' she said in anguish.

In concern, the Belgian woman said quietly, 'If your arm is broken and also bleeding, m'sieu, it is not something of small consequence.'

She opened up a workbasket and took out a pair of scissors. With great care, she cut away the jersey sleeve above the elbow. She snipped the section along its length with even greater care. The major clenched his teeth. Louise stared in horror as the cut sleeve fell away. The forearm was swollen and misshapen, and blood was seeping where a fin of splintered bone had pierced the flesh and was still protruding.

'My God, there's a mess,' said the major painfully.

The Belgian woman regarded him, her eyes dark with concern. 'M'sieu,' she said. 'I am Eloise Herriot. My husband was killed near Ypres, fighting with our army. If you are a British officer, as mam'selle has said, I must help you. I can fetch a doctor to you, but it will take time, and it's a hospital and surgeon you need. There is a hospital not run by the Germans in a place called Ixelles, three kilometres away. They will look after you there as a patient. And also, m'sieu,' she added quietly, 'as a British officer. Could you manage to walk that distance?'

'Yes,' said the major.

'But, madame,' said Louise, 'the German cycle troops will be everywhere on the roads looking for us.'

'We will not go by any road, only by footpaths,' said Eloise Herriot.

'I know Ixelles,' said Louise.

'I can take both of you there. It will be as quick my way as by any road. If you are able to endure it, m'sieu?'

'Thank you, I'm grateful,' said the major.

'Good,' said Eloise Herriot. 'M'sieu, that jersey is not very clean. I have some iodine. It will be painful, but I think necessary.'

She went out.

Louise said, 'I'm so dreadfully worried for you, m'sieu. Your arm – oh, how bad it is.'

'A mess,' said the major greyly. 'Where's Ixelles?'

'It's a suburb of Brussels, and pretty. Oh, we shall get there quickly, you'll see.'

Madame Herriot returned with a bottle of iodine, a roll of bandage and some lint.

'Bite on your tongue, m'sieu,' she said gently, and poured the iodine over the pierced, bloodstained flesh. The major stiffened and drew a hissing breath. Lightly and loosely, she applied the lint and wound the bandage. 'To keep it covered, m'sieu.'

'Thank you.'

'Now, we will go at once,' she said. She put

71

on a hat and coat. The major got to his feet. Louise fastened his overcoat by just one button. Her eyes lifted to his and he smiled bleakly. Her tears brimmed.

Madame Herriot took them out through the back door. Almost at once she stiffened. They stood outside the door, the three of them, listening to the hum of sounds that quickly became noisy.

'In there!' whispered the Belgian woman urgently, pointing to a little shed. She herself re-entered the house, taking off her hat and coat.

Louise darted towards the shed. Faintly, the major said, 'No, Louise, behind it. The Boche open every door they see.'

She remembered the hut in the woods and how they had sat undiscovered against it. With the major, she squeezed into the space between the rear of Madame Herriot's shed and a wall, the major's teeth grating and Louise suffering for him.

A platoon of the German cycle company was back, disturbing the quiet village again with the noise of a new search. Rifle butts banged on front doors and rear doors. Louise's hands were tightly clenched, her every emotion taut with concern for a comrade she had come to need and trust. She heard the Germans rampaging through Madame Herriot's house, their shouts full of angry frustration. She heard the back door open and the sound of soldiers surging out. Booted feet thumped. The shed door was yanked violently open, and she felt the little wooden edifice tremble as a rifle butt slammed it shut again. The boots and voices retreated, then comparative silence descended.

They waited. There was still a German inside the house. Through the open back door they heard his voice.

'I have seen no one, no one.' Madame Herriot spoke decisively.

The German voice snapped an abrupt response. The front door banged shut a moment later. Louise and the major stayed where they were, while the village gradually became silent again.

'Where are you?' It was a whisper close to the shed. The two fugitives emerged. Eloise Herriot, hat and coat on, smiled. 'Good,' she murmured.

'Oh, madame, you are so brave, so encouraging,' whispered Louise, 'I shall always know where to come if I'm in trouble again.'

'Come,' said Madame Herriot, and led the way out of the little alley to the rear of the village. They took a footpath that ran along the edge of a field, and travelled by a succession of similar paths, well away from any road, Madame Herriot leading, the others following. It was a long three kilometres for the major and Madame Herriot wasted no time, but walked

73

quickly, sure of her way, even by night. Louise left the major alone in his pain. She knew conversation was the last thing he wished for at the moment. Her mama had once said, 'Words console the sick, Louise, but the badly hurt can listen only to their pain.'

She could not help worrying intensely about the major's fractured arm and the tiny protrusion of splintered bone. She was sure the pain must be very very bad. But he walked with her, in the footsteps of the compassionate Madame Herriot, who moved like a black, gliding shadow ahead of them.

They reached the outer environs of Brussels at ten thirty, and when they came close to the semi-rural suburb of Ixelles, Louise knew where she was. Madame Herriot continued on, skirting a field. She stopped a little distance from the first street.

'Stay here,' she whispered, 'I shall not be long. I must first make sure it is safe for you to be admitted.'

She glided away, and Louise and the major began one more wait. Louise gently touched his right arm. He looked down at her and saw her misty, emotional smile of encouragement. He put his arm around her shoulders, and they were together in hope and faith.

Eloise Herriot was soon back, emerging silently out of the night.

'This way,' she said and led them past the

corner of the field into the street. She pointed at a cluster of four adjoining houses on the other side. 'That door. It is a nursing school and a small hospital. It is quiet and safe. The matron is English, like yourself, m'sieu. She will do more for you than have your arm repaired. Accordingly, m'sieu, you and I may meet again, for there are some of us who help her in her work. Go now.'

'Oh, madame,' whispered Louise, 'you have taken so many risks for us. Thank you, thank you so much.' Her emotion brought a rush of warmth from Eloise Herriot, the widow of a fallen soldier.

'Oh, mam'selle,' she said, 'it has been no more than a little help, and it has been given gladly. If indeed you are in need again, you know my house. May God bestow on both of you his care and protection.' She turned to the major. 'Now, go with your young friend. When the door is opened to you, say simply that you are badly hurt. "I am badly hurt." That is all.'

Thank you,' said the major, 'we shan't forget you.'

'My husband, m'sieu, was also a soldier. God go with you.'

She walked away, back to her village and her house. She was swallowed by the darkness. Louise and the major looked at each other, then crossed the street and knocked on a door.

José, the Rumanian houseboy, opened the

door. He closed it again a few seconds later, leaving a disreputable-looking man and a fair-haired girl waiting in the passage while he went to find someone who could take charge of a problem.

He found the sister on duty, an English-woman.

'There's a man arrived, Sister, with what he says is a broken arm. It might be broken for all I know, but his clothes are villainous and his looks not much better. He has given a pass-word, but I tell you, Sister, though he may say he's only down on his luck, I'd not be surprised to hear he's murdered a few people in his time. There's a girl with him. Now in her, though she needs a wash, is an angel, and we could admit her without being in any fear of having our throats cut.'

'Thank you, José,' said the sister calmly, cutting off the Rumanian's outpouring. She knew what it was all about, as she had already spoken to Eloise Herriot. She went to interview the night callers. She spoke to them in accented French, then said, 'Come with me, please.'

She took them to the clean, quiet casualty room and told the girl to sit down. Louise sat, but only on the very edge of the chair, watching in worry and anxiety as the sister opened up the major's dreadful old coat and removed the bandage and lint. The bared forearm looked terrible to Louise, and even the calm sister was shocked. The major sweated.

'M'sieu,' said the sister, 'you—'

'I'm a British officer,' he said with an effort, 'it's fair you should know that.'

'Let us concern ourselves first with your arm,' she said. 'Follow me, please.'

The major followed her out of the room. Louise rose in a rush, quite unable to simply sit and wait. The sister made no objection to her presence. She took them along a corridor, turned left and knocked on a door. Asking them to wait, she entered the room, closing the door. She came out again in less than a minute. 'Go in, please,' she said.'

They went in. Rising from her desk chair was the matron of the hospital, a slender, aristocratic-looking woman whose dark brown hair was a burnished crown beneath her white cap, and whose eyes and expression were strikingly serene.

'Good evening,' said Edith Cavell in clear English, and smiled.

And Louise knew they had found a warm haven of care.

Chapter Four

Edith Cavell was not merely an experienced nurse and a competent matron, she was a woman of intellect and compassion. And although intellect may be more enduring than beauty, and compassion more admirable, it has to be said that Edith Cavell was also endowed with good looks.

It was Dr Antoine Depage who had brought her to Brussels. A crusty surgeon but a caring man, he opened a school of nursing in 1907 with the help of his wife in four adjoining houses in Ixelles. It was the first of its kind in Belgium, and to take charge, Dr Depage wanted a British nurse. The reputation Britain had acquired since Florence Nightingale had revolutionized and upgraded the nursing profession was second to none.

Edith Cavell applied for and secured the appointment. Dedicated, and with a flair for organization, she was absolutely right for the post. She knew Brussels and cared for Belgium and its people. Before taking up nursing, she had spent several years in the city as governess to four children of a Belgian couple, and her French was fluent. She became Matron and Directress of *L'Ecole d'Infirmières Diplômées*. In time it was more commonly referred to as Edith Cavell *Clinique*.

Miss Cavell was as much of a disciplinarian as Florence Nightingale, and as much of a humanitarian. But she had none of Miss Nightingale's hypochondriac tendencies. Her pupils and nurses knew that, despite her strictness, she was scrupulously fair. She commanded unsurpassed loyalty and respect, and to anyone in trouble she was kindness and understanding personified.

She was immaculate in her appearance. Her features were fine and classical, her grey eyes quite beautiful. And she cared in an extraordinary way for people, especially those in pain or trouble.

'*Some day, somehow,*' she once wrote to her cousin Eddy, '*I am going to do something useful. I don't know what it will be. I only know it will be something for people. They are, most of them, so helpless, so hurt, and so unhappy.*'

It was these feelings which took her into nursing and which made her so caring and dedicated. Dr Depage found her supreme as a teacher and faultless as Matron. The *Clinique* was a success. The probationers she trained became the best nurses Belgium had ever turned out.

When the war crashed into the headlines in August 1914 she was in England, taking a well-earned holiday at her mother's home in Norfolk. She had been born in the little village of Swardeston, five miles south of Norwich, over forty years earlier. On hearing that Belgium was under threat from Germany, she at once made arrangements to return to Brussels.

'My duty is over there,' she said, and went.

After the Germans had finally smashed Liège with huge siege guns, and destroyed Louvain because some of its citizens were alleged to have fired on their troops, they marched into Brussels. They brought their wounded to the hospitals. They brought some to Ixelles, where Miss Cavell received a haughty German officer with a calmness that hid her dislike of the military might he represented. She accepted the order that her *Clinique* was to take in and care for the German wounded. She was known, in any case, never to raise her voice to anyone, or to show temper, and she did not argue with the German officer.

She called her staff together and told them that it was her duty and theirs to nurse the wounded of any nation. Reluctant though her Belgian nurses were, Miss Cavell's serene insistence on a rigid adherence to the basic principles of nursing was enough to ensure that duty triumphed over unwillingness. Her nurses at this time were mostly Belgian and British. Those of German or Austrian nationality had hurriedly returned to their homelands on the outbreak of war.

What would happen to British nurses in Brussels, no one quite knew. The Germans took over all hospitals in the capital and converted the Palace into another. But they left Miss Cavell's *Clinique* alone, apart from making temporary use of its facilities. Its location, in any case, was somewhat remote.

German nurses arrived to staff the occupied hospitals, and all British nurses in Belgium were ordered to report and to be sent back home. Miss Cavell and her British nurses ignored the order. And the Germans seemed disposed to leave them alone, for they made no enquiries and asked no questions. However, they did publish an edict commanding all subjects of enemy countries, except Belgium, to report without fail for registration to the Military School in Brussels. Miss Cavell and her staff ignored this too, in the hope that what the Germans did not know, they would not worry about.

Once the last of the German wounded had been discharged from the *Clinique*, its cool and redoubtable matron carried on her work as if the occupying power were an irrelevance, even if the war was not. Indeed, because of hostilities, the instruction of probationers was more necessary than ever, and the provision of qualified nurses of vital importance.

There were also other things a British nurse in enemy-occupied Belgium might be called upon to do, over and above her normal duty.

Edith Cavell knew what she must do about Major Scott: have his badly fractured arm seen to immediately, and ensure in due time that he escaped the Germans.

Chapter Five

It was very late.

'Mam'selle?'

The quiet voice and light touch awoke Louise. She blinked away sleep. The sitting-room lamps cast a warm glow. It was Madame's own room, her retreat. Everyone addressed Edith Cavell as 'Madame'. Louise had been invited to wait in this comforting sanctuary while Major Scott was in the operating theatre. Miss Cavell, after one look at his arm, had sent for Dr Depage, then taken the major up to the theatre herself.

Louise sat up. The little ornamental clock on the mantelpiece showed the time to be past midnight. She blushed.

'Oh, forgive me, Madame, I fell asleep.'

Miss Cavell smiled. 'I'm not surprised,' she said. 'Drink this, child.' She handed Louise a mug of hot cocoa, which the girl sipped with relish. Many people in Brussels knew of the English nurse, Edith Cavell, and her *Clinique*, but Louise did not. This was the first time she had encountered the renowned Directress. How calm she seemed, how fine her looks were, and how wonderful her eyes. Her matron's dress of dark blue, gathered at the waist, was given a crisp, impeccable finish by the white collar and cuffs. Her mass of rich brown hair, brushed upwards to form a crown, shone beneath the starched white cap. Her serenity made Louise feel a little emotional, for it reminded her of her Russian mother, who had always seemed far more English than she had Russian.

'Madame,' she said anxiously, 'my friend – is he . . . ?'

'Your English friend?' Miss Cavell smiled again. The girl was sweet. 'He should be asleep now. It was a difficult operation to extract the tiny bone splinters, and traction was applied with the plaster.' Miss Cavell demonstrated by pulling hard on her left arm. She had assisted Dr Depage during the operation, as was her usual practice, 'But our foremost surgeon is a man of great experience and skill. I think he has saved the arm.'

'Oh, I hope so,' breathed Louise, 'it was so very bad, Madame. To break one's arm and then to fall on it, that was very bad indeed, wasn't it?'

Miss Cavell's eyes, warm with sympathy, also showed a little light of amusement. 'I assure you, mam'selle, your friend thought he had hardly covered himself with glory. He said that to break an arm once was stupid enough, but to break it twice made him a man of no sense at all. He's a little unusual.'

'Oh, he is most unusual,' said Louise.

Miss Cavell seated herself opposite the girl. 'Mam'selle,' she said, 'you require treatment yourself, I understand.'

'No, I'm quite all right,' said Louise ingenuously, 'it was only my unusual friend.'

'I think, all the same, that we should admit you too,' said Miss Cavell gently, and Louise realized the major must have managed to say a few words about her, probably on the way up to the theatre. To know that he had been thinking of her, despite his pain, had a warm, melting effect on her.

'Madame, I may stay, you mean?' she said emotionally.

'We can admit you and find a bed for you,' said Miss Cavell. 'What is your full name?'

'Louise Victoria Bouchet. But it's only fair to warn you, Madame, that the Boche are looking for me.'

'Oh, yes.' Miss Cavell looked as if she was already aware of that. She also looked as if it worried her not the slightest. 'Well, we won't enter your name just yet. It's late, I know, but perhaps there are a few things you'd like to tell me. If you're not too tired, child?'

She was gentle in her manner. Louise repeated her story, though not with quite the same amount of detail. Warmly and impulsively she had opened her heart to the major, giving him her story at great length. She had recounted so many of the little things which had brought back the pain and sadness, yet it had also been a strangely sweet pleasure to talk about them. Mama and Papa had lived again for her. Miss Cavell listened absorbed to the same story, her clear grey eyes warming to the girl. At the end she was soft with pity and understanding.

Here was a very brave daughter of Belgium.

'Mam'selle,' she said, 'be sure now that God will have you in his care. You are an exceptional young lady.'

'Madame, you are so kind,' said Louise.

'Major Scott has commanded me to be more than kind,' said Miss Cavell.

'*Commanded* you?' said Louise, thinking of Madame's position as Matron.

'He managed to convey an air of command,' smiled Miss Cavell.

'But what did he say?'

'That you are the most courageous young lady it's been his privilege to meet, and that I was to oblige him by not doing any less for you than Our Lord might. Or words to that effect.' Miss Cavell seemed intrigued. 'In any event, I'm afraid he attempted to elevate me far above my modest capabilities. You're a patriot, mam'selle?'

Louise said firmly, 'I would never do less for

my country than I should, Madame.'

Miss Cavell regarded the girl thoughtfully. She might have asked more questions, but Louise's need of sleep was now obvious.

'If you'll come with me,' she said, 'I'll show you where we have a room and a bed for you, and perhaps we can talk again in the morning.'

She took Louise upstairs and gave her a small room to herself on the second floor. The bed was plain and practical. To Louise it was luxury. When she had undressed and washed and put on one of the hospital nightgowns, she slipped between sheets that were fresh and crisp. It was pure bliss. For a few moments she thought about Major Scott. Then her relief that Madame had taken such good care of him drew her swiftly into sleep.

A probationer brought a simple breakfast to Louise while she was still in bed. Louise was a little astonished at such service, then became aware that the probationer thought her a patient. Sensibly, she did not deny it. Almost as soon as she had finished the meal, Miss Cavell appeared. She looked, thought Louise, quite lovely in her slender grace.

'Good morning,' smiled Miss Cavell.

'Oh, Madame,' said Louise in a warm rush, 'I'm so grateful, I had such a good sleep, and look, breakfast in bed.'

'Yes, I see.' Miss Cavell looked at her. Louise, all tiredness gone, showed the colour and vitality of the young and healthy. Her hair swamped her pillow in bright gold. 'I thought it better for you not to meet the staff yet, not until you and I have decided exactly what we must do about you.'

'Please, Madame,' said Louise, 'may I know if Major Scott is improved?'

'I haven't made my round of the wards yet, child, but had there been any crisis, I should have received a report from the night nurse. I'm afraid he won't be able to escape a certain amount of pain for a while, but a man who can swear so disgracefully over a broken arm is often the sort of man who'll put up with post-operative pain quite cheerfully.'

'Madame,' said Louise in dismay and embarrassment, 'he disgraced himself so much?'

'Under the anaesthetic,' smiled Miss Cavell.

'Do people do that, talk when they are under an anaesthetic?' asked Louise in astonishment.

'Some do. They behave like people talking in their sleep. But I'm here to discuss *your* situation.'

'Oh, please don't think I wish to ask for something I shouldn't,' said Louise earnestly, 'but may I stay here until Major Scott is better? You see, there's a little agreement we have, that I'm to help him reach the Dutch border. We hope to cross it together.'

'You're to help him do that?' Miss Cavell gently shook her head. 'No, not to be thought of.'

Well, it has been thought of, said Louise to herself, and Major Scott has not actually said no.

'But, Madame—'

'My dear child,' said Miss Cavell, 'the Germans are looking for both of you, and will take a serious view of Major Scott's attack on the sergeant. And you must see that he'll need a guide who is under no suspicion, a person who has nothing to hide and can face up to German questions without fear. We must try to find someone who can help Major Scott, but you and I must both keep very quiet about it.'

'Never, Madame, would I breathe a word,' Louise assured her, but she still did not feel prepared to withdraw from the venture herself.

'Is it your own wish to leave Belgium?' asked Miss Cavell.

Louise wondered if her mind was being read. She also wondered how to answer the question. Twenty-four hours ago, despite being hunted, she would have given a resolute no. But since meeting Major Scott and experiencing the warmth of comradeship, certain pictures in her mind were not so clear. She had gone to sleep last night feeling that in the security of Madame's *Clinique* all desperation had vanished. And Major Scott had promised – well, he had almost promised – they could escape to Holland together. But Madame was bound to be dissuasive. Many people would not approve of a man and a young lady travelling through Belgium together for days, and sharing a barn at night.

'Madame, I only wish to do what I can to help Belgium.'

Miss Cavell sighed a little. The girl was heart-breakingly young and vulnerable.

Quietly she said, 'Louise Victoria—'

'Oh,' said Louise and laughed.

'What is amusing you?' asked Miss Cavell.

'That's what he calls me,' said Louise and laughed again, then blushed, for Miss Cavell was regarding her with a little smile.

'Your name amuses you?' she said.

'Oh, no. I only meant that I've always been called Louise, just Louise, and now suddenly it's Louise Victoria.'

'But they run together so naturally,' said Miss Cavell, more and more intrigued by the girl, 'something which can't be said for Edith Louisa.'

'That is your name, Madame, Edith Louisa?'

'That is what I was christened.' Miss Cavell returned crisply to what was uppermost in her mind. 'Louise Victoria, have you considered you might help Belgium by becoming a nurse?'

'Madame!' exclaimed Louise, for she herself had thought of nursing.

'Quite a good idea, I think, don't you?' Miss Cavell's voice was mellow and her smile persuasive. It was instinctive in her to look for nursing potential in any young lady seeking a career. 'I'd be happy for you to apply for admission here as a pupil. You're aware we run a nursing school.'

'Oh, yes, but—' Louise hesitated.

'But you need time to think it over? Yes, of course you do.' Miss Cavell, however, warmed to her idea. The girl not only had courage and character, she also had need of a refuge that would keep her hidden from the Germans. 'Louise, as a probationer you'd be safe from inquisitive German authorities, though it would be wise not to enrol you under your own name. You may enter the school, in fact, chiefly for your safety, and complete your training only if you decide to try for your diploma. I think you would make a very good nurse. If so, that would represent a little victory for Belgium, wouldn't it? And you could aim for no higher vocation. It's a vocation for which God has specially moulded women.'

Louise, affected though she was by the warm appeal of Madame, was still not sure she wished to commit herself. She had something else on her mind.

'Please may I think about it?' she said.

'Please do,' said Miss Cavell, and smiled. Persuasively.

Later that morning, a doctor had a few brief words with Major Scott. The major was still lethargic from the effects of a strong sleeping draught, the pain of his arm reduced to a dulled, remote throbbing. The doctor left, but a nurse remained – a slender, lovely woman in dark blue. He had never heard of the Edith Cavell *Clinique* or of Edith Cavell, until he met her. Her face, her calm grey eyes, had floated around in his dreams. His drowsy eyes opened wider and he came to. There she was, regarding him with a slight smile and professional interest.

He took her in as acutely as his lethargy would allow. An extrovert man on the whole, he became silently trapped in his survey of the blue-uniformed English nurse. She really was the most serene-looking woman he had ever encountered. Her wide eyes were clear, her features smooth and unblemished, and a faint smile parted her firm mouth. He thought of the tranquillity of an English country sky on a summer evening, with the land at peace. He reflected pleasurably on her composure, her poise, her immaculate crown of rich brown hair and the pristine whiteness of her cap. And she had the slender but unmistakably feminine figure of a young woman.

He wondered, in returning somnolence, how old she was, how many men had fallen in love with her. Men fell quickly in love with nurses.

Far more quickly, surely, with this one. Her unlined countenance defied assessment of her years. In fact, Edith Cavell was over forty, but the bright days of youth still seemed alive in her crystal-clear eyes.

'Are you photographing me?' she asked. Her voice was cultured and mellow. She was, after all, the daughter of a Norfolk vicar, from whom she had inherited a pleasing delivery as well as a sense of Christian duty.

'I'm sorry.' The major's own voice was lazy with sedation. He made an effort to rouse himself.

Miss Cavell said, 'Last night you spoke only of your young Belgian friend, and how you made such a dreadful mess of your arm.'

'I'm a jackass,' said the major. His arm, in a hoist, felt as if it was going to be the very devil.

'Dr Depage asked you how you were a few minutes ago. I'm afraid you only muttered. So I'll ask.' Again the faint smile. 'How are we this morning?'

'Grateful,' said the major, 'even if we do hurt a bit.'

'That's part of the price,' she said. 'You're aware I'm the matron here?'

'God save the angels,' murmured the major, 'never saw a more heaven-sent one.'

'Pardon me?' said Miss Cavell, not quite catching his drowsy fantasy.

'Yes, ma'am, you're the matron.'

'Miss Cavell. Edith Cavell.'

'Yes, I remember your name was mentioned.' He made another effort, his blue eyes still dreamy. 'I'm Ned Scott. Major. The Royal Norfolks.'

'A British officer, yes. And a Norfolk gentleman.' She was interested. 'From my own county?'

'I was born in Norfolk,' said the major, 'but can't say I'm always the gentleman.'

'I think,' said Miss Cavell evenly, 'it would be better, in any case, not to enter you in the records as a British officer, gentleman or not. You speak French, I believe?'

'How do you know?' The major set aside the dull, thumping ache in his growing awareness of her. There was no one else in the ward. He thought that odd. Nor were there any nurses, only Miss Cavell. He was not to know there were certain men who slept in the ward, men who weren't patients.

'Your young friend, Louise Bouchet, has advised me French is among your other assets,' said Miss Cavell.

'Met her in a ditch,' the major murmured.

'So she said.'

'A child to be cherished,' he said.

'A little more than a child, I find,' said Miss Cavell, 'but I'll do my best for her and trust you won't fault me. I could enter you in our records as Philippe Rainier, a Belgian architect who broke his arm falling carelessly off a ladder. A compound fracture. That is my considered suggestion. Before I make up my mind, however, may I hear some French from you?'

The major, under her quiet insistence, came cheerfully to life. In French he said, 'If you please, madame, where may I catch a train to Amsterdam?'

Her eyes flickered. They looked at each other. She understood the implication of the question. But she only said, 'That, I think, is an accent acceptable to any French-speaking German. So yes, an architect will do. As an architect you'll be able to wear a respectable suit, if we can find you one.'

'I don't want to be a problem.' He made another effort and spoke clearly. 'But I must try to get back as soon as I'm fit.'

To where?' she asked.

'To my regiment.'

'Then we shall have to see what we can do,' said Miss Cavell.

'We? Who are we?'

'However,' she said, bypassing the question, 'you're our patient for the moment. Perhaps for much longer than that. Your fracture will take time to mend. But as soon as you're allowed to get up, we can talk again, in my office.'

She left, moving with a crisp rustle and upright grace. The major drifted off.

Louise asked if she might see him. Quietly,

Miss Cavell asked in turn if Louise would mind waiting until tomorrow. Major Scott had been newly sedated, for it was necessary at this stage to ensure he slept and rested, to help him through the worst of his pain.

The major, fitful the second night, dozed and woke, and dozed again.

He awoke once more towards dawn. The fingers of sleep still tugged at his senses, but the blight of pain pulled him to consciousness. It was dark; the eastern horizon was not yet touched by the pale light of the new day. He became aware of the murmuring voice of the night nurse as she shook the shoulder of a sleeping man and then quietly left the ward.

Another voice murmured – a man's voice.

'Rogers, get up. And get that sleepy sod Russell on his feet. Fifteen minutes, that's all we've got. Outside her office at five thirty, you hear? Either of you not there by then, I'll saw your heads off, even if she don't. I'm off for me shave. You two stay bristly, like she said. Come on, rise an' shine, dozy.'

A mattress sighed as a body moved. A sleepy voice mumbled incoherently. The major, suspended in the fog of medicated limbo, was not sure whether the sounds were of dreams or reality. Stockinged feet padded swiftly over the polished floor of the ward. The door opened and closed.

A yawning, grumbling whisper came from a corner. 'Come on, Russ, for Chrissake.'

'Eh? Oh. Right.' The awakened man was instantly alert. His bed creaked as he divorced himself from its comfort.

Clothes rustled. The major, in subconscious thankfulness, felt himself sinking. Only brief whispers reached his closing mind, entering lazily.

'Where's the corp?'

'Shavin'.'

'Hope there's no trouble, for her sake.'

'She'll see us clear. Christ, I love that woman.'

'That'll please your missus.'

The whispers floated. The major's mind closed and he went to sleep again.

Downstairs, on the ground floor, Edith Cavell fastened her cape and waited for three men. Three men who were to be put on an escape route to Holland.

Chapter Six

During the morning the major lay pondering, as his hoisted arm throbbed. The ward floor had received its daily polishing; the beds were made. The doctor had paid him a visit, and Miss Cavell had had a few brief words with him. But, damn it, where were the other patients? Six beds in addition to his own had been occupied last night, he would swear to it, for all the sedation. Some of the occupants had gone in the night. Discharged? By night? Never.

He wondered about the whispers he had heard.

By God, those men had been British soldiers. He'd swear to that too.

The door opened. A muscular young man came in, his dressing gown neatly tied, his hair neatly brushed.

'Major Scott?' he said. 'Present my compliments, sir. Lieutenant Price of the Berkshires.'

'What?'

'I've been advised of your identity, sir. Sorry

about your arm. Pretty nasty, I understand, so no one bothered you yesterday. Miss Cavell said not to, in fact.'

'Sit down, Lieutenant,' said the major. The lieutenant took the bedside chair. 'You don't look wounded. Were you?'

'Not a scratch, sir. But came out with some of the men on the wrong side of the Ypres salient. Gave the Jerries the slip, though. Landed up here. Self and three men. The men went this morning. I'm off in a couple of days.'

'What's going on, for God's sake?' asked the major.

'Yes, sir, she thinks you ought to be put in the picture.'

'She?'

'Madame.' Lieutenant Price grinned. 'Miss Cavell.'

'I see.' The major jerked his senses into being. 'Well, put me in the picture, will you, Lieutenant?'

'The long and short of it is, sir, she's got an escape organization going.'

'She's what?' The major took sharp stock of the urbane lieutenant.

'It's a fact, sir.' Lieutenant Price grinned again.

'Holy God,' said the major, 'she's a nurse. She can't do things like that.'

'Not an army nurse, sir. She's not bound by military rules. I've been here a week. She's got me scheduled for a trip to Holland in two days. I'll tell you all I know. Won't take a jiffy.'

'Never mind a jiffy,' said the major, 'just take your time. I'm not scheduled to go anywhere myself for a while.'

What Lieutenant Price was able to tell was only part of the picture. The outline of the whole had begun to be drawn seven months ago, in October 1914. Two soldiers of the Cheshire Regiment, Colonel Bodger and Sergeant Meachin, were wounded at Mons but escaped capture, and had been hidden by a Belgian widow in her garden loft since August. In October, the Germans, tipped off by an informer, descended on the good lady to search her house and garden. However, at the first sign of the approaching Germans, Colonel Bodger and Sergeant Meachin slipped unobserved from the loft, and with the kind of audacity that serves such men well, mingled with the crowd of interested onlookers instead of bolting.

The Germans found nothing, but were still suspicious. The two Cheshire men could not endanger their guardian angel further, and two nuns took them off to a convent in Wasmes. From there they were escorted to Mons, where a photographer provided them with fake identity documents. Another Belgian friend took them to Brussels, where Marie Depage, wife of Dr Depage, recommended him to entrust the soldiers to Edith Cavell.

Miss Cavell took them in. Colonel Bodger had a wound in the foot which had had little attention and now required a major operation. Sergeant Meachin's wound was from a spent bullet, which had rendered him unconscious but left him with only a grazed forehead. However, one never knew, and Miss Cavell pursued the reasonable supposition with Sister White, who was also English, that medical examination might bring something more serious to light than a healed graze. The Germans need not be advised of these two admissions. That was understood? Sister White understood.

Miss Cavell decided to help the men escape to Holland. From the moment they were brought into her office, she was resolute in her belief she could not do otherwise. In making her decision, Miss Cavell put her own life at risk. It was a risk shared by many Belgians. Hundreds of French, British and Belgian soldiers had been on the run from the Germans since the opening battles of the war. They dotted the face of Belgium, and Belgians sheltered them, shared their limited food with them, and did their best to get them over the border into neutral Holland. It was a resistance movement – involuntary, instinctive, courageous – but it was not co-ordinated. It was the work of defiant individuals, men and women with a natural desire to help Allied soldiers in need.

A well-run escape organization was required. But who might lead it? Someone of ingenuity and authority, certainly, but not the kind of figure the Germans would automatically suspect. Someone who could command the vital qualities of courage and loyalty, who had a genius for organization and could present the perfect front.

Edith Cavell loved her country quite passionately, and had a great affection for Belgium. She could not have denied help to any Allied soldiers. She sheltered the two Cheshire men in her *Clinique* for a fortnight, and saw to it that Colonel Bodger had his operation. The co-operation she needed from her staff was given without question, and she busied herself devising ways and means to get both men safely on the journey to Holland. That meant making contact with Belgians she knew and could trust. With their assistance she arranged for Colonel Bodger to travel part of the way by barge, since he was still lame, and for Sergeant Meachin to go on foot.

Miss Cavell herself took them on the first leg of their journey and handed them over to their guides. By their separate ways they reached Ghent. Joining up, they entered an *estaminet* with their guide. While there, Germans burst in. Sergeant Meachin and the guide escaped; Colonel Bodger, not so mobile, was captured. Sergeant Meachin continued on, crossed into

Holland, landed in the welcoming arms of the far from neutral Dutch, and subsequently reached England.

One captured, one home to fight again. An escape organization had come into being, for the venture had been a planned and co-ordinated one. Impressed Belgians spread whispers. Individuals sat up and took notice. Almost at once other Allied soldiers on the run began to arrive at the *Clinique*, brought discreetly by people who had heard that Madame would take care of them. Miss Cavell, having committed herself, refused help to none. Those with wounds were genuine patients; others simply acted the part. Funds necessary to the organization were donated by well-wishers, and such was Edith Cavell's personality that she actually persuaded her nurses to give up their salaries to the cause.

Prince Reginald de Croy and his sister, Princess Marie, who lived in a medieval chateau at Bellignies, just a few miles inside an occupied part of France, despatched Allied soldiers, in the care of guides, with dangerous regularity to the *Clinique* in Ixelles. Whether or not Edith Cavell felt the regular comings and subsequent goings of such men could not escape notice, she displayed no anxiety. She had made up her mind what she should do, and she did it with the cool resolution of a woman fearless of the consequences.

Fugitives put on the escape route to Holland were taken from Brussels to Vilvoorde, then to Malines. From Malines it was either north-west to Antwerp, or north-east to Turnhout or a little place called Overpelt. It was from Antwerp or Turnhout or Overpelt that the final dash to the border was made. Most of the men were successful.

The soldiers all risked capture; the guides risked their lives. They had great nerve and courage, these men and women who were so loyal to Edith Cavell and the cause of the Allies. Perhaps she alone could have commanded men and women of this calibre. She herself escorted soldiers when they left the *Clinique* to rendezvous with the guides, usually setting out between five and seven in the morning, when most of Ixelles was still sleeping.

Inevitably, Miss Cavell became the most important person in the organization. She ran the *Clinique*, which provided such suitable cover. And she was the great symbol of hope to all those men who wished to get back to their countries and renew their fight against Germany. She was warmly affected by the courage of these soldiers willing to return to the horrors of the war.

Every member of her staff was faithful to her but fearful for her. The risks she ran were frightening. How was it possible for such a venture to escape notice and discovery indefinitely? Miss

Cavell said that whatever happened, she was in the hands of God.

Her probationers knew nothing of the organization. She did not want any of them involved in the smallest way. Her responsibility to them was to turn them into efficient nurses, not embroil them in intrigues they might have been too young or too unsophisticated to cope with. She cherished their innocence, for her own years of growing up had been carefree.

Germans did call at the *Clinique* one day. They searched the place, but found no fugitives. A prearranged warning system had operated perfectly, and British soldiers resident at the time were either spirited away or accepted by the Germans as genuine patients of Belgian nationality.

But the German visit, perhaps, meant someone had begun to talk.

'So that's it, is it?' said Major Scott when Lieutenant Price had finished his account of a deadly dangerous enterprise, which he obviously thought just a cracking adventure yarn. 'Holy God, man, does she realize what she's doing?'

'I think she's got her head well screwed on, sir.'

'I hope it stays there. How many men is she sheltering here at the moment?'

'Sixteen, sir. In here and other wards.'

'Well, keep them away from the gunpowder, Lieutenant.'

'Sir?' said the lieutenant. Then he grinned. 'Oh. Yes. Right, sir.'

Louise was given permission during the afternoon to visit Major Scott. At the same time, Miss Cavell advised her it would be wise if no one else in the *Clinique* knew her real name. She must assume another. Between them they decided on Anna Marie Descamps.

'And Major Scott,' said Miss Cavell, 'is to be known as Philippe Rainier. When you need to, for the benefit of others, that's what you must call him.'

A nurse took Louise up to the men's surgical ward, which contained only two patients. One, his head bandaged, was just leaving. Seeing Louise, he was tempted to stay, but a pointed glance from the nurse sent him on his way. The other patient was lying on his bed, looking at the ceiling. His left arm, plastered and bandaged, was high in a hoist. Louise tiptoed up as the nurse left her.

'I see you,' said Major Scott.

'Well, that isn't fair, not when you're looking at the ceiling. Oh, m'sieu, your arm, it's enormously wrapped up. Is it very painful?'

During his fighting days in Flanders and his subsequent wanderings, he had become tanned and weathered. Beneath his tan was now the pallor of pain. The plaster was open at the point where part of the surgical wound had been left unstitched to allow the pus to escape. But the major smiled at his young friend. 'Oh, I've been patched up very professionally,' he said, 'and they've taken care of you too, haven't they?'

'You've noticed my appearance has improved, m'sieu?'

'I didn't think there was all that much room for improvement,' he said, 'only that, like me, you were in need of a wash.'

Louise smiled. She was so glad his arm would get better. It must be awkward for him, hoisted up like that, as well as painful, but he seemed quite cheerful.

'To be truthful, I was in need of a bath,' she said, 'and I've had two.'

'Oh, a pretty picture, Louise Victoria.'

She had been given a complete change of clothes and underwear. A green frock with a white collar ran softly over her astonishingly good figure. The major, dwelling on her rounded bosom, remembered the warmth of her body close to his in the ditch. He frowned at himself. Good God, what was he thinking of? She was not long out of school.

But Louise, though she might have blushed had she been privy to his thoughts, would not have been displeased. She was very feminine. And in the week that had culminated in her walk through the darkness with him, she had grown up.

'You are sure your arm is satisfactory?' she asked.

'Well, I liked it better before I broke it,' said the major, 'but it'll do. Won't you sit down, chicken?'

Louise seated herself.

'They have looked after both of us, haven't they?' she said. 'See, they have even given me new clothes – oh, and such a pretty petticoat because my own was – well, rather torn—'

'How pretty?' asked the major solemnly.

'I am to show you?' blushed Louise.

The major could not resist that blush. 'If you insist,' he said.

'But I am not insisting,' protested Louise, 'I – oh, you are joking with me.'

'Not at all.'

'*Mon Commandant*, I ask you to take my word for it.'

'That it's pretty? Very well.'

She laughed, then said, 'Oh, what do you think? Madame says I should enrol here as a pupil and become a nurse. Do you think I should?' She asked because she had no one else to turn to. She had cousins in Belgium, and relatives in England and Russia, but they were all inaccessible. She also had a widowed paternal grandmother, who had gone to live in the South of France when war broke out, wanting nothing to do with its horrors and privations.

'It's a first-class idea,' said the major. 'You must say yes to Miss Cavell.'

'The truth is, *mon Commandant*,' confided Louise, 'I don't think Madame is inclined to let me say no, especially as she feels I'll be safe from the Boche as a pupil here. We have decided I might enrol under the name of Anna Marie Descamps. Anna Marie is the name of a family servant.'

'Anna Marie sounds a nice, safe name,' said the major, 'though I like Louise Victoria better. You think highly of Miss Cavell? She's a striking woman, isn't she?'

Louise thought Madame a figure of professional elegance. 'Oh, perhaps, in her own way,' she said.

'Exquisite shape,' murmured the major, and Louise thought him a little far away. What was the matter with him? He was speaking as if Madame were a young woman. It was true she had the figure of a young woman, but—

'Of course, she wears very well, m'sieu,' she said. She considered her own figure quite as good as Madame's, if not better. She sat up straighter, and her bodice adjusted noticeably to her prouder posture. But the major had his eyes on the ceiling again. It quite piqued Louise. It also disturbed her a little. She had never before wished to have a man look at her in a special way. Such feelings were very new to her.

'Exceptional woman,' said the major.

'Yes,' said Louise, 'and she will have to be very exceptional in her discretion concerning you, won't she? I mean, you are English. She will have to keep both of us hidden from the Boche. You and I,' she added with a little smile, 'we are still rather in the same boat together, aren't we?'

'Except that we shall have to let Madame do the rowing.'

'It is to be hoped the water doesn't get too rough,' said Louise. 'Will you be able to get up when the pain has gone?'

'I'll be up when the doctor says so, and Madame allows it.'

'Oh,' sighed Louise, 'we are trapped, both of us. You must obey Madame, and I must do as she suggests. But, of course, we must not forget our agreement.'

'What agreement?' The major found it better to be talking with her than having only the pain as company.

'M'sieu, when we were walking together in Brussels, we agreed you and I should go to Holland, and perhaps from there to England or Russia.'

'Dangerous,' said the major, 'very dangerous. The Boche are on to you, and they'll have circulated a description of you. Louise Victoria

Bouchet, seventeen, with big brave eyes, fair hair and beautiful.'

'Beautiful?' Louise's big brave eyes opened wide. 'Who is beautiful?'

'All seventeen-year-old girls are beautiful, Louise Victoria. Some more than others, of course, which makes them very easy to spot.'

'You are joking again,' she said.

'Was your mother as beautiful as you said?' asked the major.

'Oh, yes,' said Louise.

'Well, there you are, then. You're her daughter. You're very distinctive. The Boche will pounce on you. So you must stay here and not try to cross borders. And there are pupils in the school, I imagine, girls near to your own age.'

'*Mon Commandant*,' said Louise, 'it isn't in the best interest of comradeship to throw me to the lions.'

She made the remark seriously. He considered it seriously.

'The pupils are lions?' he said.

'Among them, I shall only be a lamb. I shall be eaten.'

'Be of good cheer, Louise Victoria,' he said, 'they'll soon discover they're biting off far more than they can chew.'

Louise laughed, her eyes bright. But there was a little emotion beneath the brightness. She had acquired a comrade, a man who could lift her out of sadness and bring her to laughter again.

'Matron,' said the major the following morning, 'where are the other patients?'

'I think you know about certain other patients,' said Miss Cavell, 'for I presume you aren't referring to some sick civilians in another ward. We have a reading room. Men not receiving treatment congregate there most of the time.'

The reading room, a recreational retreat for fugitive soldiers, was on the ground floor and at the rear of the *Clinique*. From there the men could effect a quick exit into the garden if an emergency arose, and make their getaway over the garden wall. It was not possible for Germans, or anyone else, to enter the *Clinique* by the rear.

'You're a cool one,' smiled the major.

Miss Cavell regarded the patient in her unruffled way. If everything Louise Bouchet had told her was true, he was a fairly cool character himself, and good to have around in a crisis. He had a strong, rugged face, and a mouth of masculine determination. He would want a woman to be a woman, but shake his head if she proved a helpless one. His blue eyes were frank and direct. She felt a little regret that so many years had been so full of dedication.

'There are things one must do in wartime,' she said.

'You're at risk,' he said.

'So are you, Major Scott. So are many people. Because of the war, that is unavoidable.'

'I don't give a damn—'

'Now, Major Scott.'

' – for the right people being at risk. You're a nurse. You're far more necessary to this unholy world than I am.'

'I am a very inadequate person,' said Edith Cavell.

'I don't think so. When can I get up and talk to you?'

'In a fortnight, perhaps.'

'Holy angels,' said the major, 'a fortnight?'

'I shall look forward to it,' said Miss Cavell, her smile warm. 'I really must go now. You're a commendable patient, Major.'

'You're an exceptional matron,' said the major.

Chapter Seven

Five weeks had passed, and Louise was now a probationer. Having given the question of enrolment earnest thought, she came to the satisfying conclusion that it would do no harm to receive tuition, even though it might be for a short time only. Primarily set on escape now, she could complete her training elsewhere. As a qualified nurse she would be able to work in a Belgian field hospital. King Albert was still in command of the surviving Belgian forces, providing them with the leadership and inspiration which kept them fighting with the French and British.

She did not really think that when Major Scott made his bid for the Dutch border he could justifiably leave her behind. They were comrades; he had said so. Comrades should be together. In any case, the Boche were quite capable of reaching into the school and pulling her out. Madame was not omnipotent. She could not guarantee that any wanted pupil would be safer in the school than on an escape route with Major Scott. Major Scott was so resourceful. If anyone could get her to Holland, he could. And if anyone could show him the way, she could. She did not want to desert Belgium. But she wanted to help, and becoming a nurse at the Front would be her best way of helping.

She enrolled as Anna Marie Descamps, and Miss Cavell, such was her affection for the orphaned girl, squeezed time out of her busy days to give her extra lectures. Louise quickly caught up with the most recent intake of pupils. Most of the other probationers were Belgian. The war had killed the school's normal international flavour.

She was somewhat dismayed, however, by the strictness of the rules. She was unable to visit Major Scott except at very fixed times, and then only when a sister or Madame herself gave permission. She was unaware that the rules ensured there was no possible way probationers would discover certain patients had nothing wrong with them. Miss Cavell did not want Louise to be burdened with the knowledge that there were other fugitive soldiers in the *Clinique* besides the major.

The restrictions aroused mutinous impulses in Louise. Madame spoke just a little firmly to her. Louise sighed. It was only that Major Scott was a very special friend—

'Yes, I know,' said Miss Cavell, 'but you do see him from time to time.'

'Oh, Madame, I hardly like to say so,' said Louise, 'but from time to time seems very infrequently.'

'Does it?' Miss Cavell considered that with a gravity that hid her smile. 'Well, you may visit him this afternoon, then.'

'Thank you, Madame,' said Louise with deep gratitude, and Miss Cavell wondered about the extent of the girl's devotion to the major, and whether its emotional nature might not lead to heartbreak. Louise was so obviously in need of love.

Miss Cavell managed to get a letter smuggled out to her cousin Eddy in England. Towards the end of it she wrote, *'There are other things besides nursing to do here now and I am helping in a way I may not describe to you. There are many things I may not write until we are free again.'*

It meant she was fully committed to the escape organization. As a Red Cross nurse and not an army one, she was not bound by the terms of the Geneva Convention, which prohibited all military medical personnel from playing any part in war except ministering to the wounded. It was neither against her code nor her conscience to do what she could for Allied soldiers on the run. And what she was doing was giving them the opportunity to rejoin their units in the fight against Germany.

By mid-June she was still sheltering all the men brought to her, still maintaining necessary contact with associates, and still taking upon herself the responsibility of escorting fugitives to their rendezvous with guides.

Lieutenant Bergan, an officer of the German secret police, was not entirely ignorant of the Edith Cavell *Clinique*. But he was a busy man, and his time was taken up with investigations into the activities of suspected spies or Belgian underground movements. It was a while before he was able to spare a few minutes to confer with Detective Henri Pinkhoff on the subject of the *Clinique*. They decided it might be worth checking.

Which meant the drums had begun to roll for Edith Cavell.

Miss Cavell, dedicated and absorbed, did not hear them.

Major Scott was up and about. His splintered bone was healing very slowly, still giving trouble, but at least he was not tied to his bed. He was able to see more of Edith Cavell. Her serenity, her purposefulness and her complete lack of fear for herself, all fascinated him. In turn, she warmed to him and gave him time she was always sure she could not spare, but did.

On her behalf, he kept a sharp eye on the

behaviour of resident soldiers. Some were inclined to be rowdily and indiscreetly high-spirited.

The reading room was noisy one morning with horseplay. A Belgian nurse was begging for peace and quiet. A young French officer, putting his arm around her waist, reduced her pleas to incoherence as he attempted to swing her into a waltz to the improvised music of whistling men. It was quite against all the regulations, as well as Miss Cavell's unwritten code. It stripped from the nurse her necessary and precious cloak of authority.

There were a dozen men present, two French and the rest British. They were a special breed of men, the kind who had used inventive determination to evade capture, who preferred to live dangerously in their attempt to return to France or Britain. They could have given themselves up and settled for the safety of a prisoner-of-war camp. But that meant sustained boredom. To them, war and the fates were a challenge. And a pretty nurse was fair game. In high spirits, they tilted at the windmill of regulations and orders, and uproar prevailed.

'Stop it, please,' gasped Nurse Duval, spinning in the arms of a Frenchman, 'stop it!'

The door opened and Major Scott walked in. He came to a halt. The uproar subsided. The silence touched a nerve or two, and a soldier shuffled his feet. The major's arm was in a sling, his dressing gown old and a faded grey, but he was the senior of the three officers currently resident, and he looked what he was: a man who knew how to command others. He fixed a cold blue eye on the French officer. The Frenchman released the nurse. She, flushed and embarrassed, turned to the major.

Before she could speak, he said, 'I apologize for my colleagues, nurse. Will you leave them to me?'

Nurse Duval smiled. Major Scott was an officer of breezy, rugged cheer. But she knew it was a mistake to think he could not be formidable.

'Willingly,' she said and made her exit, closing the door behind her.

The major addressed the men.

'You're a rabble,' he said.

'Sir,' said an uneasy soldier, 'it was only—'

'Only? Only what? Nothing short of damned disgrace. What the devil d'you think you're up to? You know what they're doing for us here, don't you?'

'Just a bit of a lark, sir,' said a man of the East Surreys.

'A bit of a lark? I'll knock your damned head off,' said the major. 'All right, a nurse is pretty. All right, hold her hand, if she'll let you, and read her a sonnet—'

A man guffawed. The cold blue eyes silenced him.

'Sorry, sir,' he said.

'You'd better be,' said the major. 'Nurses are special, you know that. Particularly, they're special to us, to every soldier. That doesn't mean you can't flirt with them. That's a traditional pastime, and they'd think there was something wrong if you gave it up. But, by God, when they tell you to behave, you'll behave. When they tell you to shut up, you'll shut up.'

The young French officer, dignity outraged at having to take all this in common with other ranks, drew himself up, his face flushed.

'*Mon Commandant*, you – you—'

'Yes?' said the major icily.

'I apologize,' said the Frenchman, coming sensibly to earth.

'That's a good fellow,' said the major generously.

'I—'

The door opened again, abruptly. Nurse Duval reappeared, her expression tense. 'Two Germans are here. Quickly!'

The men were out of the room within seconds. Moments later they were running through the garden, mounting the walls and leaping behind them. The major, not up to leaping walls, went quietly back to his ward to become a Belgian patient by the name of Philippe Rainier, with a forged document to back up his identity and enough facility with French to convince any German.

The two German callers did not appear in the wards, however. A sister put her head in after a while to signal that all was clear, and the major asked her if he might see Miss Cavell. Miss Cavell received him almost at once. It was a concession on her part, since every day for her was a full and busy one. But she had made such concessions previously to Major Scott, and to Louise too.

She asked him to sit down. He did so, and they regarded each other over her desk. He felt the visit of the Germans must have alarmed her, but she gave no sign of it. Her look was one of calm enquiry.

'Well, Major Scott?' she said.

'May I ask, Matron, what those two Germans wanted?'

'It was just a routine call,' she said, 'to ask a few questions.'

'What about?'

'The administration of the school and *Clinique*, the composition of the staff and which doctors gave their services. They also made a routine check of our records. They were quite polite, and it was all very harmless.'

'Hm,' said the major. 'I don't like it. Were they from the German army?'

'No. From the police department.'

His look was enquiring, searching. Miss Cavell's clear eyes seemed quite untroubled.

'You're hedging,' said the major.

'I'm doing no such thing. Oh, you mean which department? I believe the badges they showed identified them as members of the German secret police.'

'Oh, my God,' said the major.

'Major Scott, it was purely routine—'

'It always is, to start with. Aren't you worried?'

'We are in God's hands,' said Miss Cavell confidently.

'What if you find yourself in German hands, not his?' said the major, at which she shook her head gently, as if reminding him that whatever happened her Maker would not desert her. The major sighed. She was flying a capricious kite, and flying it high. In the first real storm it would plunge broken to the ground. 'Matron, there are fifteen of us here at the moment. I suggest you allow us all to leave this evening. Some of us might be caught, but I fancy the prospects of most.'

'Without the right help,' said Miss Cavell, 'the prospects for all of you are dismal.'

'I'm more worried about you than about any of us.'

Her smile was warm.

'Thank you,' she said, 'but you must see that just as you have a duty to escape, I have a duty to help you.'

'Miss Cavell, your duty is to the sick.'

'And to my country, Major.'

'Escape work is for others.' His concern was

intense, born of a deep regard for her.

'It's for all who wish the Allies well,' she said gently. 'Please be a dear man, please believe in me and let me do what I can for you and all the other men who want to get to Holland.'

'I believe very much in you,' said the major.

'Thank you,' she said again. 'You know, of course, your arm must take its time, that we can't get you away until that bone is strong again.'

'I shan't fret too much,' he said cheerfully. He got to his feet. 'It means I'll be able to keep my eye on you all the time I'm here.'

'I've never thought I needed a keeper,' said Miss Cavell.

'No, just a close and caring friend,' he said, which raised a slight flush in her. 'I think I'll take a walk one day. I haven't been outside this place since I arrived.'

'You have your identity document,' she said, 'be sure to take it with you. But be very careful, wherever you go.'

'Now there's a shining example of the drowning sailor warning the sinking passenger,' he said.

She was smiling as he left the office. Major Scott was not a man of elegant social graces, but his personality was warm and likeable. And he had a distinctive air of command. The girl, Louise, perhaps saw him as her cheerful Rock of Gibraltar.

*   *   *

Lieutenant Bergan, on receipt of his men's report on the Edith Cavell *Clinique*, did not feel anything very significant had come to light, except the revelation that its matron was British. That was hardly a major discovery. Perhaps it was interesting, though. He made a request to Detective Pinkhoff. Someone might find out, perhaps, if the matron, Edith Cavell, had registered as an enemy alien.

Well, it was not a request, of course. It was an order.

Louise, having finished some evening work in one of the women's wards, walked to the stairs that led to the students' rooms. A man appeared, wearing a dressing gown over shirt and trousers. A patient. She was quite willing to obey the rule which precluded her from socializing with male patients, as long as Major Scott remained the exception, and so she tried to continue on her way. But the man detained her. He was dark and hollow-chested, his dressing gown loose on his thin figure.

'Nurse,' he said with a friendly smile, 'how pretty.'

'If you please, m'sieu,' said Louise, 'I wish to pass.'

'Of course,' he said, his French fluent, but he made no attempt to stand aside. Instead, he began to talk to her as if they had been friends for years. He expounded on the merits of her uniform, on the age of his dressing gown, the comforts of the *Clinique*, how well he was being looked after and how angelic the nurses were. Why, with such angels he could fly. His appreciation of their qualities was enormous. He was a Pole, he said, a subject of the Tsar of Russia, and had come by a roundabout way to the *Clinique* after escaping from a working party of other prisoners from Russia. He put a finger to his lips and winked. To be so far from home in occupied Belgium, he said, would have been very uncomfortable had it not been for the kindness of Madame and her staff. Madame was the kindest of ladies. And to run into so pretty a nurse now was a joy. Who was she?

Louise might have been more receptive to so friendly a man had she been less intelligent than she was, and if recent experiences had not taught her to look twice at people. She decided the Pole was too friendly to be true. And his bright eyes were inquisitive in a way that was at variance with his smile.

'I'm a probationer, m'sieu,' she said, 'a student nurse.'

'Ah, you are one of those being taught by Madame. How tireless she is, how busy, with so many different things to look after, and so many patients coming and going, nearly all of them men. Have you seen how they come and go? What do you think of it all?'

Louise knew nothing of Allied soldiers who came and went. She knew only that Major Scott was British and that one day Madame would help him escape.

'Patients do come and go, m'sieu,' she said.

'Between you and me, mam'selle,' he said, with another wink, 'I'm grateful Madame took me in, for I'm Polish, as I said. We're fighting with the Russians against the Germans.'

'Madame would be concerned only with your health, m'sieu, not who you were,' said Louise.

'True, true,' he said, and looked strangely subdued.

Another man appeared. It was Major Scott, on the trail of the Polish man, who a soldier had said was wandering about.

'Koletsky, what are you doing here?'

Louise thought the major quite without his usual warmth. He looked cold, even dangerous, in the way he eyed the Pole.

'I'm doing nothing, nothing at all,' said the Pole, but his eyes shifted around uneasily. 'I'm merely passing the time with this young nurse.'

'Go to your ward,' said the major.

'There's no harm done, I—'

'Do as I say.' The major was icy. The Pole, nervous departed.

'You frightened him,' said Louise.

'I don't trust the fellow,' said the major.

'M'sieu?'

'Come in here, chicken,' he said, and took her into a small room with a single bed. It was the room Louise had occupied during her first days in the *Clinique*. 'What was the fellow saying to you?'

'Oh, he was so talkative it was like a gabble,' said Louise with a smile. 'All about the *Clinique*, what a fine place it was, how gracious Madame had been to take him in, especially as he was Polish, and how busy she was with so many men patients coming and going—'

'A fox, damned if he isn't,' said the major.

'M'sieu, what did he mean about Madame taking him in despite his being Polish?'

'He's a capering idiot as well,' said the major, 'that's the meaning.'

'I said Madame would be concerned only with his health, not who he was.'

'Louise,' he said, giving her a smile, 'you're the best and most intelligent of all young ladies. The fox says he's Polish. He may be. It's a safe nationality for a planted informer to assume, with genuine Poles about as plentiful here as water taps in a desert.'

'What are you saying?' asked Louise in astonishment. 'That the Germans have sent someone here to spy on Madame and her patients? Oh, on you, perhaps. Someone has talked about you? Oh, if so, we must go—'

'No, don't worry, sweet girl.' The major's smile was wry. He had used his tongue too freely in front of his young comrade. He must remember that Edith Cavell did not want innocents involved. 'I simply don't like the fellow.'

'Nor I,' said Louise. 'Madame must send him packing. *Mon Commandant*, you and I have much in common. We agree on many things, we are both good at eluding the Boche, we both respect Madame and we both dislike the Polish man.'

'Yes, that's all something to remember, Louise.'

'To remember?' Her brightness dimmed. 'Does that mean you are going to leave?'

'Not yet,' he said, and he looked at her and wondered about her, about the years that had meant so much to her, and the year that had been so tragic for her. He wondered about the Germans, who wanted her. When he eventually went on his way to Holland, could he take her with him, could he risk it? She was not really safe here, for her compassionate guardian, Edith Cavell, was not safe herself. He felt deep concern for both of them. He was acutely conscious of the youth of one and the blind devotion to duty of the other. 'Perhaps, Louise Victoria, we should go together, you and I.'

Louise drew a deep breath and said, 'I would rather face all the dangers of escaping, m'sieu, escaping with you, than just be left with memories.'

She moved to the window. The evening was

lovely. Summer was casting its fragrance and showering its gold. Belgium was full of warmth and colour. She wished she might walk where Ixelles opened out into green fields, with the major beside her. Her parents had loved to walk, especially together. The people who would not go from one house to the next without taking their carriage did not know what they were missing. She had grown up enjoying the pleasure of walking over paths and fields, cliffs and hills.

The major joined her at the window. He said nothing; neither did she. But she did not feel it was because they had nothing to say. Ixelles was quiet too. And the only movement was that of a man slowly sauntering.

'What are you thinking of, Louise Victoria?' he asked, after a while.

'Only about what a lovely long walk it will be.'

'To where?'

'To Holland,' said Louise, 'by way of Overpelt, where I have friends who could help us cross the border.'

Chapter Eight

Major Scott dressed, putting on a dark grey suit supplied by Miss Cavell. Appropriate civilian clothes for her soldiers materialized by ways and means she never disclosed. No one asked. It was accepted that the less everyone knew about all her contacts and sources of help, the better.

Coming down the stairs from the men's wards, the major saw Louise in the ground-floor corridor, talking to another probationer. Louise at once persuaded her to depart upstairs. She approached the major, her eyes bright. He looked like a professional man in his suit, collar and tie. A homburg hat was in his right hand. His left arm was in its sling.

'Hello,' he said, 'where have you been lately?'

Louise looked around. There was no one about, and so she indulged in a little indignation. 'Where? Where? In my prison, in the school. Yes, and you helped to put me there, and I don't have a moment to myself. Oh, that's a sad thing, *mon Commandant*, putting one's comrade into the clutches of people who simply work one to death.'

The major did his best to keep his face straight. He failed. 'Chicken, your feathers are showing,' he smiled.

'I'm not surprised, I'm always being ruffled up,' said Louise. She was happy to see him, and wondering if she might ask Madame if she could spend an hour or two with him. 'Madame has said I'm showing exceptional promise, but I still can't visit you unless I get permission. If things go on like this, we shall begin to forget each other.'

'I doubt if I'll forget you,' said the major.

'Oh, remembering one's comrade is important, isn't it?' said Louise earnestly. 'For a woman of my age – I am eighteen – well, I'm almost eighteen – it's not easy to know what are the really important things of life. Of course, I am sophisticated in some things—'

'Such as?' asked the major, intrigued.

'In the domestic sciences, I have an admirable sophistication. Also, I am very learned in languages and in painters of the fifteenth and sixteenth centuries. If you were ever interested in buying canvases of the old Flemish and Dutch masters, I could give you the most valuable advice.'

'Ah,' said the major, 'I'll remember that.'

'However, *mon Commandant*,' she went on, 'to

be learned in the arts is not necessarily to be learned about life. As you are a little older than me, you will have found out, perhaps, if friendship is important?'

'Quite as important as domestic sciences and old masters.'

'Comradeship is also special?' she said gravely.

'Very special, Louise Victoria.'

'Oh, I think so too,' she said warmly. '*Mon Commandant*, you have a hat in your hand. Are you going out?'

'I am.'

In sudden anxiety, she said, 'You are only going out, you are not going away?'

'I'm only going out,' he smiled.

Anxiety fled. Shyly she said, 'Please, may I come with you? It's a day off for me at last.'

'It's Sunday, when you're often free, aren't you?'

'Oh, I have no day absolutely free,' she said, 'and you would not believe what can be found for us to do on Sundays. Oh, may I come with you, please?'

'Of course you may. But you'd better ask Miss Cavell first. I'll wait.'

Louise sped away. She was back within two minutes, and in delight. 'Madame has said yes, and that it will be a good thing for me to be with you. I am to put on my uniform and give you my protection.'

'Are you sure Madame said that?'

'Oh, she holds you in high regard,' said Louise, 'and warms to the sound of your name. She said that in my uniform I'm unlikely to be stopped and questioned, which means you'll be safer with me than by yourself. She would not want you to get into trouble. So I must go and change. Oh, you will wait for me, won't you?'

'Gladly,' said the major, and watched her in affection as she picked up her skirts and ran. The hem of her petticoat ran frothily with her. She reappeared ten minutes later, looking fresh and crisp in her probationer's uniform. The dress was blue, with a white collar and white linen sleeves. Her white cap was a Sister Dora. Her cape was blue. The blue set off the gold of her hair and crept, it seemed, into her hazel eyes. The major wondered if life would ever be kind enough to give him a daughter as delicious as this girl,

'I am ready,' said Louise.

'Well, other young ladies could have taken twice as long without looking half as pretty.'

'Sometimes,' said Louise, as they left the *Clinique* and walked along the rue de la Culture, 'sometimes you are really very nice to me. But at other times I'm in dread that you will go back on your promise.'

'What promise?' he asked warily. There were occasions when Louise Victoria, for all her youth, could place her foot on the ladder of demure feminine guile.

'That we will go to Holland together.'

'Louise Victoria, you're a Turk,' he said, 'I promised no such thing.'

'I misunderstood?' Louise's white cap bobbed to her walk. 'Of course, even though I'm getting on, I'm still not mature enough, perhaps, to realize that when an English officer says one thing, he really means another. You will excuse my gaucherie, *mon Commandant*? It's a regrettable fault in many young ladies.'

'I haven't noticed it in you. As to Holland, what I said was that we'd think about it.'

'Well, I have thought about it a lot myself,' said Louise, 'and I'm sure it's better for us to go together. I know the best way to reach the border, from a little place called Overpelt, where I told you friends of mine live.'

'Then,' said the major, enjoying the air, the sunshine and the enchantment of Louise, 'your Uncle Scottie will have to give it more thought himself.'

Louise wrinkled her nose. She may have been unsure of some things, but she was positive she was not going to accept him as an uncle. She might have needed a father. She did not need an uncle. She had uncles, in Russia and England, and she had a family affection for them. She did not think it was a family affection she had for Major Scott. She preferred to call him '*mon Commandant*'.

Ixelles was peaceful. People were out because the day was sunny, but no one disturbed the quiet. Louise was as bright as the summer, carrying herself with an airy grace, linking her walk to the major's saunter. They took a tram into the centre of Brussels. There were Germans on the tram. They looked at her. Louise, suddenly, was tense. But they looked only because they saw in her a young nurse of captivating charm.

Leaving the tram, she strolled with the major to the Grande Place, the square which was one of the most beautiful and interesting in Europe. Here the people liked to sit or walk, to relax or browse, to watch life go by or be a part of it. But it was not the same these days as it had been. The Germans had taken it over. Naturally, the Grande Place provided the most imposing arena in which Kaiser Wilhelm's victorious soldiers could show themselves. Their grey-green uniforms dominated the square. They looked well fed; the outnumbered Belgians looked hungry, but they did not shuffle along. They behaved as if they were not aware of the conquerors. If they were stopped, if they were questioned or even searched, their faces became impassive or stony. They had a great deal to put up with.

There were no newspapers. Newspapers had

been censored on the arrival of the Germans, and then prohibited. *La Libre Belgique,* the underground paper, gave them some consolation, however, and a little pride. The telephone service had been taken over, and Belgians had no access to it. People could write to each other, using the postal service, but all letters had to be left unsealed to facilitate the work of the censors. Trams were run by the Germans and mostly for the Germans. Belgians needed a pass to travel on them. In fact, they needed a pass to travel anywhere. Louise and the major had passes. Faked ones.

No bicycles were permitted. The food situation was bad enough to necessitate soup kitchens being set up. Belgium, which imported as much as eighty per cent of its grain, was receiving only a fraction of its needs. The British naval blockade was largely responsible for this, but the Belgians, loyal to their allies, appreciated the reasons behind the blockade.

Louise put on an air of self-assurance, though her heart beat a little faster each time a German soldier looked at her. She saw all eyes as suspicious, not admiring. However, she was in her uniform and cape, and she had her stalwart British comrade beside her, looking, perhaps, like a patient of hers with his broken arm. He seemed far more interested in the Grande Place than in the Germans. His cheerful indifference to them gave her heart and confidence. He commented on the architecture of the Hotel de Ville, which dated back to medieval times, as Louise explained to him. But she apologized for everything being rather depressing now. The cafés were no longer the stimulating meeting places they had been, the rendezvous of lovers, sweethearts, talkers, drinkers and dreamers. War and the Boche had robbed Brussels of its verve, its excitement and its colour; the people exchanged none of the greetings they used to, and the cafés lacked their former atmosphere of gaiety. They had little to offer customers, which was sad.

'But it's so bright, normally,' she said, 'oh, just as much as Paris. You should see it when it is alive, *mon*—' She did not complete that. Instead, quite carefully, she said, 'M'sieu.'

'Very wise,' murmured the major, 'one has to think of a thousand ears.'

Indeed, there were Germans to spare close by. Those who were off duty looked around. Those who were on duty looked at the people. They distrusted the Belgians, who could not be regarded as at all reliable. They could not be relied on to co-operate or to exercise obedience. They could not even be relied on to read the German edicts posted up in the streets. And many were addicted to helping Allied soldiers, harbouring spies, encouraging resistance and practising sedition by publishing or reading *La Libre Belgique*. All this had to be stopped. An example had to be made of some of them.

Louise, despite one or two little butterflies in her stomach, enjoyed being out. Perhaps she and Major Scott were rather flying in the face of the enemy, but it was a happy excursion all the same. And she was sure the major would get them out of trouble if trouble arose. Not that it was really likely. She was a nurse. Well, on the way to being one. And her uniform made her inviolate.

She was surprised into shock when two German soldiers did stop them. Far from considering her inviolate, both of them barred her way to look very keenly at her. The major suspected at once that they were interested in fraternization and nothing else. They spared hardly a glance for him. They had eyes only for Louise, who had the sparkle of champagne rather than the wryness of medicine. One of the Germans, speaking enough French to make himself understood, asked her who she was and where she and her companion were going. Fortunately, she and the major had already decided what was to be said in answer to such questions. Louise improved on the agreed formula, and was so crisply credible that not even the major knew how rapidly her heart was beating.

'Who am I? Who am I? I'm a nurse. Do you think these are the clothes of a tram driver? Do you think tram drivers nurse wounded

Germans at the Palace hospital? This gentleman is M'sieu Rainier, who is an outpatient, and is simply walking with me. M'sieu Rainier, show them your papers.'

'That isn't necessary, mam'selle,' said the German, with something of a grin for her pertinacity, 'I only wish to know your name.'

'I am Anna Descamps,' said Louise haughtily.

'Ach, so?' The German was undoubtedly already an admirer of Anna Descamps. 'Then permit me, Nurse Anna Descamps, to call for you when you are next off duty at the Palace. When are you next off duty?'

'Please call whenever you wish, when you can ask for me,' said Louise, 'but I warn you, a certain German army doctor isn't going to like it.'

'Ach, those medical officers, they get all the prettiest nurses, leaving none for a good soldier.' And the German grinned again, gave a good-natured shrug of disappointment, then moved off with his comrade.

'Well done, you sweet girl,' said Major Scott as he and Louise walked on, 'that was a rattling fine performance.'

'Oh, but I was terrified,' said Louise, 'didn't you see me shaking?'

'Didn't see you even bat an eyelash.' The major wanted to put his arm around her and give her a squeeze of pride and affection. 'I don't know what kind of a future you'll enjoy when the war's over, but I'll be surprised if it's less than historic. I cherish you, little Belgian nightingale.'

'Cherish me, m'sieu?' said Louise as they walked amid strolling Germans and hungry Belgians.

'That's the least of it,' said the major.

'Oh, it was nothing, really,' she said slightly pinkly, 'only a little bit like standing on a trembling earthquake.'

The major laughed. A buxom woman in a black hat and black dress glanced at him as she passed. Her eyes then turned on Louise, who was looking up at him with a smile and a warm glow. The woman blinked, stopped, looked after them and put a black-gloved hand to her mouth. Then she hitched her dress and positively ran to catch them up. She swept round in front of Louise.

'Oh, ma chérie! Ma petite mam'selle! Ma petite comtesse!'

She threw her arms around Louise and wept tears of emotion. Louise stared. Her eyes lit up.

'Elizabeth! Oh Elizabeth!' she cried, and they hugged each other. People looked and Germans peered as they passed by. The major stood beside Louise with the protective air of an uncle, or father, or simply a man who was sympathetic to all her emotions. Louise was showing wet eyes and the woman was openly weeping. Silently, the major handed Louise a handkerchief that was white and clean. She dabbed her nose with it, then passed it to the woman, who thoroughly dampened it before handing it back.

In French, Louise said, 'M'sieu, this is Madame Elizabeth Dupont. She and her husband have been in our family's service for years. I haven't seen her since I went to live with Aunt Tilli. Our tears are embarrassing you?'

'Shall we try to find an *estaminet* that might serve us something?' suggested the major on a cheerful and practical note.

'Oh, that is such a good idea,' said Louise, who never found it difficult to agree with her English comrade. 'One near the Palace, in case Germans question us. If we are near the Palace we can think up very good answers. Elizabeth, this is a friend of mine, a good friend, so please don't look him up and down.' She whispered the last words to Elizabeth alone.

Madame Elizabeth Dupont was indeed regarding the major with eyes suspicious and searching through their rapturous wetness. The major smiled politely. His suit and sling were inspected, his rugged countenance surveyed and his cheerful blue eyes peered into. Ah, he thought, here is the family warhorse ready to chew my ears off in defence of the innocent foal.

'Come,' said Elizabeth, not too unhappy with

her conclusions, 'we will go to the *estaminet* where Jacques will perhaps find some weak coffee to serve to us. Oh, sweet child,' she said to Louise, 'how happy I am to have found you. Come, come.' She was dark in her mourning clothes, but bright in her possession of Louise. Willing to tolerate the major, she led them to a café near the Palace. They went inside, out of sight of parading Germans, and found a corner table. They secured the furtive help of a waiter called Jacques, who brought them coffee. Coffee was controlled by the German commissariat, and, with exceptions, was available to German patrons only in many cafés.

They were able to talk.

'I am going to whisper everything to Elizabeth. It will be quite safe to tell her,' said Louise to the major. And she told Elizabeth, who had known her since infancy, about Aunt Tilli, the soldiers hidden in the cellar, and Aunt Tilli's defection. She recounted the details of her flight, her meeting with Major Scott and her enrolment as a pupil at the *Clinique* in Ixelles. Elizabeth spent the entire time clasping her hands prayerfully, uttering little sighs and looking at Louise with loving and mournful eyes. At the end she turned to the major.

'So, you are a good man, m'sieu, you saved our precious comtesse—'

'Elizabeth, please,' said Louise in confusion.

'Louise Victoria is a comtesse?' murmured the major.

Elizabeth looked shocked. 'You question it, m'sieu?' she said. 'Is she not the daughter of the late Comte and Comtesse de Bouchet, and heiress to their estate?'

'Louise Victoria?' said the major, understanding now some of Louise's more piquant moments and her faultless manners.

Louise looked slightly embarrassed. 'Oh, it was not a deception, m'sieu,' she said, 'I gave it no thought – and what difference would it have made?'

'None,' said the major, 'for it would hardly have altered the circumstances or the shape of the ditch. You'll agree, I think, Madame Dupont, that some young ladies are to be cherished, whether they're comtesses or not?'

'M'sieu, in my time I have cherished the whole family – oh, such tragedy, so cruel for my little one.' Elizabeth sighed. 'Even more cruel now, for she cannot enter her own home.'

She explained. She and her husband had been in service with the family for twenty years. They still lived in the family residence in the rue Royale, for they had the responsibility of looking after it until Louise, having come of age, would be independent of her aunt and return home. It was terrible that her aunt had acted in such a way as to make Louise fly for her life. And she could not use her house in Brussels,

for the Boche had called several times, looking for the young Comtesse de Bouchet on the
grounds that she had assisted Allied soldiers to
escape.

'Yes, Elizabeth, I thought the Boche would
do that,' said Louise, 'so I kept away. Did my
aunt get in touch with you?'

'No.' Elizabeth could not hide her disgust
for a woman who had betrayed her country's
honour and, when all was said and done, even
her own niece. 'Oh, it is good you are at that
place in Ixelles as a probationer. You will be safe
there. The Boche took away two photographs
of you. Oh, little one—'

'Elizabeth, I'm not little,' said Louise, who
wasn't.

'Fuss, fuss,' muttered Elizabeth.

'It's you who are fussing.'

'Yes? Yes?' Elizabeth's whisper was chiding,
'Well, who else is there to fuss over you, tell me
that? Oh, you are so young.'

'I'm not, I'm almost eighteen,' said Louise.
'So, please, be calm, or we shall embarrass
Major Scott – no, we must be careful to call him
M'sieu Rainier here.'

Elizabeth leaned forward and whispered, 'He
is really an English officer? You are sure?'

'He's not a horse thief, if that's what you
mean,' said Louise firmly.

'I am only wanting you to be sure,' murmured
Elizabeth, 'one cannot be too careful—'

'Elizabeth, be quiet!'

The major, hearing it all, rubbed his nose thoughtfully. Louise glanced at him. He smiled. It told her he only found Elizabeth amusing. Louise returned his smile. Elizabeth saw the warmth in her eyes and muttered to herself.

'What are things coming to, what are things—'

'Elizabeth, now what are you saying?' asked Louise.

'Nothing,' said Elizabeth, but made another inspection of the major. An English officer he might be, but Louise was the Comtesse de Bouchet. The major suffered the new inspection with disarming urbanity.

Three German officers entered the *estaminet*. They sat down at the next table. They exhibited a polished correctness as they removed their caps and gloves. Their eyes alighted on Louise. One officer scrutinized her with Teutonic deliberation. It made Louise worry a little.

'Why is he looking at me like that?' she whispered.

'My little one,' sighed Elizabeth, 'you are right, you are no longer little. You have grown up. That is why he is looking at you. M'sieu,' she said anxiously to the major, 'you will see she is taken good care of? She will not be able to come home until the war is over and the Boche have gone. Keep her safe in the *Clinique*. She must not visit the city too often.'

'She'll be taken great care of,' said the major earnestly.

They left the café. Elizabeth wept a little as she said goodbye to Louise, who promised to send messages to her in some way or another, which made Elizabeth ask why she had not done so before.

'Because I didn't know whether the Germans were watching the house or not,' said Louise sensibly. 'I didn't know if they were stopping everyone who called. It might have meant trouble for you, Elizabeth. But I hadn't forgotten you, no, of course I hadn't. Go on your way now and give my love to Pierre.'

'Oh, that husband of mine, he will dance with happiness, knowing you're safe,' said Elizabeth. 'There, I've cried enough. Look after her, m'sieu, she is so young.'

She hurried off, a matronly figure in black, happy to have found Louise but in deep mourning for the girl's parents.

Louise and the major walked to catch a tram back to Ixelles. The major was thoughtful.

'Young lady,' he said, 'I'm afraid I connected you too much with your aunt's house in Dendermonde. I should have remembered your mention of your Brussels home. It was careless of me to bring you here. You might have been recognized by a member of the German secret police. They have photographs of you, and I imagine they lurk around

146

Brussels, peering into every face that passes by.'

'Oh, but they would not have been looking for a nurse, m'sieu,' said Louise, 'and it was so good to meet Elizabeth. It's also so good to be out that you should not reproach yourself for your carelessness.'

'Thank you,' said the major gravely. 'I think, by the way, that we should let Miss Cavell know exactly who you are.'

'But she'll think I want special privileges.'

'I don't fancy you'll get them. But a comtesse, by heaven!'

'Oh, you must believe me,' she said, 'it was not at all important. A title, m'sieu, on occasions like that, is quite insignificant compared with a trout.'

'Well, insignificant compared with Louise Victoria herself,' he said, which, for some reason, made her eyes look slightly moist.

They turned into a street, wide and long, and made their way towards a tram stop. A man in a black waterproof raincoat and a black, peaked cap was coming their way. He had the gait of an idler. His eyes turned to Louise, as other eyes had. But the other eyes had been admiring; his were curiously speculative. His look was not lost on the major. The man passed them, walking silently. That meant rubber soles. People usually bought rubber soles because they were cheap, and easy to glue to a boot or shoe. But there were some people who used them because they could walk silently in them. The major was instinctively alerted.

A shop window cast glittering reflections. He stopped. Louise turned and saw him gazing into the window.

'What are you looking at?' she asked. The shop sold millinery. Its window contained a single exhibit: a brown velour hat, with ornamental hatpin, against a background of angled mirrors.

'Is this a hat you would wear?' he asked. Louise joined him at the window and looked at the hat. But he was not looking at it himself. His eyes were on the street scene reflected in one of the mirrors. A little way down the street, the man in the black waterproof had stopped and turned. He began to retrace his steps.

'M'sieu, that is a hat for a lady of forty,' said Louise.

'There's a tram coming,' said the major, taking her by the elbow and walking quickly away with her.

'We shall miss it,' said Louise, seeing the tram slowing down on its approach to the stop.

'Not if we run. Louise Victoria, run.'

She knew then that something was wrong. She ran. That was neither too pointed nor too suspicious in itself. Many people ran to catch trams. The major, with his left arm in its sling, ran with her. They caught the tram, boarding it in the wake of some German soldiers and a civilian. The major took Louise through the long vehicle. The man in the waterproof, sprinting, reached the step and swung himself aboard. Very neatly, the major slipped out of the rear exit, Louise with him, and a second later the crowded tram clanged away. The man in the waterproof shouldered his way along, peering at the passengers, standing and seated, as the major and Louise eased themselves out of sight on the blind side of another tram, which had come to a fortuitous halt on the adjacent lines.

'We are safe now from whoever it was?' breathed Louise.

'Not yet, I imagine. He'll stop the tram and jump off the moment he realizes we're not on it. Come on, sweet girl, we must move fast.'

They crossed to the pavement. They saw the tram come to a halt two hundred metres away. Adroitly, the major put himself behind Louise, covering her, for in her uniform she was dangerously distinctive. He took off his hat. That could, be picked out too.

'M'sieu—'

'Walk,' he whispered, 'walk to the next turning. I'll stay behind you.'

She asked no questions. She was not too afraid as long as he was with her. She walked quickly, the major close behind, his hat held in front of him. It was a short walk but a nerve-racking one. He did not make the obvious mistake of looking back, but he could not escape the spine-prickling sixth-sense feeling that the hunter had eyes on him and was moving at speed. The pavement was now crowded. He and Louise threaded a fairly easy passage, but he would have been happier with a lot more people about. One could quickly get lost in a crowd. He shielded her as she reached a corner and turned into a side street. Across the street, a little way down, was a bookshop that was open. He took her over to it.

'Go in,' he said, 'look at some books and be as invisible as possible.'

Again she asked no questions, though he knew she badly wanted to. He blessed her aptitude for keeping a cool head in a crisis. She went in. There was a positive library of books filling the shelves and stacked on tables. On one table at the far end was a great pile of second-hand titles. She quickly rustled her way through the shop and put the table and its literary mountain between her and the door. The proprietor ventured over and she began to talk to him, the while stooping to examine titles at the bottom of the pile. The major, watching her from inside the shop doorway, saw her completely disappear. He turned then, and through the glass corner of the shop window began an observation of the entrance to the street.

The man in the black raincoat appeared

almost immediately. He looked hot. He stopped, obviously undecided about whether to keep straight on down the main boulevard or enter the minor thoroughfare. Brussels took on an ominous quiet to the major, the sounds of the city receding from his consciousness to leave him in a silent void created by his tense awareness of the hunter.

The man made up his mind – he entered the side street. The major vanished from the doorway and darted into the shop. He joined Louise behind the huge pile of books. The slightly startled proprietor looked down at him as he stooped beside Louise.

'My niece,' he said in explanation. He did not enlarge on that. He knew his French must have a non-Belgian accent. Louise shot him a look in which worry was edged with momentary indignation. Then she talked loquaciously to him about what good bargains some of the second-hand books were, without making it necessary for him to say a word himself. The proprietor, prolific in his knowledge of literature, joined in.

'And that one, mam'selle, do you see, is an edition of Voltaire's *Candide* published in 1798.'

'1798?' said Louise. She and the major stooped lower in search of the title. They found it. 'But why is it in such indifferent company, m'sieu?'

'Indifferent, mam'selle?' said the proprietor, quite unaware of the tenseness this nurse and her companion were sharing.

'There are good books here,' said Louise, 'but also many which are surely very indifferent compared with anything written by Voltaire.'

'To be frank, mam'selle,' said the proprietor, 'its value is not what it might be. There are four pages missing.'

The major was listening, waiting for the door to open and for the sound of a voice asking questions about a nurse and a man with his arm in a sling.

The proprietor, intrigued by Louise's comments – who wouldn't be? the major thought – crossed to a shelf to select some exceptionally fine works for her interest. The major straightened up and strolled to the door. Louise trembled for him, but it was an all-or-nothing situation. Through the window he had a view of part of the street. Opposite, a little way down, the hunter was entering a jeweller's. He was out again after a few moments, scanning the street before entering the next open shop, his every movement quick and purposeful. He was obviously no fool. He had made up his mind his quarry had turned down this street, and that they could only have got out of sight by entering a shop. Undoubtedly, he was going to thrust his nose into every one.

The major, returning to Louise, said casually,

'I must be off, little one, but you can take your time. Another five minutes, if you like. Then go back to Madame. I'll see you there later.'

Her eyes clouded a little as he walked through the shop. She said nothing, nor did she run after him, though she wanted to. He had seen something that meant a new tactic must be tried. She was to leave the shop in five minutes, not before. That was his message, and part of the tactic.

Outside, in the doorway, the major saw the hunter emerge from another shop to take his quick look up and down before darting into the next. The major stepped from the doorway and marched at a fast pace towards the main boulevard. When he reached the corner he stopped. He looked back. The hunter was there, on the pavement, staring, and at a distance of sixty yards he recognized the major. Negotiating the corner swiftly, the major drew the man after him, past the bookshop and off the scent of his real quarry. The hunter was in pursuit of the decoy. The major had no doubt he was expected to lead the man, directly or indirectly, to Louise Victoria. Undeniably, the young Comtesse de Bouchet had been recognized.

From the moment he turned the corner, the major gave himself no more than ten seconds before the hunter would have him in sight again. He could not run without attracting the suspicions of strolling Germans, unless he had a good reason. A reason clanged by in the shape of a tram. He ran into the road after it, his hat in his right hand and his left arm jolting in its sling. People stared, for his chase was a hopeless one. But it looked more stupid, perhaps, than suspicious. He gave up and crossed the road, hurrying into the rue Belliard, his stride long and devouring. When he reached the first side street, he looked back. The hunter had not been lost. He was coming at a run. Moreover, there were two German soldiers with him.

The major walked smartly down the side street. He saw a doctor's brass plate beside a door. He went up the three front steps and rang the bell. Another ten seconds of grace was all he had, no more. The door opened. A housemaid gazed enquiringly at him. He stepped into the hall, smiling at her, and casually closed the door.

'Dr Bonnier is in, mam'selle?' he said. Bonnier was the name of a French general, and the only name he could think of at this moment. 'I have no appointment, but I was told he might see me.'

'M'sieu?' The housemaid, a comely young woman, looked perplexed. 'Dr Bonnier?'

'A friend of mine recommended I should consult him while I was in Brussels. Is it possible you could ask him if he would spare me a few minutes? I have a card, I think.' The major put his hat on the stand and began to dig into his waistcoat pocket.

'There's no doctor of that name here, m'sieu,' said the housemaid. 'This is the surgery and residence of Dr Leroy.'

'No, it isn't Dr Leroy I want. I am sure he's an excellent practitioner, mam'selle, but for my complaint – no, not my arm, but my back – I was assured by my friend that Dr Bonnier is a specialist in the field.'

'He does not specialize at this address, m'sieu.' The housemaid might have been more brusque, but the major's warm smile drew from her words of regret that she was unable to help him. She added, 'Dr Leroy might know of him, but unfortunately he is out with his family.'

The major stopped digging for the non-existent card.

'Undoubtedly, mam'selle, my friend has mixed up the addresses. I am sorry to have troubled you.' The major picked up his hat and turned towards the door. But he needed more time before he felt it would be safe to open it and show himself. He paused. 'Ah, would you perhaps have some register here of Brussels doctors? If so, would it be permissible to refer to it? To find Dr Bonnier's address in it?'

She liked his smile and the crispness of his French. 'I'm so sorry, m'sieu,' she said, 'but the doctor's consulting room is locked, and that is where the register would be.'

'Ah, yes. Of course. Thank you all the same, mam'selle. I must make enquiries elsewhere.'

Since his every instinct told him not to emerge yet, he blessed the delay the housemaid offered him as she said thoughtfully, 'There is Dr Humbert in the next street, the rue de Treves, m'sieu. Although he does not receive patients on Sundays, he may help you.'

'Sundays, yes.' The major shook his head at himself. 'How foolish of me to make my call on a Sunday. But I'm only in Brussels for a short while. There is a chance, perhaps, that Dr Humbert may spare a moment?'

'He may, m'sieu.'

'Then I'll take the chance and go round to see him. I really would like to obtain Dr Bonnier's address. Would you have heard of him yourself, mam'selle, and what his reputation is as a specialist?'

'To be frank, m'sieu,' said the housemaid, 'I've not heard of him at all.'

He turned again towards the door, smiled at her and said, 'That will completely ruin things for me, mam'selle, if I've not only got his address wrong but his name as well. However, thank you for being so kind. Thank you very much.'

'I am sorry I can't help you more, m'sieu.'

She reached to open the door for him, then

said, 'It is possible Dr Humbert may not be at home, either, but as Dr Leroy and his family are expected back in twenty minutes, would you care to wait, m'sieu?'

'How kind, mam'selle, how thoughtful. I will wait with pleasure. One doctor will always know the whereabouts of another doctor, isn't that so?'

The housemaid, not disagreeing, took him into the waiting room and saw him comfortably seated. She lingered, ostensibly to talk, but he supposed it could be because she thought he might not be what he seemed. She was not going to risk having him make off with the polished waiting-room table. With confidence, however, in the cut and quality of the suit Edith Cavell had found for him, he passed ten minutes conversing with the young woman. At the end of that time he glanced at the waiting-room clock.

'Heavens, the time!' He rose quickly to his feet. 'I almost forgot. I came in only to make an appointment with Dr Bonnier. I can't stay longer, after all. There's my dear wife – she'll be waiting – mam'selle, my empty head – imagine almost forgetting one's wife – it's as bad as almost forgetting one has a wife at all.'

The housemaid, who had found his company much more pleasurable than that of the cook, was disposed to giggle, but put a hasty hand to her mouth and coughed instead. If she thought he had shot very springily to his feet for a man with a bad back, she made no comment. She saw him out. He thanked her again and she expressed the hope he would find Dr Bonnier. She closed the door behind him. The major put on his hat and walked down the steps into the street.

Louise left the bookshop five minutes after the major, obeyed his instructions and hastened to a tram stop. She produced her pass on the vehicle, and that was the only incident of note during her journey back to Ixelles. On arrival at the *Clinique*, she did not go up to the probationers' quarters. She went into the waiting room. There she sat in worry and impatience. A sister looked in.

'Nurse, what are you doing here?'

'I am waiting for my friend, Sister.'

'Oh, your friend.'

'Madame has given me permission to be with him today.'

'I see.' The sister nodded and withdrew. She came back after a few minutes. 'Anna, your friend is out.'

'Yes, Sister, I know. That is why I'm waiting for him.'

It was an anxious wait. Ten minutes seemed very long. Twenty minutes seemed an hour. Forty minutes seemed an eternity. She went out into the street. There was no sign of him.

She returned. She sat down. Her heart felt leaden.

She looked up as someone entered.

'What has happened, Louise?' said Miss Cavell. 'Where is Major Scott?'

Chapter Nine

Louise came to her feet, her worry undisguised. Madame's expression clearly indicated that she too had anxieties.

'Madame – oh, I'm so afraid—'

'Major Scott has been arrested?' Miss Cavell's fine features were taut with anticipation of the worst.

'No – that is, I don't know—'

'You did not return together, I understand. Louise – my dear – if anything has happened, you must tell me.'

'Oh, you see, Madame,' began Louise in a rush, 'we were—'

She was interrupted as José put his head in. 'Madame,' he said, 'the patient is coming down the street.'

Louise rushed out. Miss Cavell swept after her. José opened the front door for them, and as they emerged into the street they saw Major Scott walking with cheerful briskness towards the *Clinique*. Relief engulfed Louise in hot, melting bliss, and Miss Cavell drew a deep breath. She glanced at Louise, saw the moist brilliance of her eyes and the flush on her face.

'I think you want to talk to him,' she said quietly, 'so you may use my office. I'll see him later.'

She turned and went back into the *Clinique*. José, as he often did, gave her a little bow as she passed him, and then followed her.

The major came striding up. Louise wanted to throw her arms around him. He, for his part, was cheerfully himself, his blue eyes surveying her with affection and satisfaction. She was here, where he had expected her to be, for he had been confident she would not panic but make her way back to the *Clinique* as he had told her to.

'Good girl,' he said and smiled at her.

'Oh, *mon Commandant*, I—' She stopped, her emotions making it so difficult for her. The sunny street was quiet, but her heart was not. It was pounding noisily. The nature of her feelings, so new and so strange to her, was more disturbing than ever. It was not a need for comradeship, it was something quite different, something far more necessary to her welfare and happiness. It was a wanting that was physical as well as emotional. She desired to be touched. Colour rushed and flooded her.

'Louise Victoria, I knew you'd be here,' he

said, and he smiled as if there had been no worries, no anxieties, no dangers, only a rather lively kind of afternoon. It piqued her.

'Yes, I am here,' she said stiffly. 'Please can we talk in Madame's office? She has given us permission.'

In the office they talked. She told him how she had left the bookshop, made her way to a tram stop and reached Ixelles without trouble. He told her what had happened to him. She lost much of her pique in her delight at his specious entry into the house of Dr Leroy, and his even more specious entry into the confidence of the housemaid. When he finally came out, he told her, the hunter and the two German soldiers had disappeared. He took a cautious, roundabout route to reach a suitable tram stop, and his ride back to Ixelles had been as free of incident as her own.

Louise asked questions, and he answered them, and she understood exactly why it had been wise to run and to stay out of sight. Because the man was almost certainly German, and a police agent at that, and because he might have recognized Louise as a wanted person.

'And because he came after us,' said Louise.

'Indeed he did,' said the major.

'Oh, we were very elusive, weren't we?' she said. 'We are really quite good at that sort of thing, don't you think? Of course, it can be a little desperate, and rack one's nerves.' She felt emotional again. Her smile came and went, came and went. She steadied herself. 'But what made you tell the bookseller I was your niece? I felt so embarrassed.'

'Embarrassed? Why?' The major was intrigued.

'Why? Why?' Louise sounded as if he was requiring her to explain the obvious.

'Yes, why?'

'Who would not be at such an absurd fabrication?' she said.

'Absurd? Did you think so?' The major was far more concerned about the fact that she'd been recognized than resolving what seemed an issue of inconsequence. His smile hid the concern. 'But it helped an awkward moment, I thought, and sounded fairly reasonable.'

'Well, I did not think so,' said Louise, and rushed into reasons why. 'Anyone could have seen I was too old to be your niece, and the bookseller must have noticed there was no family resemblance at all. It would have been much more believable if you'd said I was your—' The flow stopped.

The major did not ask her to finish. He wanted to see Edith Cavell, urgently. He said, 'I think no more excursions, Louise.'

'But, *mon Commandant*—'

'Wiser not to, you know. I don't intend to let you get caught. You're precious.'

Her colour rose again. 'Oh, I—'

'Too precious to land up in the hands of the Boche.'

'Very well, *mon Commandant*,' she said, 'we must not go into the city again. It really means, don't you think so, that if we can't go out without being chased, we should seriously consider going to Holland as soon as your arm is no more trouble.'

'We'll consider that very seriously, Louise Victoria.'

'Oh, yes,' said Louise Victoria, but the pique returned ten minutes later when Miss Cavell arranged for him to take tea with her in her sitting room. Louise felt painfully excluded.

Miss Cavell took tea in her sitting room every afternoon at four o'clock. It was her most welcome break of the day. For once, she had delayed it in order that Major Scott could join her. She received him with a smile; her natural reserve was always inclined to melt in his presence. He was no matinée idol, but he had a warm, rugged masculinity many women preferred to mere good looks. It was necessary, however, for any woman of character to watch that he did not take over her life as well as her affections.

'Please sit down, Major Scott.' Her mellow voice was an encouragement to informality. 'You don't mind taking tea with me?'

'A decided pleasure,' he said as he sat down.

'Thank you for asking me, especially as I wanted to see you.'

She poured the tea. Her Belgian sheepdog, Jackie, lay beside her chair, lazily thumping the carpet with its tail. Edith Cavell adored dogs. She had a feeling for people and all living creatures. If her sense of duty had become almost a religion, it only hid her human feelings, it did not smother them. She was neither frigid nor puritanical. She loved music and the theatre. She had a weakness for jewellery, and for good clothes. She especially liked good shoes. A natural cosmopolitan, she enjoyed foreign travel. Her work and the war had curtailed that. But in Major Scott she had found a man with whom she could enjoy her love of conversation.

Taking the cup and saucer, Major Scott felt trapped, as usual, by the fascinating quality of her peerless looks and the mesmerizing clarity of her eyes.

'You've given up your adventurous idea of moving my patients out in a body?' she asked. She smiled as she put the question.

'I wish they genuinely were your patients.'

'Well, you're quite genuine yourself,' she said.

'Oh, reckless and wilful woman,' he said, shaking his head, 'to whom has been given beauty but no sense of discretion.'

She coloured. 'Major Scott—'

'Can't help your protests, Matron,' he said cheerfully, 'I stand on my declaration. But I'll tell you this. If I had half your kind of courage, I'd have a shot at something very necessary.'

'A deed of unusual daring, Major Scott?'

'Very. I'd tie you up the moment you took one risky step too many, and parcel you off to a nunnery.'

'A nunnery?' Amusement warmed Miss Cavell's eyes. Major Scott in a cavalier mood was characteristically himself, but not to be taken seriously. 'A nunnery, Major?'

'A convent,' he said. 'There are quite a few in Belgium. I came across one during my time on the run. I received food and kindness, and a candle was lit for me. I'll bundle you off there. Just the place for a nurse who needs taking in hand.'

'Shall we be serious?' she smiled.

'I am serious. I care for your safety, Edith, I care for it very much.'

A flush tinted her smooth face. It might have been because of his use of her name, or his words. The major was thirty, but had the maturity of a man who had seen a great deal of varied life, and his own quota of war and suffering. She had an unlined countenance and eyes as clear as the eyes of youth, and he had a look of warmth and strength.

'I shall take no unnecessary risks. I never do,'

she said in her quiet way. She put out a hand for his cup and saucer. She refilled the cup. It seemed necessary to her at this moment to busy herself a little. He thanked her. Their eyes met, hers not quite as calm as usual. 'You must not worry about me,' she said.

'Can't help it,' said the major. 'Especially with men like Koletsky around. Caught him snooping about a few days ago.'

'Yes, you mentioned it,' she said, and looked thoughtfully into her cup.

'Shall we face up to the fact that he may be an informer?'

'We need not concern ourselves,' she said, 'he's gone. He left early this afternoon, without warning and without advising anyone.'

'I hate the sound of that,' said the major, frowning.

'Nurse van Til found some things he left behind in his hurry, including a letter he'd written but not finished.'

'Do you have it?'

'Yes.' She took it from her pocket and gave it to him, rather as if she would like to have his opinion of it. The major read it. It was an account of the day-to-day running of the *Clinique*, the work of the staff and the treatment of male patients. There was a reference to the efficiency and kindness of Madame, and an illuminating sentence that leapt to the major's eyes:

'Madame's house is good and I find it impossible to do any of the things required of me.'

'Oh, hell,' said the major.

'That is a very uninformative comment, Ned.'

'Is it? Edith, this isn't a letter. It's an account of things, a report.'

'But it says nothing that could go against us.'

'It might have, if he'd finished it,' said the major, 'but his heart wasn't in it.'

'In what?' Miss Cavell showed just a little concern.

'If he wasn't planted here by the Germans, then I'm Alexander the Great. But I misjudged him to some extent. He wasn't quite the fox I thought. He was obviously so impressed by you that he decided he couldn't inform on you, and got the wind up about what his German paymaster would think of his lack of heart. So he departed at speed.'

'You're very imaginative,' she said.

'Edith, will you close up shop for a while?'

'How can we when men still need our help?' she said, and he saw in her a dedication that was as much to do with warm affection for her soldiers as with her sense of duty. 'Ned,' she said, 'what happened this afternoon that had Louise so worried about you? She was back a little after three. You didn't return until a little after four. I began to worry myself, then.'

168

'Louise was the reason I wanted to see you,' he said. 'The Germans have a description of her, and also two photographs. She was recognized this afternoon.' He recounted the incident. Miss Cavell listened, giving him a little smile of approval for his own part. 'And I have to tell you,' he said, 'that she's actually the Comtesse de Bouchet, even if she is an orphan. She didn't consider her title important. I think it is – to the Germans. It's the reason why they sent platoons of soldiers looking for her the day I met her. She's a young Belgian aristocrat who's had the nerve to defy them, and because of that they want her badly enough to make a salutary example of her. They'll put her in prison for years.'

'A girl so young?' said Miss Cavell.

'Yes, a girl so young,' he said, and they looked at each other, but left unspoken that if the Germans could be so severe on a girl, what might they not do to a mature woman of such professional stature as the Directress of this *Clinique*?

'Thank you for telling me,' said Miss Cavell. 'I know now why Louise has little ways of her own. Yes, the Germans will be furious with her. But she'll be safe here, though she considers you have chief responsibility for her, not I. Whenever I try to discuss her future with her, she usually says she'll see what your opinion is. She has no parents, no father.'

'She has intelligence and courage,' said the major.

Miss Cavell smiled. 'It isn't a question of her intelligence and courage, but her needs. You must come to understand that.'

'Meanwhile,' said the major, 'we have to consider that she's not as safe here as we think.'

'You feel the Germans will come here looking for her?'

'Louise was in her uniform. The Germans will assume she either acquired it as a disguise, or that she really is a nurse. They'll have a file on her, they'll know her age. She's unlikely at seventeen to be a qualified nurse, and so they'll start looking for a probationer.'

'Which means they'll investigate hospitals with training facilities,' said Miss Cavell, 'hoping to find her in one.'

'Yes,' said the major. 'They'll begin by making enquiries at the hospitals in Brussels. Then they'll think of this place. I'd say they'll be here by Tuesday at the latest.'

'Looking all over the *Clinique*? That,' murmured Miss Cavell, 'would be most inconvenient. But we'll see what can be done.'

'Inconvenient?' The major regarded her with a whimsical eye. 'Inconvenient, Edith?'

'Yes, Ned, very.'

'You wouldn't prefer to call it worrying or alarming or even frightening?'

'One word or another, is that important?' she

smiled. 'It's more important, isn't it, to decide what to do for Louise.'

'And for you too,' said the major, 'and anyone else who's liable to be investigated.'

'Yes, of course.' Her smile was gracious. 'You'll be a splendid help, Ned. First, I suggest Louise should be moved out.'

'Agreed,' said the major, and they put their heads together to discuss what other steps to take.

Chapter Ten

The square, a cabinet-cluttered office at police headquarters, was blue with cigarette smoke. The ceiling was brownly stained with it. Through the haze, two members of the German secret police eyed each other. Both men were ambitious and both accordingly sensitive about dues and credits.

'I think,' said Lieutenant Bergan, 'it's time a few positive facts were established about that place in – in – where is it?' He looked enquiringly at his subordinate, Detective Henri Pinkhoff.

'Ixelles,' said Pinkhoff. He was quite aware that Bergan was testing his Monday morning alertness.

'Ah, yes, Ixelles.' Lieutenant Bergan, heavily built and fleshily jowled, was a man of varying moods and expressions, but no one ever knew whether a smile truly reflected good humour or a frown was symptomatic of dissatisfaction. It confused some suspects during interrogation, and confused suspects were easy to break down. When they began to contradict themselves, Bergan could smile and raise his voice, or frown and gently murmur. It all hid a man addicted to prejudging a suspect and subtly intimidating him.

Detective Pinkhoff, on the other hand, looked what he was – a dark, human ferret. The sly cast of his features, a facial birthmark, and the inquisitive thrust of his nose above a heavy black moustache, disturbed people with secrets to hide. Nor were innocent people entirely at ease when his unblinking eyes alighted on them. Pinkhoff was a professional. He had actually found his way into the British army earlier in life, serving for several years and trading in the right quarters for classified military information on behalf of Germany. Subsequently, he took on the respectable front of a travelling umbrella salesman in Paris, where he again did some useful espionage work for Germany. He was an excellent linguist, and he interpreted for Lieutenant Bergan whenever necessary during an interrogation. Lieutenant Bergan, whose foreign language accomplishments were limited to a few words of French, was not always too happy to have his subordinate exercise a gift he did not own himself.

Lieutenant Bergan seemed fussy, but was subtle. Pinkhoff was devious but diligent. They made a formidable pair, though it was doubtful if they liked each other. It was doubtful if Pinkhoff liked anybody.

'*Herr Leutnant*—'

'What's the position at the moment?' asked Bergan. He meant, how much information had the department acquired?

'To begin with,' said Pinkhoff, 'the official title of the place is *L'Ecole*—'

'Not the inessentials, please,' said Bergan.

'Essentials, then,' said Pinkhoff. 'It's run by a nurse called Edith Cavell, undoubtedly of British nationality.'

'Undoubtedly,' said Bergan, putting his cigarette out, 'but that's not news.'

'You didn't ask for news, *Herr Leutnant*, you asked for—'

'I know.' Bergan waved a hand. 'Continue. You'll allow me a comment or two.'

'There's a training school for nurses and a hospital for patients. Fräulein Cavell is in charge of both. There's no record, however, that she ever registered as an enemy alien.'

'I don't suppose she bothered,' said Bergan amiably. 'Probably regarded it as unnecessary. Probably considered herself too busy.'

'Unnecessary? Too busy?' Pinkhoff's dark brows grew together. 'It was a special order, *Herr Leutnant*, issued by—'

'I know that.' Bergan shuffled fussily in his chair. 'I said that for certain probable reasons she failed to register. I didn't say I approved. Continue.'

'The rest is rumour, *Herr Leutnant*.'

'Yes, a rumour that it's a dispersal centre for Allied soldiers. I think we should take greater interest in the place. Some periodical surveillance should be sufficient to lay the ground for a full investigation.'

'We're short-staffed,' said Pinkhoff.

'I said periodical surveillance. A man or two, here and there, now and again.'

'When we have them to spare?' Pinkhoff nodded. 'That's to our advantage. It's a very quiet area. Post the same men too often and they're bound to be noticed.'

'We don't want that,' said Bergan, lighting another cigarette. 'If there's anything stinking in the house of Denmark, we don't want the queen alerted.' He smiled at Pinkhoff. 'I thought we had an inside man at work?'

'We have. I was coming to that.'

'Of course. You have a report from him you were also coming to?'

'I've had nothing at all,' said Pinkhoff impassively. He had the consolation of knowing that when expected information did not materialize, Bergan's frustration, however well hidden, was worse than his own.

Bergan, with a fleshy smile, said, 'Is he an incompetent, then?'

'A collaborator, and the best we could find at

the time. He did say if he couldn't get information out to us, he'd let us have it when he left.'

'There's a certain incompetent for you. He knew his limited ability would make him of limited value.' Bergan regarded the ceiling through a puff of smoke. 'A good inside man could do our work for us.'

'I'll look into it,' said Pinkhoff. '*Herr Leutnant*, have you considered arresting Fräulein Cavell for failing to register as an enemy alien?'

'Of course not. We don't want her brought in on a comparatively minor charge if there's a possibility of catching her out in far more serious misdemeanours. Watch her, but allow her the pleasure of remaining unmolested. For the time being.'

A few minutes after Pinkhoff had left the office, another detective came in.

'*Herr Leutnant?*'

'Yes, Heilmann?' said Bergan, sounding benignly receptive.

'I've a report to make.'

'Concerning?'

'Concerning the Comtesse de Bouchet,' said Detective Heilmann.

'Who's she?' asked Bergan, sitting back.

'Her file, *Herr Leutnant*,' said Heilmann, and placed a folder on the desk.

'Oh, yes. The Comtesse de Bouchet. I remember. What about her?'

'I think she's in Brussels,' said Heilmann. 'I'm almost sure I saw her yesterday.'

'Almost?' said Bergan very benignly.

'No, certain,' said Heilmann.

'You're suddenly quite sure, are you, not almost?'

'The reactions of the suspect have convinced me.'

'Ah? You arrested her?' said Bergan.

'I regret—'

'You failed to arrest her, although you were convinced?'

'If I may recount what happened, *Herr Leutnant*?' suggested Heilmann.

'It might be as well,' said Bergan.

The detective made his report. He and the lieutenant then discussed the case of the Comtesse de Bouchet, wanted for assisting the escape of enemy soldiers.

At eleven on Tuesday morning, two Germans arrived and asked to see the Directress of the establishment. They were shown into Miss Cavell's office. While she was receiving them, words of warning flashed around and fugitive soldiers effected their usual vanishing trick.

The two men produced badges which identified them as members of the German secret police. They both spoke French. Without saying why, they asked to see the register of probationers, and their cards. The register and cards were brought out by the nurse who had shown the detectives in, and who remained to give support to Miss Cavell.

Detective Heilmann, the man in the black raincoat, examined the register with care, checking that there was a card corresponding with each entry. The personal details on each card were examined with equal care. His colleague stood by, looking around the tidy office and noting the calm demeanour of Miss Cavell. Heilmann noticed it too. It was hardly the reaction of a woman who was harbouring a known suspect in her training school. He asked questions of her.

How many probationers were under training?

Twenty.

How many were registered?

Twenty, naturally, as the register would show.

There were cards for all of them?

There were twenty cards. They could be counted.

Were there any other cards?

Only of probationers who had received their diplomas and left the school. They were on a separate file, which could also be inspected, if required.

At this point, Detective Heilmann put the register and cards aside. He looked at his colleague, then spoke again to Miss Cavell.

'Assemble your probationers.'

Miss Cavell regarded him in cool silence.

'If you please, Madame,' he added, not un-impressed.

Where did he wish them to assemble?

'Here,' said Heilmann.

Could the reason be given?

'Not at the moment,' said Heilmann.

'Nurse,' said Miss Cavell, 'will you fetch them down, please?'

The nurse left the office. The probationers arrived a few minutes later, filing with a rustle of curiosity into the presence of the Germans. Heilmann and his colleague looked at the group, and Heilmann began a careful inspection of each pupil. Miss Cavell remained at her desk, her expression quite calm. Heilmann moved from girl to girl, showing his keenest interest in the blondes. These came under very close scrutiny. It made some of them colour up. The silent man began a lip-moving count. He murmured something to Heilmann at the end of the inspection. Heilmann turned to Miss Cavell.

'Twenty was the number, Madame. There are only nineteen assembled.'

'Nurse?' said Miss Cavell.

'Oh, I'm sorry, Madame, I didn't think to check,' said the nurse.

Miss Cavell addressed her wondering pupils.

'Who is missing?' she asked.

'If you please, Madame,' said a girl called Yvette, 'it's Nurse Descamps. She's on kitchen duty.'

'Ah,' said Heilmann, a glint in his eye. He turned to the nurse to ask her to fetch the missing probationer, changed his mind and said, 'Take us there.'

The nurse glanced at Miss Cavell. Miss Cavell nodded her assent. Heilmann let the briefest smile flicker. Undeniably, this slender and handsome Directress had a natural aptitude for playing the *grande dame*. It had to be acknowledged, she had the poise of an aristocrat. He had had no luck yesterday afternoon when going the rounds of the city hospitals. Today he needed to produce something for Lieutenant Bergan. It was Bergan who had told him all the possibilities had not been exhausted, to go to Ixelles and try *L'Ecole d'Infirmières Diplômées*.

So, there was one probationer working in the kitchen. That information had come not from the nurse or the Directress, but from a probationer. Interesting.

He and his colleague followed the nurse. The staff in the kitchen looked up. So did a young lady in a probationer's uniform. She was scouring a pot. She was very fair; Heilmann strode across to her. His manner made her drop her eyes nervously. But he was quite gentle as he put his hand under her chin and lifted her face. His gentleness came of triumphant anticipation, an anticipation that changed at once to frustration.

She was young and she was fair, but she was not the Comtesse de Bouchet.

'M'sieu?' she said, flushing.

'Your pardon, mam'selle,' he said abruptly. He went back to the office with his colleague. There he spoke again to Miss Cavell. He described the young lady his department was interested in, though he did not name her or mention what she had done.

'Well, as you have seen, she is not here,' said Miss Cavell truthfully.

'When she was last observed, Madame, she was wearing a uniform and cap very much like your own pupils wear. You have been most co-operative, and if you could help us with further information of any kind—'

'I can only tell you it would be the easiest thing in the world for her, if she was taught dressmaking at school, to make herself a nurse's uniform. She may have made several, all with little differences, if she thinks any of them would create the perfect disguise.'

'Or she might have acquired a uniform?' said Heilmann.

'Feloniously?' said the calm Miss Cavell. 'We should know if one had been taken from here.'

'What if one of your probationers had got to know her and decided to help her out?' said Heilmann's colleague.

'Our supervision is too strict to allow any of them to part with one item of their official wear,' said Miss Cavell with quiet conviction. 'However, I will make discreet enquiries and get in touch with you if I find I have something to tell you.'

'Thank you, Madame,' said Heilmann, and he and his colleague left, to return to Lieutenant Bergan with empty hands.

Major Scott appeared on the ground floor ten minutes later. Nurse Duval, Belgian and fair-haired, was just leaving Miss Cavell's office. She was wearing a probationer's uniform.

'Ah, clever and courageous Annette, you did it,' he said, his eyes at their most cheerful.

'But all the morning in the kitchen,' sighed Nurse Duval, 'cleaning, scrubbing and scouring pots.'

'Well, it might have been all day, you sweet girl, it might even have been all week,' said the major, and kissed the tip of her nose.

Nurse Annette Duval blushed, then said, 'Only my nose, m'sieu? Is that all it was worth? A peck on the nose?'

Miss Cavell, coming out of her office, stopped in her tracks. Major Scott was kissing Nurse Duval warmly on the mouth.

'Nurse?' The mellow voice vibrated a little.

Nurse Duval broke away, blushed, gasped and stammered, 'Madame – oh, I'm sorry – but it was the triumph, you see – the excitement—'

She fled.

'It was my fault,' said the major.

'Major Scott,' said Miss Cavell coolly, 'you—'

'Yes, I understand,' he said. 'Bad breach of discipline.' He followed her back into her office and closed the door. 'You'd better carpet me. But spare Nurse Duval, won't you? It took nerve on her part to fool the Boche. And yours.'

Miss Cavell let a smile come. 'I'm only too relieved it worked out so well for us. It went exactly as we hoped it would.'

'It went exactly as you planned,' he said, in admiration.

'As we both planned,' she said. She sat down at her desk. The slightest of tremors shook her.

'Edith?' The major showed concern.

'Just a little reaction,' she said. 'There was only one risk, that the Germans might have asked for the missing probationer to be brought from the kitchen to my office. All I could have done then was to have sent the other girls back upstairs before Nurse Duval came in. Whether the Germans would have been too suspicious to allow this, I don't know, but I do know that if the other girls had seen Nurse Duval in Louise's uniform, their surprise might have been dangerously obvious.'

'A close thing, but a victory's a victory,' said the major, 'even if you only achieve it by the skin of your teeth.'

She eyed him a little uncertainly, for he looked quite capable of kissing her too. She picked up a pen from its stand and regarded the nib critically.

'When Louise returns,' she said, 'her colleagues will ask her where she was last night, and why she spent so much time in the kitchen this morning. They'll tell her about the Germans who came to inspect them for some reason or another. They know nothing of Louise's real identity and what she has done.'

'Louise can say she spent the night helping one of your nurses with a private case,' suggested the major. The *Clinique* offered a nursing service for patients in their own homes. 'And that you gave her kitchen duties today for reasons of your own.'

'Ned, you've a facile intelligence,' she smiled. 'I shall leave it to you to advise her on how to answer questions and satisfy curiosity.'

'You have your own virtues, Edith. Shall we wait until this evening to have Louise brought back? When it's dark?'

'How is your arm?' she asked in seeming irrelevance.

'Sore. Tender. Fragile.'

'That's an improvement on wanting to take it off and throw it away. I asked because eventually you'll have to leave us. I shall miss your support, Ned. Yes, we'll have Louise brought back when it's dark. You know, if we should fail that sweet girl at any time, I'm sure God will not.'

Louise was in an empty house not far from the *Clinique*. There was only a discreet and loyal caretaker looking after the place. It was sometimes used for briefly lodging young Belgians who wished, with Miss Cavell's help, to enlist with King Albert's fighting men in Flanders. Louise had been there over twenty-four hours, in a state of restless anxiety. Not until darkness had fallen did a sister arrive to take her back to the *Clinique*. On the way, she asked quick, worried questions. When she heard what had happened she wanted to dance with relief. No one was in trouble. The Germans had been and gone, Madame having convinced them they must look elsewhere for whoever it was they were after. The sister had no idea why that person was probationer 'Anna Descamps', nor did anyone else on the staff. It was enough that Miss Cavell had said certain action was necessary. Only Miss Cavell and the major knew the truth about Louise, and Miss Cavell was keeping it so.

Louise was required to go to Madame's office when she reached the *Clinique*. It was not Miss Cavell who awaited her there, however, but Major Scott. As she closed the door and saw him standing by the desk with a smile of welcome on his face, Louise almost gave in to an impulse to fly to him. She felt she had been away an eternity and she was poised on feet that were winged.

'Well, little Belgian nightingale, was it very boring?'

She let her impulse cool down and approached him quite soberly. '*Mon Commandant*,' she said, 'it was better to be bored than arrested, yet the boredom was nothing compared with my worry. I thought of the danger you and Madame must face if the Germans came. All the questions and then the suspicions. If they had discovered you were an English officer, they would have taken you away and arrested Madame for hiding you. It was excessively worrying. My freedom would not mean very much to me if you and Madame had lost yours.'

Her earnestness was intense.

'Fortunately, everything worked out very well,' said the major, 'and all due to our remarkable and ingenious Madame, and her loyal staff. You can say, in fact, that the day was well won by all concerned.'

'But especially by Madame?' said Louise. 'You have a great admiration for her?'

'Indeed I have,' he said, and Louise winced. The major, observing her, said, 'Louise, are you all right?'

'Quite all right, m'sieu,' she said stiffly.

'Are you sure?'

'Quite sure, m'sieu. I will say goodnight.'

'Before you do, I thought I'd mention that the other girls may bombard you with questions—'

'I am aware of that,' said Louise. The major, however, commenced to make suggestions about what she should say. She assured him she had already given thought to questions and answers; there was no need for him to worry. She would take care of the probationers' curiosity, without giving away any secrets concerning him and Madame and herself. She would never, in any case, talk indiscreetly, and it was not at all necessary to caution her in respect of this, since he ought to know by now that he could trust her to be as sensible as any woman.

Woman?

'Louise Victoria,' he said, 'I've declared my belief in your intelligence more than once. Of course I know you'd answer any questions sensibly, but it's natural, isn't it, that you and I should first talk about it? Just to make sure?'

'That is why you waited to see me? Just to make sure? I see. I understand, m'sieu.' She was very formal. 'I will say goodnight now.'

'Louise Victoria?' he said as she walked to the door.

'M'sieu?' she said, keeping her back to him.

'Come here, Louise Victoria,' he said. Aloofly, she returned to him. He put his arm around her shoulders and squeezed her with warm affection. 'What's wrong, sweet girl?'

Louise, her stiffness melting under his fondness and concern, said in a small voice, 'There's nothing really wrong, *mon Commandant*, except that sometimes I am much more stupid than sensible, after all.'

'As are most of us. So be of good cheer, comrade, for you're in excellent company.'

Chapter Eleven

Lieutenant Bergan listened to Detective Heilmann's report.

'So, you've had no luck?' he said.

'None, *Herr Leutnant,*' said Heilmann.

'Hm,' said Bergan and lit a cigarette. He made a study of the curling smoke. 'However,' he said.

'Yes?' said Heilmann.

'As far as your memory serves you, the uniform worn by the suspect you saw on Sunday was most like that worn by the probationers at Ixelles?'

'I'd say so, *Herr Leutnant.* Her cap, I'm sure, was identical with theirs.'

'Interesting,' murmured Bergan. 'The establishment, now, is run by – let me see – by – um – ?'

'By its Directress, Fräulein Cavell,' said Heilmann.

'Ah, yes,' said Bergan, happy, apparently, to receive the information.

'A very helpful woman,' said Heilmann.

'Which makes her a welcome phenomenon in a country full of people who are usually no help at all,' said Bergan. Heilmann, obviously, had not realized his helpful woman was British. Well, that was something the department did not want to become general knowledge. General knowledge in the department had a habit of becoming common knowledge among people outside. It was better for Edith Cavell not to know that rumour had pointed the finger of suspicion at her. Heilmann, had he been aware of her nationality, might have conducted his enquiry with the kind of hostility that would have alerted a guilty woman. And if she was guilty, if she was assisting Allied soldiers, Bergan did not want her warned off. He wanted her to hang herself. It really would have been very interesting if Heilmann had discovered she was harbouring the Comtesse de Bouchet. 'What was it you said, Heilmann? The cap worn by the suspect was identical?'

'I'm positive, *Herr Leutnant.*'

'Then the helpful Fräulein Cavell could be right in suggesting the young lady was clever enough to make herself the uniform. Having had the wit to elude us as she has, she would make no mistakes about details of design. And she would think about the esteem in which nurses are held. We've been known to suspect the credibility of a person wearing a nun's habit, but not a young lady in nurse's uniform. Can it be true, Heilmann, that we have more feeling for those who minister to our physical ailments than for those who minister to our spiritual needs?'

'Pain makes us groan louder for help than our sins do, *Herr Leutnant.*'

'On the other hand,' mused Bergan frowningly, 'the sweet pigeon, frightened by your recognition of her on Sunday, may simply have flown the coop.'

'But which coop?' asked Heilmann.

'Ah, yes, which? What did you think of Fräulein Cavell? Did you see in her a shelterer of our kind of pigeon?'

'Frankly,' said Heilmann, 'I felt her to be a lady of integrity.'

'Indeed?' Bergan seemed receptive to that opinion. 'Now, the man with the broken arm, whom you say was with the young nurse whom you say was the Comtesse de Bouchet, might lead us to her. Ask at the hospitals tomorrow for details of all men recently treated for a broken arm. The right arm, was it?'

'The left,' said Heilmann.

'You might as well make Ixelles your first call this time, instead of your last,' suggested Bergan. An afterthought followed. 'Oh, and while you're there, why not have another look at the probationers?'

'*Herr Leutnant?*' said Heilmann, then nodded. 'Ah, yes. I see.'

'If the pigeon was being sheltered there,' said the lieutenant, 'she may by tomorrow have flown back. But in any event, be sure to treat Fräulein Cavell with courtesy and respect.'

José, standing at the open door of the institute and enjoying the look of the bright morning, saw two men turn a corner and enter the rue de la Culture. Rapidly he slipped inside, for he had seen them the day before. They were members of the German secret police. The alarm system, based on brief code words, gestures and signals, went into immediate operation and the soldiers disappeared. The major, about to make himself inconspicuous, went on a quick search for Nurse Duval instead. He found her and spoke urgently to her.

Louise was plucked out of the lecture room by Nurse Duval on a pretext. Swiftly, they changed uniforms. Louise hid herself under a great heap of sheets in the linen room, and Nurse Duval sped back to the lecture room, sidling in with the flair of a young lady who had a natural genius for tactical unobtrusiveness. The droning doctor scarcely noticed her. A flutter, that was all. True, three or four student nurses looked at her a little puzzledly.

'Your attention, please, young ladies,' said the doctor, observant at least of turning heads.

Downstairs, Detective Heilmann and his colleague, Detective Mayer, were received once more with calm politeness by Miss Cavell, though this time she had the worry of not knowing whether anything was being done about Louise. Relief submerged the worry when Heilmann explained they were trying to trace a man with a broken arm. He apologized for taking up Madame's time again. He described the man and how he was dressed. From his look, he could be a professional gentleman, he added. His left arm had been in a sling. Did Madame's records indicate whether the *Clinique* had recently treated a man with a broken left arm?

It did not seem to disconcert Miss Cavell that the German was obviously talking about the major. She gave the enquiry some thought, went through a selection of neatly indexed cards and extracted one.

'Could this be the person?' she asked, showing the card. 'Philippe Rainier, an architect from Bruges? This is the address he gave. He broke his arm while inspecting a building in Brussels. His arm was set here in April – there is the date. He returned to Bruges the same day, I believe. As you can see, he did not attend here as an outpatient.' She yielded the card to Heilmann, who made a note of name and address. He thanked her.

'Oh, by the way,' he went on casually, 'while

I'm here I'd like to see your probationers again.'

A frown clouded Miss Cavell's serenity. 'Naturally, if you insist,' she said with quiet reproof.

'A formality, Madame, I assure you,' said Heilmann, and his colleague gave him a pitying look for his softness.

'They're at a lecture,' said Miss Cavell.

'Where?' asked Detective Mayer.

'A nurse will take you,' said Miss Cavell, 'but I should like you to appreciate it's a doctor's lecture. He—'

'We shan't interrupt, merely look in,' said Heilmann, quite convinced, in the face of such dignified charm and such help in the matter of a man with a broken arm, that Fräulein Cavell was not concealing the Comtesse de Bouchet.

A nurse was summoned. She took the two Germans to the lecture room, while Miss Cavell remained at her desk and composed herself to await the outcome. She looked up as the door opened and Major Scott slipped in. She rose quickly to her feet, showing alarm for once.

'Ned! You should be out of the building.'

'Yes. But had to let you know that Louise is well hidden. Nurse Duval is sitting in for her at the lecture. Thought you ought to know, thought you deserved to.'

'But the risk,' she breathed, 'when it's you they're after as well now.'

'Oh, I've been lurking around very quietly – shall I duck into your sitting room?'

'Yes, but out of sight. Quickly.'

He went in and closed the door. She sat down again. She touched her cap, patted her hair and waited. In a little while Heilmann and his colleague were back. They had drawn another blank. Heilmann showed no disgruntlement, however, even if his colleague did. He felt Madame had given him a lead on the man he had seen with the Comtesse. He thanked her for her help and co-operation.

'My probationers,' said Miss Cavell, 'will be wondering at your interest in them.'

'Explain to them,' said Heilmann, 'that we were professionally motivated.' He thought Lieutenant Bergan could not have bettered the subtlety of that. He and Mayer departed. Miss Cavell rose from her chair, looked at her watch and opened her sitting-room door. Major Scott straightened up from behind the sofa.

'Gone?' he asked.

'Yes,' said Miss Cavell.

They smiled at each other and sat down together. 'They're getting closer, you know,' he said.

'Everything is back to normal.'

'I think you mean the abnormal. You must stop your good works, Edith. And Louise and I must go.'

'There's no need for that,' she said. 'The

Germans went away satisfied. Louise should be quite safe now, and what we must do for you is to change your name again and get you a new identity card.' She explained how forthcoming she had been with the Germans about 'Philippe Rainier'.

'I see,' said the major. 'They've been coming to more conclusions and making more deductions.' He laughed. 'That'll keep them busy, trying to find me in Bruges, and trying to locate a building in Brussels said to have been inspected by an architect in April.' He looked at her and became serious. 'You know, I'm not sure whether your flair for this sort of work isn't giving you a dangerous feeling of invulnerability.'

'I assure you, Ned, I know all my weaknesses. I know I'm very vulnerable. But my faith is strong. Shall we talk of other things for a change?'

'If you can spare the time,' he said, 'let's talk about Norfolk, to which we both belong.'

'I should like that,' she said.

He had touched her on a soft spot. Her mellow voice was warm as she began to describe Swardeston, the little village of her birth, and her childhood there. In her memories of the peace and beauty of the village and the countryside, and the joy she found in walking the quiet lanes and fields with her family, the major discerned the great love she had for Norfolk and her country.

She had one brother and two sisters, and the whole family was close-knit. From her father, the vicar of Swardeston, she received due instruction in the love of God. From her mother she learned, by example, the practical Christian ways of caring for people. In all things her father was just and devout, her mother compassionate and human. Her father too could exercise practical Christianity. She and the other children were required to carry helpings from the Sunday dinner table to needy parishioners. Eventually they sat down to what was left, in the knowledge that they had shared God's bounty with their neighbours. However, she said with a smile, it meant they spent a gruellingly hungry time before they came to the table.

Her parents were devoted to each other, which was the happiest thing, for it created a harmonious family atmosphere so important and necessary to the children. She enjoyed her years of growing up. She practised the domestic sciences, the useful and the humdrum as well as the creative, and there were pursuits such as sketching, painting, needlework, embroidery, tapestry, pottery, music and dressmaking. Life was never dull. Indoor activities came into their own during the winter, when a parlour was made cosy by the blaze of a fire, when the sounds were of conversation or music, the snipping of scissors or the snapping of threads. The house shut out the wind and the rain, and chestnuts were roasted and devoured.

The major said little. He listened, and he watched the changing light of reflected memories in her eyes.

The summers were beautiful, she said.

The summers, he remembered, had been beautiful for Louise too.

The countryside around Swardeston saw nature at its most prolific and colourful every summer. Sometimes, as a special treat, there were picnics. Picnics were sheer heaven to all children, and even enjoyable to some parents. And during the holiday periods, the family went every year to a resort on the Norfolk coast.

'Even to Cromer, perhaps, which isn't far from where my family have their farm?' said the major.

'Even to Cromer, Ned.'

During such holidays she spent much of her time with her cousin Eddy. They were as compatible as cousins could be when they were irresponsibly young, when high spirits and impossible dreams could not be diminished either by inclement weather or what lay behind the cautious words of parents.

'Yes, I know,' said the major, thinking of the days which had been sweet for Louise. 'The days of our youth always remain our days of Utopia.'

'The days of our youth, Ned, remain our days of innocence, when a toothache was the worst disillusionment suffered by innocence.'

Because of her smile he said, 'You have never lost the best of your youth.'

'I've lost all my youth and so much else, Ned, for I married my profession.'

Refugee soldiers continued to arrive at the *Clinique*, and the escape organization continued to help them get to Holland. But because of the visits of the German secret police, and because there was a growing feeling of strangers occasionally hovering in the near vicinity, the atmosphere was uneasy. Miss Cavell was the only one who seemed unperturbed.

The major remained in residence. Miss Cavell refused to consider sending him on his way until his compound fracture was fully healed. Three times it had been freshly plastered. Louise was in no hurry for him to go, unless he took her with him, though she felt very unhappy about his deepening relationship with Madame. He gave her the impression at times that he was in love with Miss Cavell.

A man arrived at the *Clinique*, a man who said his name was Jacobs and that he needed help. He had escaped from a German labour camp. Now he wished to escape from Belgium.

Miss Cavell wanted to know who had sent him to her. He was unable to be specific. He could not remember their names. He thought perhaps they hadn't told him. But what people were they? Ah, yes, he was able to tell her that. They were some peasants who had befriended him near Mons. Yes, he was sure that was so. Some peasants.

From a farm?

Well, they worked on one of the farms, he thought. They had mentioned her and her reputation for being kind to fugitive soldiers of the Belgian army.

Had he served in the Belgian army, then?

Oh, yes.

Did he not know the agreed password?

No, he had been told nothing of any password, only to come to this *Clinique* and ask for her.

Miss Cavell hesitated. Jacobs begged her to believe he could not afford to be recaptured by the Germans: they would shoot him.

Always inclined to be swayed by that kind of plea, she gave him the benefit of the doubt and took him in.

The new arrival quickly came to the attention of Major Scott. In his determination to keep an eye on things, the major exercised the kind of authority that allowed no one to argue it with him. His interview with Jacobs was an interrogation. Jacobs was as vague about his contacts as he had been with Miss Cavell. He was just as vague about his soldiering record. The major was inclined to bury the fellow in a hole in the ground. Instead, he went down to talk to Miss Cavell.

The prolonged mending process was trying his patience, he said, but what was trying his patience more now was Edith's injudicious Christian pity. It had led her to admit an informer as obvious as Jacobs. The man was a palpable liar, without the smallest credibility as a refugee Belgian soldier, and had never seen a rifle in his life.

Miss Cavell knew by now that the major's judgement of a man was not something she could ignore. His opinion of Jacobs confirmed her uneasy assessment of the Belgian.

'Oh, dear,' she said, 'have I made a mistake, Ned?'

'You aren't a woman of mistakes, Edith, only of too much feeling for people,' he said. Her belief in God's love and dispensation, and her devoutly Christian attitude, especially to men and women in need, kept her outside the murky corridors in which crept cheating, lying, villainy and murder. She saw all people as God's creatures. No sinner was incurable. She was incapable of believing that some man to whom she gave shelter would betray her. And even if she had believed it, she would have done nothing except wait in the hope that her Judas

Iscariot would suffer a miraculous change of heart and throw his thirty pieces of silver away. It occurred to the major that the man who called himself Koletsky had done just that.

'Ned,' she said with a smile, 'you're prepared to accept the consequences of being a soldier in wartime. I must be prepared to accept the consequences of being committed to my duty, and to any mistakes I make.'

'That's a philosophy which in your case equates duty with suicide. My very dear Edith, get rid of Jacobs, won't you?'

'Yes, Ned,' she said quietly, and for once her lashes fell to hide her clear eyes.

Jacobs was sent to the Dutch border a day or two later, in company with some other men. It was a great pity that Albert Libiez, a lawyer and a member of the escape organization, had not been aware that Jacobs had been admitted to the *Clinique*. For Albert Libiez knew Jacobs; the man had worked for him during the early months of the war. Libiez became suspicious of his activities and contacts, and, eventually, convinced that the man was collaborating with the Germans. So he had sacked him.

Jacobs allowed himself to be escorted over the border into Holland. He subsequently recrossed the border and made his way to Turnhout.

'Where's Detective Pinkhoff?' asked Lieutenant Bergan, as if he didn't know.

'I believe you sent him off somewhere,' said Detective Heilmann.

'Ah, yes. To Turnhout. Correct.' Bergan seemed happy with his recollection. Heilmann wondered why the lieutenant simulated so much forgetfulness. The habit was becoming an addiction, as if he were drugged by his own subtlety. One would think the lieutenant's main interest in life was catching everyone out, felons, suspects and colleagues alike. 'It's to be hoped,' continued Bergan, 'that Pinkhoff has more luck in Turnhout than you did in Bruges. Philippe Rainier has never been heard of at the address Fräulein Cavell gave you, eh?'

Wishing to be fair to the elegant and impressive Directress, Heilmann said, 'It was the address he gave her. But no, he has never been heard of there.'

'Were you surprised?' asked Bergan amiably, but with a frown.

'Experience, *Herr Leutnant*, has taught me—'

'It's taught us all. You were not surprised. Fräulein Cavell, of course, can't be blamed.'

'I felt her incapable of lying,' said Heilmann.

'Ah, you're a conscientious policeman,' said Bergan, 'and a recognizer of good and helpful women. Your colleague, Mayer, distrusts everyone, and would even look under the wings of an angel to see what heaven had hidden there.'

'Men like the one who calls himself Philippe Rainier, and people like the Comtesse de Bouchet, are all slippery, they all wriggle.'

'Those two have wriggled away from you, that's true,' observed Bergan acidly.

'I'll find them, *Herr Leutnant*,' said Heilmann. 'Is Pinkhoff now on the case too?'

'Which case?'

'The case of the Comtesse and the man who—'

'That's your case, Heilmann,' said Bergan, his heavy jowls spreading in a large, friendly smile, 'you can bring both of them in when you find them. Pinkhoff hasn't gone to Turnhout to look for either.'

No. Pinkhoff had gone to Turnhout to meet the man called Jacobs.

Miss Cavell's daily workload was immense. The training of nurses, her regular evening lectures to them, her duties as Matron, her assistance in the theatre, her administrative tasks and responsibility for catering, all these and other things occupied her. In addition, she was involved in a host of activities for the escape organization, including seeing to the provision of fake documents, maintaining coded contact with guides and associates, raising funds to finance the cause, conducting soldiers on the first leg of their journey and supervising their upkeep while in residence.

She alone knew of everything that was done, and she alone knew all the members of the organization. Which meant, in the event of her arrest, her certain indictment as its head.

Lieutenant Bergan now had her *Clinique* under periodical surveillance. He had never met the renowned matron. But as he sat slowly spinning his web, he felt the pleasure of coming face to face with her might not be long delayed.

An entirely agreeable refugee reached the *Clinique*. He was a tall, handsome Frenchman, Captain Gaston Quien. He had been sent by Prince Reginald de Croy. Miss Cavell could have arranged for him to start for Holland the following day, in company with some British soldiers, but the captain, unfortunately, had a bad foot. Inspection revealed he was suffering from an ingrowing toenail, which necessitated a stay at the *Clinique* for treatment.

Quien quickly made himself at home, wandering about and dispensing an inordinate amount of Gallic charm, which he poured over staff and inmates alike. He was interested in everyone and everything. He flashed smiles as generously as an unclouded sun, and at staircases and cupboards, as well as people. Major Scott thought him more like an exile from the *Comédie Française* than a French officer on the run from Germans.

He had been cut off from his regiment, he said, during the battle of Charleroi, and by a stroke of luck had run into the Prince and Princess de Croy of Bellignies, who helped him to reach Brussels.

'Cut off, you say?' said the major.

'In an instant, *mon ami.*'

'And ran like hell?'

'Faster than the devil himself,' said the amicable Frenchman.

'With an ingrowing toenail,' said the major, 'that must have hurt.'

'One endures, *mon Commandant*,' said Quien modestly, 'because sometimes one has to. But then one reaches a place like this, a haven of charity, presided over by a nurse of great sympathy. Madame is altogether a delightful and estimable lady.'

The major's eyes flickered. He remembered Koletsky, who had had a lot to say about the fine qualities of Madame.

'Yes, entirely estimable, Captain Quien, and the kind of lady whom I hope none of us would ever betray.'

Quien's dark eyebrows rose in astonishment. 'Is it possible, *mon Commandant*, that anyone would consider such a thing?'

'I hope not,' said the major, 'but Belgium is an occupied country and a hungry one. The Germans have food, money and favours to dispense. Some men whose souls are dark enough would sell Christ again for a loaf of bread and twenty marks.'

Quien sighed. 'There are many kinds of people,' he said, 'the good and the bad, the sad and the cheerful. They echo life itself, for life can be good one day, bad the next. But I refuse to believe our beautiful Madame inspires anything but devotion at all times.'

Undoubtedly, Quien was a likeable fellow. He had a Frenchman's weakness for the ladies, and most of the nurses found him irresistible. Quien's dark eyes seemed in perpetual pursuit of pretty faces, and his charm and personality carried him along on a tide of flirtation. But Miss Cavell's liking for him cooled considerably because of the liberties he took with her nurses and her female staff. His philandering ways undermined discipline. He frequently wandered out of the *Clinique to* talk to people he met, and wandered back again looking as if life, however, many bad days it burdened other men with, bestowed only the good on him.

In the *Clinique*, he showed the exploratory interest of a house guest so enchanted by everything that he could not refrain from discovering what the probationers' quarters were like. They were out of bounds, but that did not deter the intrigued Frenchman. He found the restroom. There he gave the impression of a smiling fox among startled chickens. His eye fell with particular pleasure on Louise, whose hair was tinted with gold, whose eyes were quick with life and whose mouth was kissably delicious. Louise, however, ushered him firmly out. Who was he? Did he not know he was breaking one of Madame's strictest rules by being here? Smiling, he said he was a patient. More firmly, she ushered him towards the landing and stairs, her action instinctive. She had not forgotten Koletsky, the Polish man who had wandered about and aroused icy anger in Major Scott.

On the landing, Quien said, 'It is true, mam'selle? It is actually forbidden for gentlemen to meet Madame's charming pupils?'

'It is rigorously forbidden for gentlemen to invade us, m'sieu,' said Louise.

'Even for me? I am Captain Gaston Quien of St Quentin.'

She stared at him. His easy disclosure of his name and rank came as a little shock. 'It makes no difference, *mon Capitaine*,' she said, 'you are still forbidden in this part of the institute.'

The handsome Frenchman sighed, smiled and shrugged. 'Of course. Yes,' he said. 'I am stupid. Naturally, Madame could not permit even the most praiseworthy gentleman to invade the precincts of her pupils. You must forgive me. But I am not completely penitent, for my intrusion has given me the pleasure of meeting one who I am sure must be the most charming of them all. You are smiling, mam'selle?'

'No,' said Louise, who wasn't.

'Ah, you think I'm flattering you, that I'll flirt with you.'

'All that is also forbidden in this area,' said Louise. Gallants like Captain Quien had called on her parents, kissed Mama's hand and flashed winning smiles, then turned their eyes to her too and named her the budding bloom of the family. They had even professed adoration and she had laughed silently at such silliness, thinking them the kind of men who could not grow up. They had not impressed Louise any more than they impressed Mama. Mama had said that any lady who had known the flirtatious flamboyance of Russian men could easily resist the flattery of others. Mama had always made very adept use of her fan, behind which she had hidden her smiles at the importunities of the gallants. Papa had generally made a practice of leading them to more eligible ladies, and Mama had never been displeased that Papa could still be jealous.

I am like Papa, thought Louise, I suffer from jealousy. I wonder, could *mon Commandant* suffer from it too?

She came back to the present, to hear Captain Quien confessing with a frank smile that he found all pretty nurses impossible to resist.

'It is their air, mam'selle, their sweet dignity. I am quite outrageous, for I should find no difficulty in kissing them all. Not at the same time, you understand.'

Louise smiled. He had quite an air himself. He was not unlikeable, although he did not have the vigorous freshness of Major Scott.

'You must go, *mon Capitaine*,' she said.

'At once, hand on my heart. But first will you tell me who you are?'

'Nurse Descamps,' said Louise.

'It is forbidden, is it, to meet you in the garden?'

It was, unless she got permission. But it might be interesting to find out what he had to say. Was he someone else who wanted to know things about Major Scott? There was an atmosphere in the *Clinique* these days. She had a feeling it was something to do with people like Captain Quien and that other man, Koletsky.

'You are French?' she asked.

'Ah, whisper it, mam'selle,' said Quien, and somehow she thought a secretive wink would follow. It didn't, but she made a decision.

'I am sometimes allowed to go down into the garden in the evenings, if there's no lecture,' she said. 'I may perhaps be there this evening.'

'Then, mam'selle,' said Quien warmly, 'I shall most certainly be there myself.'

One of the Belgian nurses, Jacqueline van Til, was out on an errand for Miss Cavell that afternoon. She was to deliver a letter from Miss Cavell to Philippe Baucq, a prominent member of the escape organization and an extremely versatile guide. As she approached his house she saw Captain Quien nearby, talking to a German officer. Nurse van Til was one of the few who did not like Captain Quien. Wisely, she decided not to deliver the letter. Suspecting Philippe Baucq's house to be under surveillance, she did not turn in her tracks and hasten away. That would have been too pointed a reaction. She continued on her way for a few steps, then knocked on the door of a house in which friends lived. To her utter dismay, when the door was opened she was informed that two members of the family had that day been arrested for sheltering French soldiers.

Although that had nothing to do with Madame, Nurse van Til returned to the *Clinique* worried and depressed. She saw Philippe Baucq leaving as she approached. He hurried away, giving her no chance to speak to him. She refrained from telling Miss Cavell what had happened, not wanting to add to Madame's burden of worries, and said only that Philippe Baucq had not been at home, so she had brought the letter back. She wondered later if she should tell Madame she thought Baucq's house was being watched, but kept silent in the hope that she was mistaken. Unhappily, she was not. The diligent Henri Pinkhoff was himself active in Ixelles, pursuing a thorough official investigation. He had made contact with Jacobs, who had given him useful information. Pinkhoff now had full authority to take all steps necessary to uncover the escape organization they suspected was being run by Edith Cavell. Pinkhoff had some names listed. At the top was Edith Cavell's. Philippe Baucq's was also prominent.

Pinkhoff was not proceeding impatiently. He was a policeman of methodical technique. Lieutenant Bergan wanted a foolproof case, and he would get one. The hunt was on, the main quarry sighted and the trap being carefully set to catch everyone else.

Major Scott, standing at the window of the reading room, saw a halo of white and the gleam of the evening sun on fair hair. It was Louise, entering the garden. That French coxcomb, Quien, rose from the seat to greet her. Faintly, the major caught the sound of her laughter, and saw them sit down together.

Louise, smiling, glimpsed the figure of the major at the window. She was sure he was frowning. Dismayed at times by the closeness of his relationship with Madame, she wondered if he was now feeling similar dismay at her rendezvous with the dashing French officer. She turned her eyes soulfully on the captain, and simulated utter absorption in his flirtatious advances.

The major, looking on, conceded it was natural. Louise was snatching a moment to enjoy the company of the most handsome man in the place. Yes, it was natural: a girl who was lovely and a French officer who was irresistible. The major's frown grew sombre, however, and he wondered why he suddenly felt an active dislike for Quien, why he even felt a little sad.

Quien had begun to ask questions of Louise about herself. For Louise, it meant inventing a personal history. It did not hurt her conscience too much as she plunged into fabrication.

'I'm very ordinary, *mon Capitaine*—'

'I challenge that.'

'But I am. I was in service many years before enrolling here.'

'Many years?' Quien laughed. 'Impossible. You are still so young.'

'I am almost twenty,' said Louise, crossing her fingers.

'Ah, remain almost, mam'selle. It's better on most voyages of life to linger than to actually arrive.'

'But then one would always be at sea,' said Louise.

'Always at sea? Ah, how delicious you are.'

'I was in service with an admirable family,' said Louise, her eyes glancing upwards for a fleeting observance of the frowning major. 'They were extremely good to me, but then the war came and I thought I should become a nurse. And so here I am, and that is all. I told you I was very ordinary.'

'But you're not, no. You have so much grace and such fine hands.'

'You've been in the war?' said Louise, attempting to keep her hands out of reach. But he had a long arm. He took hold of her right hand, pressed it and caressed it. It did not excite her, but it made her wonder what Major Scott was thinking.

'You are really quite lovely,' smiled Quien.

'Have you been in the war?' asked Louise again, and felt just a little nervous at his closeness and his persistent stroking of her hand.

'It was difficult to escape it,' said the modest captain.

'You were wounded, of course, which is why you're here. The Boche will come for you when you're discharged?'

'Do they come here, then, to take wounded soldiers away?' he asked, his smile oblique.

'I suppose so,' said Louise.

'Ah, the miserable Boche,' said Quien, and laughed. Louise thought him as handsome and dashing as her father had been, but her instinct told her she would not have placed herself as trustingly in his hands as in the major's. 'Sweet nurse, you worry about me, so you must be saluted.'

He saluted her with a kiss on the lips.

The major turned from the window and strode from the room.

Louise, agitated, sought to free her lips.

Quien smothered them. She put her hands against his chest and furiously thrust him off. She sprang to her feet.

'I did not like that!'

'Mam'selle—'

'And I do not like you!'

'Is a kiss so dreadful a thing?' asked the mortified Quien, quite unused to this kind of rebuff.

'When it isn't wanted or asked for, yes!'

'Wasn't it wanted? Wasn't it asked for with your eyes?'

'Oh!'

'Nurse!' A voice called sharply.

Louise turned. Sister Wilkins had appeared, her expression angry. Major Scott had informed her of the garden tête-à-tête. He had wanted to go down himself, to knock Quien's handsome head off; wisely, he had held himself in check.

'Sister,' said Louise, flushed and unhappy, 'I—'

'Go in, please,' said Sister Wilkins.

'Yes, Sister.' Louise, her ears burning, left the garden and made her way upstairs. She was called down a few minutes later for Sister Wilkins to begin reading her a severe lecture. With some relief, Louise realized that at least her superior had not seen her being kissed.

'But, Sister, I went down into the garden and there he was.' It was the truth, but not quite all of it. Louise thought her mama would concede she had not actually told a lie.

'You know the garden is out of bounds to all student nurses except when you have permission, and you also know the rules concerning patients.'

Louise, with her lively mind, had long begun to wonder why the rules prohibited contact only with male patients, but she accepted she should not argue.

'I'm sorry, Sister.'

'What were you talking about?'

'About me, that's all. I'm sorry.' Louise could not explain. It was all to do with her curiosity about Captain Quien, and with Major Scott, and with her regrettable little jealousies. 'Please, am I allowed to ask if Captain Quien, as a French officer, will be handed over to the Germans when he's discharged?'

'So you did not talk just about yourself?'

'Oh, he only told me who he was, and so I wondered about him.'

Sister Wilkins fretted about what to say. The girl had posed an awkward one, especially as she knew that Major Scott was British. The presence of another Allied officer was bound to make her wonder. But it was Miss Cavell's firm wish that no information of any kind relating to fugitive soldiers should find its way to any student nurse.

Sister Wilkins dealt kindly and tactfully

with the matter. 'Listen to me, Anna,' she said. To everyone except Miss Cavell and the major, Louise was Anna Descamps. 'Captain Quien is French, but although we can take care of his wound, we have no control over what might happen afterwards. You find him attractive, don't you? Well, he's a great one for flirtations, which means you mustn't take him too seriously. And if the Germans come for him, they'll only make him a prisoner of war, nothing worse.'

Louise, who had thought the captain dashing and gallant, did not think that now. His lips had been so greedy, so amorous, turning the kiss into an assault.

'Yes, I see,' she said. She hesitated, then added, 'I just wondered if he really was a French officer.'

'Anna?' Sister Wilkins looked startled.

'You see, there's my friend, Major Scott.' Louise dropped her voice to a discreet whisper. 'He's English, and perhaps the Germans have heard about him being here, perhaps they've sent someone to spy on him—'

'No, of course not.' Sister Wilkins was brisk and decisive. 'If the Germans had heard about any British soldier being here, they would have come and taken him away, not sent spies to search him out. You mustn't worry about Major Scott. We are taking good care of him.'

'Madame said—'

'I think Madame asked you to keep very quiet about him.'

'Oh, I've said nothing to anyone, nothing,' said Louise in her earnest way.

'Good. That's all, then, Anna.' Sister Wilkins found it almost impossible to sustain a strict attitude with this endearing Belgian girl.

'Thank you, Sister.'

'Oh, yes, please go down to the garden again. Your friend wishes to speak to you. You have permission.'

'Oh, thank you so much,' said Louise.

She sped down to the basement in a flurry of whisking skirts, but after a moment or two she restrained her eager rush. There was the dreadful fact that Major Scott had seen Captain Quien kiss her. Her face grew hot. He had witnessed the inevitable consequence of her foolishness. Captain Quien had clearly thought she wanted to be kissed. In her desire to make Major Scott jealous, she had acted stupidly, and Captain Quien had treated her as a coquette.

Oh, what will *mon Commandant* think of me? she wondered.

In the garden, the major waited for her. It had been almost three months since he had sustained his compound fracture. It had taken a long time to begin its real mend, but he was in good physical shape now. It was his emotions which troubled him, for he was torn between his duty to escape and his compulsive desire to stand with Edith. She aroused in him feelings he had not known before, and he wondered if he was in love with her.

Louise Victoria walked slowly up to him.

'*Mon Commandant?*' she said hesitantly.

He was not sure what to say to her. In talking to Quien, she had laid herself open to hearing things which Edith Cavell sought to keep from all the probationers. In being kissed by the Frenchman, she had experienced what any pretty girl might in his company. And if she was drawn to him, that was not unnatural. The man was all too likeable, and the friendliest fellow.

Koletsky had been just as friendly.

The major frowned. Louise, unhappy, dropped her eyes.

'*Mon Commandant?*' she said again, praying he would not be angry with her. But that was foolish too. She had wanted to make him angry and jealous.

The major put aside his doubts and smiled at Louise. 'You're growing, aren't you?'

'Growing?' She glanced uncertainly at him. It was not the opening she had expected.

'In only three months, you're taller.' He might also have said shapelier. Louise was visibly a young woman. 'You're a prettier picture each day, Louise.'

'I am Louise now? What has happened to Victoria?' It was said with a slightly nervous smile. She was sensitive, in any event, about the major's own way of naming her.

'Oh, Victoria is never behind Louise,' he said.

'We're together most of the time.'

'Did Sister Wilkins make it hot for you?' he asked.

'Because of Captain Quien?'

The major wondered exactly what she meant by that. 'You know he's a French officer?' he said.

'Yes.' Louise was on terrible edge, waiting for words she knew were going to hurt her badly.

'The fact is,' said the major, 'he was admitted with a wounded foot. Miss Cavell has her duty as a nurse, d'you see.'

'Which she puts above her obedience to German orders,' said Louise, the evening sun deepening the gold of her hair. 'I think, *mon Commandant*, I am beginning to understand what that means.'

Yes, he thought, she would. Young as she was, she was neither simple nor unperceptive.

'Well, we must stand with Madame, you and I,' he said. 'But, my sweet girl, be careful of men like Captain Quien.'

Emotion swept her. Shame burned her. She

bent her head. What must he think of her, a coquette?

'Be careful not to fall in love with him, you mean?' she whispered.

'Almost every nurse here has.'

'It would not be to your liking if I did too?'

'No. Louise Victoria, he's a man who's in love with all of you.'

She burst into penitence. 'Oh, *mon Commandant*, I did not want him to kiss me – I – I – oh, I was so silly – please never think badly of me for it. However much he's in love with all the nurses here, he's not a man I'd ever fall in love with myself – oh, I am so ashamed.'

'Ashamed? Ashamed, you precious girl?'

'Oh, I am ten thousand times ashamed.'

'Because he kissed you? But you're the most kissable nurse in the place.' The major smiled at his sensitive young comrade.

'But – but you did not like him kissing me, did you?' she asked anxiously.

'No,' said the major frankly. He had, in fact, hated it.

'*Mon Commandant*,' she said, feeling a little better at that, 'you do not know how stupid I was.'

'Louise Victoria, I'll never believe you stupid. You're far from that, and you'll make one of Madame's finest nurses.'

'There's something else I'd much rather be,' she said impulsively.

'What's that?' he asked.

'Oh, something you would say was absurd. If it won't offend you, I'd prefer to keep it to myself.'

'I'm not offended,' he said.

'Your arm will be quite better soon?' she asked.

'I think so.'

She was silent for a few moments, then said, 'I understand how dangerous the Boche are and what might happen, I understand you might have to leave very quickly and that it might not be possible for us to go together. But will you please promise me you will never go without first telling me, that you will not simply disappear without a word?'

'Louise Victoria, I'd never leave this place without first saying goodbye to you.'

Louise looked shocked. *'Mon Commandant,'* she said, 'I hope that is only a careless answer. Who is talking of saying goodbye? I am not. I am only saying you must tell me if you have to leave suddenly.'

'If I have to leave as fast as that,' said the major, 'I'm not sure it wouldn't mean you'd have to leave just as fast yourself. In which case, we'd make a run for it together.'

'Thank you,' she said, 'I feel happier now.'

'My careless answer upset you?' he said, and his teasing smile and his obvious belief that she was not a coquette meant far more to Louise than all the gallantries of Captain Quien.

'Yes,' she said.

'Louise Victoria, you are my inseparable comrade.'

'Then we could never actually say goodbye to each other, could we?'

Chapter Twelve

Edith Cavell conceded that the *Clinique* might be under observation. But there were well over twenty fugitive soldiers in residence, and she was resolved to put them on the road to freedom, like all the others before them. The strain, however, was beginning to show. And the behaviour of Captain Quien caused her unusual irritation.

It was Major Scott's opinion that Quien was so much the ladies' man that he had probably quit the battlefield at Charleroi to go in search of drawing rooms and boudoirs.

'You don't like him, Ned?'

'Oh, he's a pretty fellow,' said the major caustically. 'Found him making eyes at Louise a couple of days ago.'

'Was that what you didn't like?' said Miss Cavell, pouring tea and handing him a cup. He had several times shared this moment of relaxation with her.

'I wasn't precisely overjoyed,' said the major.

'Well, we shall have him out of her way to-morrow,' said Miss Cavell. 'He's fit enough now to make the journey to Holland.'

'Good,' said the major with frank relief. 'I'd like to see you get everyone else out of the place. Edith, it really can't go on.'

Her serenity wavered a little. She was tired. 'It has to go on, Ned.'

'You need a rest from it all,' he said, 'you need to enjoy a month of doing precisely nothing.'

'A month away from all my work? How can I possibly do that?'

'By taking a holiday in a quiet village some-where. I'll go with you. We'll tramp around the countryside together and find places the Germans never bother about.'

The temptation was there, pulling at her. She was silent for some time, thinking about the peace and quiet in a green and untroubled area of Belgium. Then she said softly, 'Thank you for always being so thoughtful, Ned. It's a sweet idea. When we've dispersed all the soldiers here at the moment, we'll talk about it again.'

He doubted, however, if she would do more than that. She was so committed to the cause, so devoted to the soldiers of the Allies. To her, their wish to escape, to get back to the Western Front, meant they were willing to face again the carnage of war. She considered that what she was doing for them was far less than what they were ready to do for the Allies.

She was not going to desert them.

Gaston Quien, in departing from the *Clinique*, left moist feminine eyes behind him. Miss Cavell stood apart from the lamentations. His constant pursuit of females, and his familiarities, had long since spoiled whatever charm he had had for her in the first place.

She was up very early in order to take him to his guide. It was still dark when they left. José, the houseboy, accompanied her, as he often did. Some distance behind, another man followed quietly. It was a long walk to the guide's house, but Miss Cavell insisted on silence. As there was every good reason for that, the Frenchman complied, though he had a hard job to keep his tongue clamped.

When they arrived at the house, she and Quien were admitted, and she introduced him to the guide, Philippe Baucq. She wished him luck and said goodbye. Quien was profuse in his response. As she came out of the house to rejoin José, who was keeping watch, the houseboy lightly touched Miss Cavell's arm and pointed. In the dim light of the breaking dawn, a man was approaching, his arm in a sling.

It was Major Scott. He came up silently but cheerfully.

'What are you doing here?' Miss Cavell whispered.

'I was awake,' he said, 'and found myself thinking. I decided I'd like to keep the pretty fellow close company.'

'The guide will do that.'

'All the same, I'll go with them. I want to see Quien across the border. It's been on my mind these last few days that the fellow's too smooth by half.'

Miss Cavell, slenderly handsome in her cape and uniform, looked hard at him. 'Ned, you intend to cross the border too, to escape with him?' she asked.

'I ought to. But my arm's still not my most reliable asset. I can't crawl about or swim rivers, but I can keep an eye on Quien, and I mean to. Until we reach the border, he'll think I'm going all the way with him. Let me do this, won't you?'

'You'll be so handicapped,' she said, but she smiled faintly in assent.

'My right arm's very useful,' murmured the major, looking up and down the silent, greyshrouded street. 'Don't know how I'm going to stand his Gallic verbosity, but that's not important. Once I'm sure he's going to cross the border, I'll be on my way back to you.'

'It will be very risky if you return on your own.'

'We'll see,' he said.

'Take great care,' she said, and he thought how poised she looked and yet how vulnerable she was. He took both her hands and pressed them. She smiled. 'Thank you, Ned, I know why you're doing this. I must have a word with the guide about you.'

She went back into the house, and the major followed. She introduced him to Philippe Baucq, her friend and associate, a strong-faced, handsome man. Quien looked surprised but not unhappy about having the major for extra company. Miss Cavell, saying goodbye again, with the slightest of smiles for the major, began her return to the *Clinique* with José beside her. From the door the major watched her. Her figure was upright, her walk calm and unhurried. Her cape stirred in the warm breeze, her serenity as tangible to him at a distance as close to. He felt great pride for her. He also felt a poignancy. He quietly closed the door and rejoined Quien and Baucq. They left for the border a few minutes later.

'It's time,' said Lieutenant Bergan through wispy smoke.

'What for?' asked Detective Pinkhoff.

'A call.'

'On Ixelles?'

'We've enough information to justify a search,' said Bergan. 'Our new friend has been very helpful. Jacobs gave you a few names.

This man has given you information.'

'If we find enemy soldiers in hiding there, *Herr Leutnant*, I don't recommend arresting Fräulein Cavell.'

'Did I say we should?'

'Arresting her would make her contacts disappear overnight.'

'I hope we're all capable of drawing that obvious conclusion. To scare the lady should be enough. She'll dispatch her staff in all directions, carrying warning messages to her associates. Watch her. Watch them.'

'That is the plan? To panic Fräulein Cavell into alerting her associates?' Pinkhoff was dubious.

'And leading us to them. Jacobs gave us a few names. You've established a connection exists between them and a few others. I'm convinced that those we could accordingly lay our hands on now represent only a small part of the organization.'

'So far, neither Fräulein Cavell nor any of her staff have led us to obvious contacts,' said Pinkhoff. 'She herself calls only at houses where nurses of hers are looking after private patients. Philippe Baucq and others, yes, they're different. Baucq calls at the *Clinique* from time to time. He calls on certain other people from time to time. He disappears from time to time. He's disappeared now.'

'You've lost a man high on your list of

suspects?' said Bergan, acid on his tongue, but a smile on his face.

'We haven't the men available to watch any of them all the time. But Baucq will be back.'

'Has he ever been observed leaving the *Clinique* in company with men?' asked Bergan.

'No, *Herr Leutnant*,' said Pinkhoff. 'Incidentally, should I go on this raid? At this stage, I'd still prefer to remain in the background.' Pinkhoff, certain that Edith Cavell was a woman of cunning, had no desire to take charge of a search. He felt he would draw the kind of blank that would do his reputation no good at all. He favoured persistent and diligent surveillance.

'Raid?' said Bergan. 'Raid? Noise and disturbance? The arousing of the whole of Ixelles? The organization would melt away at once. I said make a call. Conduct an official but quiet search. Send just two men, including Detective Mayer. Mayer knows something of the place. He's been there twice with Heilmann, looking for the Comtesse de Bouchet. Fräulein Cavell won't like him turning up a third time. But he's to arrest no one, except any Allied soldiers he might find.'

'I'll send Mayer and another man,' said Pinkhoff.

'Yes, do that.' Bergan nodded. 'By the way, tell Mayer not to make the same mistake as Heilmann.'

'What mistake?'

'Tell him not to fall in love with Fräulein Cavell.'

Detective Otto Mayer needed no such advice. Whereas Heilmann had been impressed by the demeanour of Edith Cavell, Mayer had felt her serenity too good to be true. In company with a colleague, he made his call on the *Clinique* in a mood of officious determination. He was advised that Madame was out, making one of her regular rounds of private patients. Sister Wilkins received the two Germans. She did not know either of them. Mayer looked around her room. She asked him what he wanted.

Casually, Mayer asked, 'Have you any more left?'

'No, none,' she said, assuming he was asking if there were any nurses available for private patients. The *Clinique* could rarely meet all the demands in this field.

'What, no more Tommies?' said Mayer caustically, and showed her his badge. Sister Wilkins, realizing she was in the presence of two members of the German secret police, felt prickles of alarm, but she resolutely denied knowing what he was talking about. Mayer, expecting such a response, was not put off. He began to rummage through her desk, then abruptly asked to be taken to the men's wards. Sister Wilkins silently led the way.

It was a day when fortune smiled on the brave. The patients were all genuine cases, all Belgian civilians, and the ranks of resident soldiers had been reduced to four men only. And these four were in the reading room. Mayer and his colleague began to question the patients, and Sister Wilkins managed to convey the warning signal to a nurse. The nurse slipped quietly out. A minute or so later, the four soldiers had disappeared over the garden wall.

Mayer, finding none of the patients suspect, became coldly angry. At this moment Miss Cavell returned. He pounced. He shot questions at her, all concerning the use of her *Clinique* as a shelter and a rendezvous for Allied soldiers attempting to escape to Holland. Miss Cavell answered all his questions calmly, without giving anything away, and put one of her own. Had he discovered any soldiers in the *Clinique*? That was not the point, said Mayer. Surely it was the whole point, she suggested. He brushed that aside, and asked more questions. Miss Cavell, her unshakeable coolness hiding the strain of the confrontation, still managed to give answers that admitted nothing.

Mayer, his search fruitless and his questions answered, had no further terms of reference. He left in a mood of frustration.

At once, Miss Cavell was persuaded by her nurses to embark on her first real act of self-preservation. With their help she destroyed all papers and documents likely to incriminate her. What she did not do was to turn her staff into messengers of fear and send them running in all directions. She was too clear-headed a woman to make a move as obvious as that.

During the rest of that day and the whole of the next, Pinkhoff and his surveillance team watched the *Clinique* in vain. Lieutenant Bergan had overlooked what she might do with incriminating papers; Mayer had been instructed only to search the place for refugee enemy soldiers and to ask questions. He had not been told to seize any papers.

Louise, leaving Miss Cavell's room in company with other probationers after an evening lecture, saw Sister Wilkins in the corridor. She broke away to speak to her.

'Sister, may I please visit the patient or meet him in the garden?' It was the accepted opening. Sister Wilkins knew which patient was meant, and that the girl was occasionally allowed to spend time with him.

Worried and preoccupied because of events, she said, 'Your friend, nurse? He's gone.'

'Gone?' Louise could not comprehend such an answer, nor its casualness.

Sister Wilkins, looking round, said quietly, 'To the border. A few days ago. You won't ask me to say more.' Indeed, there was little more she could have said, for she only knew what

Miss Cavell had told her – that Major Scott had gone on the escape route with Captain Quien.

Louise looked stunned, incredulous. Sister Wilkins hurried away. The young Comtesse did not move. She could not, she was frozen. *Gone?* He had gone, without telling her, without even that contentious goodbye – after all he had said, after all they had both said?

The pain of his cruel defection knifed through her frozen body. Her teeth caught on a lip that had begun to tremble. She turned and walked out of the *Clinique* into the evening sunshine, across the street to fields of potatoes, careless of who might see her. No one did. The nearest surveillance man was walking along the rue de Berkendael, away from the *Clinique*, going off duty.

The tears began to run as she blindly walked a path between the fields.

Lieutenant Bergan, almost out of temper because Edith Cavell had made none of the moves expected of her, cooled down after a day or two. He dispatched two other men to the *Clinique*. The tactics now were to harass her into panic. Bergan meant to round up every member of the organization. Jacobs had managed to come up with four names, including Edith Cavell's. Pinkhoff had collected other names, of people called on by suspects like Philippe Baucq. But, as Pinkhoff himself admitted, such people might only be innocent friends. What was wanted was a move by a scared Edith Cavell which would lead them to undoubted members of her organization.

The two policemen made no search, nor did they question Miss Cavell, They merely informed her they wanted to take Sister Wilkins to headquarters for interrogation. Miss Cavell showed a visible concern.

At headquarters, Sister Wilkins was questioned for two hours. Bergan stood by, listening to the interpreter. He asked no questions of his own and let Pinkhoff conduct the proceedings. Bergan was saving his own style of interrogation for Edith Cavell. Sister Wilkins, despite all her fears and anxieties, proved an exemplary lieutenant of her matron. She denied all knowledge of an escape organization. She, like Miss Cavell, gave nothing away. She was partly helped by the nature of the questions, which seemed to indicate the Germans had no facts, only suspicions. She was released. But completely alarmed now, she hurried back to the *Clinique* and begged Miss Cavell to vanish. She must go, at once, to any place that would provide security – Holland, France, or even some remote little spot in Belgium. Miss Cavell firmly refused to consider it.

To go meant an abdication of her duty and responsibilities. After all, she argued, had there been any real danger, had the secret police been in possession of proof, they would have taken her to headquarters as well, and neither of them would have been released. It was unpleasant, perhaps, to have the Germans breathing so persistently down their necks, but it only meant everyone had to take more care than usual. No one must worry unnecessarily.

She was reassuring, she was even serene, but there were deepening shadows around her eyes.

She knew the drums were rolling. She could hear them now.

Bergan's men made an organized raid at last, a few days later. It was entirely typical of Miss Cavell that, despite her awareness of the closing net, she had received several British soldiers under the cover of darkness since the last German visit.

Pinkhoff himself appeared, in command of the raid. The interrogation of Sister Wilkins had again failed to panic Miss Cavell. So, Bergan had said, it was time for a very positive move. He had finally realized Edith Cavell might possess papers listing names of all her contacts. Her *Clinique* must be turned upside down for such documents, and Pinkhoff was to supervise the search.

Pinkhoff emerged from the shadowy background as dark and as dangerous as a hungry wolf. The moment he entered the *Clinique* with his men, Sister Wilkins, an astute and courageous woman, went into action. Swiftly she withdrew to communicate alarm. With the assistance of several nurses, she quickly rounded up the resident British soldiers. They sped down to the basement and out through the door that led into the garden. In their awareness of the situation they asked no questions. They would have jumped off the moon for Miss Cavell and her nurses. The garden wall was a minor hazard and they were over it in seconds.

Pinkhoff and his men ransacked every room in the *Clinique*. The first thing they discovered was that there was not one Allied soldier anywhere in the place. That was a blow to Pinkhoff, but not an unexpected one. Heilmann had felt Miss Cavell was too gracious a woman to break the law; Pinkhoff felt she was far too intelligent to be easily found out. The most valuable exhibits the prosecution could bring before a court – Allied soldiers apprehended on the premises – did not materialize.

He turned to the business of finding other evidence: papers, documents, diaries, anything. The search was destructively thorough. In her office, Miss Cavell, lips compressed, looked on silently as the Germans wrenched pictures from walls, and scattered drawers and papers, files and cards. Then they ravaged her sitting room. They left the *Clinique* looking wrecked. The innocent probationers, taking notes at a lecture in their own side of the institute, were troubled by the noise but they were left alone. Had Detective Mayer thought to look in on them, he might have noticed a sad-eyed nurse corresponding to the description of the Comtesse de Bouchet.

Pinkhoff discovered not one paper or one document of value. He departed in savage silence, without a word to anyone. His men followed him out. One, however, remained in occupation of a front room, his presence a warning and a threat. The raid was harassment of a brutally abrasive kind. It had the nurses near to tears.

Miss Cavell, pale but still incredibly calm, restored much of the morale of nurses and staff. She spoke to them as if the incident had been of no more importance than any of their everyday problems. She thanked them for their loyalty, their courage and their steadfastness. Times were difficult, of course, but so they were for all people in Belgium these days. Salvation lay in God's love, and comfort lay in prayer. A few smashed windows in the wards were of no importance at all.

These quiet, reassuring words resulted in a grand gesture of defiance. The entire staff attacked the chaos until the *Clinique* again looked as it always did – a picture of tidiness and cleanliness. Perhaps the gesture was an emotional one, an involuntary demonstration of the devotion Edith Cavell inspired, and perhaps she appreciated the practical turn it took.

That night the wind blew strongly from the south-west. Louise, lying awake, like other people in the *Clinique*, though not for the same reason, heard the sounds of the great guns of war from the Front. In Brussels, people got out of their beds and looked from their windows at the distant night sky. The flash and glare of the gunfire could be seen. Louise did not get out of her bed. She lay awake, consumed by the heartache of new loneliness.

Three of the British soldiers quietly returned during the night. Miss Cavell got up, and under the nose of the sleeping German policeman she took them to the house of Philippe Baucq, whose family received them. They were taken out of the house before Brussels was awake, and turned over to a guide.

It was a long walk to and from Baucq's house for Miss Cavell that night. With the persistent sound of the guns, she had had little sleep at all. She entered the *Clinique* unnoticed by the snoring German sentry at six o'clock, the dawn hour.

Dawn was the immutable hour of destiny for Edith Cavell. Almost, perhaps, in her feeling for the inevitable, she was waiting for it.

Chapter Thirteen

A boy called at the *Clinique*, asking if he could see Miss Cavell. He had a letter to give her and could give it to no one else, he said. He was taken to her office. A polite little fellow, he doffed his cap to her and executed a small bow. This gesture of courtesy, from a lad of ten, brought a misty smile to the face of the nurse who had shown him in. Grave youth at its politest before dearest Madame made a picture to remember. Madame smiled back and the nurse left.

'Madame?' said the boy.

'Young man?'

'I am to ask, Madame, if you know Nurse Anna Marie Descamps.'

'I know her. She is a student here.'

'Then, Madame,' said the lad with the utmost gravity, 'I am to give you this letter, if you please, and to ask if you will pass it on to her.'

He produced the letter. The sealed envelope was plain, inscribed with neither name nor address. Miss Cavell looked into his brown eyes, his earnest face, and she smiled again.

'Very well. I will pass it on to her.'

'Thank you, Madame.' He bowed again, put his cap on and went to the door.

'Goodbye,' said Miss Cavell.

He turned and looked at her, his gravity masking his shyness. Her gentleness was very reassuring. He smiled.

'Goodbye, Madame,' he said.

Miss Cavell gave the letter to Louise a little later, catching the girl as she left the classroom.

'Brought by a boy for Anna Marie Descamps,' murmured Miss Cavell.

'Oh? Thank you, Madame.'

Miss Cavell glanced questioningly at her. Louise looked a little low.

'If the letter means a problem of some kind, come and see me,' she said.

'Yes, Madame. Thank you.'

Louise took the letter up to her room. She shared it with three other girls, but it was empty at the moment. She began to slit the envelope without much interest, then she suddenly wondered why it was blank, thought of Major Scott – and tore it open quickly.

But it was not from him. It was from Elizabeth, a note accompanying a letter which had found its way into Belgium through Holland, and been opened by the German censor before being delivered. It was from Louise's grandmother in Petrograd. Elizabeth explained in her note that she had not been able to bring it herself, for she was sure she was being followed whenever she went out. So she managed to arrange for a dear young friend to bring it. She sent Louise her fondest love and begged her to take every care.

The letter from Grandmama was one of anxious, loving enquiry. She begged Louise for some news, for some assurance that she was all right. She had heard nothing from her since her father's death at Liège. It was the dreadful war, of course, but was it not possible to get a letter through somehow to one who loved her and worried about her? Was it not even possible, perhaps, for her to get to Petrograd, which would be so much better than occupied Belgium? Her grandmama dearly wished to see her, to take care of her.

Louise wrote back in a mood of sadness. Miss Cavell promised she would ask someone to take the letter to Holland and post it there. She was about to ask Louise if anything was worrying her, for the girl seemed so dispirited, when Sister Wilkins came in, and Louise drifted away.

'What is the matter, Anna?' asked her friend, Yvette, that evening.

'Nothing,' said Louise.

'Yes, there is. You're so unhappy.'

'It's nothing,' said Louise. There was no one she could talk to. Except Madame, perhaps, but Madame had her own worries. Everyone knew, the whole of Ixelles knew, that for some reason the Germans had turned the *Clinique* upside down. Perhaps they'd been after Major Scott. Perhaps that was why he'd gone; perhaps Madame had known the Germans meant to arrest him, and she had got him away. They were very close, Madame and Major Scott. Perhaps they were in love.

No, she could not talk to Madame.

'Anna, please let me help,' said Yvette, 'I know you're unhappy.'

'I am going to try to get to Russia,' said Louise flatly, 'and live with my grandparents there. In Petrograd.'

'You have grandparents in Russia?' said Yvette in astonishment.

'There's nothing against that, is there?'

'No, of course not,' said Yvette, but wondered why her friend, who usually said little about her family, should suddenly claim Russian grandparents. 'Anna, are you in love?'

'That's a silly question,' Louise said, turning away.

'Have you met a nice boy somewhere?' asked Yvette, thinking perhaps Anna had fallen for someone who did not return her affection.

'A nice boy? A boy?' Louise, suffering, thought

that even sillier. 'I've grown out of boys, I should hope.'

'I only meant—'

'Please excuse me,' said Louise. She could stand no more of Yvette's curiosity, nor continue with a conversation that was twisting the knife of pain. She went up to an empty room on the top floor and stood at the window, looking at the potato fields opposite, where she and Major Scott had waited that night while Madame Herriot had gone to make sure all was well.

She should not feel lonely. But she was, despite the friends she had made. The major had deserted her on her eighteenth birthday. That made his defection so much more painful, because at eighteen one was a woman.

She lay awake again that night.

Before breakfast the next morning, Yvette hastened down to see Miss Cavell on a matter that was alarming her.

'Oh, Madame – Nurse Descamps – she can't be found.'

Miss Cavell, disguising her immediate concern, applied a calming note to the probationer's agitation.

'Well, I'm sure there's an explanation. She retired to bed with the rest of you last night?'

'Yes. But she wasn't in her bed when we got up. Madame, she talked to me yesterday about trying to get to Petrograd, where she said she had grandparents.'

Miss Cavell, recalling Louise's recent look of depression, began an immediate investigation. It did not take her long to realize that whatever had been troubling Louise was serious enough to have made her walk out of the school to heaven knew where. Could it really be Petrograd she had in mind?

The girl was gone; that was painfully certain.

Miss Cavell, distressed, searched her mind for clues that might tell her the route Louise would have taken to reach the Dutch border. She knew the country, but the Germans wanted her badly. She would be at great risk for all her knowledge.

The following day, Major Scott returned, entering the *Clinique* just after midday, his sling discarded and his left arm free. He went at once to report to Miss Cavell.

He had found the venture spiced with moments of danger but, under the guidance of Philippe Baucq, neither he nor Quien had lost confidence. They had travelled mainly on foot. Baucq was so familiar with every landmark and, at times, even with every blade of grass, that his relationship with the whole route was one of comforting intimacy. For the most part he chose byways that kept them clear of Germans.

He made them wait outside some villages, which he entered alone. When he returned he usually brought a little food and wine, but which houses he visited and which families supplied him with the food, he did not say. The major knew he would not, even if asked. Quien, however, was more curious and less tactful.

'M'sieu,' he said on one occasion, 'what's the name of this particular village?'

Philippe Baucq looked thoughtfully at the Frenchman. 'I don't know,' he said with pleasant deliberation, 'and as I don't know, nor do either of you, which is better for all of us.'

'Ah, yes,' smiled Quien, 'of course.' But he asked similar questions on other occasions. Always, Baucq's reply was uninformative.

At night, they slept in the open or in barns, when the ache in the major's arm was a nagging reminder that it still needed care. But he took the sling off one day, stowed it in his pocket, and put the arm to swinging exercise as he walked. Quien, on the whole, gave no trouble at all – probably because he was out of reach of women – and was a pleasant companion. He made the trek more tolerable than the major had expected; but his determination to keep an eye on the Frenchman was unchanged.

Only when it was unavoidable did they enter urban areas. Since this meant they were under the eyes of the Germans, they split up, Quien in company with either Baucq or the major. There were no crises, and they reached Overpelt safely. But here there was so much German activity that a border crossing was out of the question. They turned south-east to a point where, on the other side of the Meuse, lay Maastricht in Holland. The bridge was tightly guarded by the Germans on the Belgian side. At this stage, Baucq transferred the major and Quien to the care of another guide, who knew the bargemen and where to get escaping soldiers under the wire and down the bank to the water.

The bank was patrolled with dangerous regularity by German soldiers, but the guide knew the moments to choose. Under cover of darkness, the three men broke through, evading the sweep of searchlights. The guide gestured Quien to follow him and keep close behind him on the descent to the water and a waiting boat.

The Frenchman whispered to the major, 'Not you, *mon Commandant*?'

'One at a time, and you first,' murmured the major, who had no intention of going.

The guide, aware of the major's plan, gave him a brief smile and vanished with Quien. The major heard the slight rustle of their movements, then silence descended. He waited, stretched out on the ground, while the probing lights restlessly streaked earth and sky, and German patrols passed by nerve-rackingly close. His left arm took on a sensitive tenderness, a feeling of peculiar susceptibility, as if the damaged bone would crumble in brittle fragility at the first violent movement. He persisted with his waiting brief, however. If Quien slipped away, the guide would be back. When there was no sign of either man after thirty minutes, the major climbed slowly and cautiously to his feet, judged to a nicety the moment to break clear, and made his dash. Under the wire, and out of range of lights and patrols a few minutes later, he began his journey back to Ixelles, and to Edith Cavell and Louise.

Miss Cavell listened to his story without interrupting him, then said, I'm very glad you're safely back, Ned, and to see you again.'

'I'm just as glad to see you,' he said, 'and I have to confess it was slower coming than going.'

'Without a guide, it was bound to be,' she said. The shadows of increasing strain were around her eyes. In a moment, she was going to have to tell the major that Louise had gone.

'But I've learned how to get to the Dutch border by myself, if I have to,' he said.

'Yes, that was part of the exercise, wasn't it?'

'Edith, you look tired. Has anything happened?'

Two things: the devastating raid by the Germans, and the disappearance of Louise. But she only said, 'We are carrying on in our usual way.'

'Your usual way means something highly dangerous in my book,' said the major. It was Edith, not Quien, who had really occupied his mind during the journey. 'Are you sure there's been no trouble?'

She hesitated before making a small admission. 'I think the Germans are watching us. Most of my nurses are certain they're being followed whenever they go out.'

The major grimaced. 'I'd better go,' he said. 'Being here is no help to you.'

'You're quite wrong, Ned, if you think I'd rather you went in order to make it safer for me. And there are always other soldiers here beside yourself, so your presence makes no difference. However, if Dr Depage says your arm is all right—'

'I think he'll only say I can't yet swing a club with it. Edith, you won't take time off for a rest, I know, but will you at least assure me that if there's a crisis, you'll be ready to fly?'

'If there's a crisis, Ned, I must stay to fight it,' she said. 'I can't leave my nurses to face it for me.'

'Your nurses aren't in it as deeply as you are.'

'All the same—'

'Oh, the devil,' said the major.

'We try,' said Miss Cavell, 'to keep that dark gentleman out of our institute.'

'Oh, I think he's looked in occasionally,' said

the major, thinking of people like Koletsky and Jacobs.

'Ned, I must tell you,' she said. 'I must tell you, I'm afraid, that Louise is missing.'

'*Missing?*'

'It seems she got up before dawn yesterday and walked out. She had talked to another student nurse about going to Petrograd to be with her Russian grandparents. She hasn't been her usual self lately, and I meant to call her in and talk to her, but I've been so terribly busy. I blame myself bitterly for not having spared her a little time at least. Ned, I think she missed you more than she cared to say. How did she behave when you told her you were going with Captain Quien to the border?'

'Oh, my God,' said the major, and looked stunned.

Miss Cavell eyed him in disbelief. 'You didn't tell her?'

'No. I should have, of course I should, but I don't have direct contact with your pro-bationers, especially not at five in the morning. Edith, I thought you would tell her.'

'And I thought you would, naturally,' said Miss Cavell in distress. 'Ned, you could have left a little note for her or at least given me a message to pass on to her.'

'I allowed myself no time to write her a note.' The major paced the office. 'Oh, my God, I've let her down, and badly. She must have thought I'd gone for good. Didn't she ask?'

'No, I'm afraid she didn't. I think your going must have made her feel questions were useless. But I'm to blame as much as you. I should have talked to her, spared her a few minutes. It's very possible indeed that she's going to try to get to Petrograd from Holland. Her grandparents there are dear to her, and she needs to belong to someone she feels close to.'

'I must go after her,' said the major decisively.

'In which direction?' asked Miss Cavell.

'Direction? My God, the infinite variations frighten me. But I wonder – her house in Brussels? If she's risking a journey to the border, she might first have risked going there to see the family servant, Madame Dupont. Edith, I'm off to Brussels.'

'You realize the Germans may be watching her house, looking just as hard for you as for her?' she said.

'Yes. But I must go. It's our one chance of getting a lead on her.' The major's mouth became tight, his expression full of bitter self-reproach.

He took a tram into the city. He was dressed these days in new clothes Miss Cavell had found for him: a dark blue jacket, grey trousers and a straw boater. They went with his new identity.

Brussels wore its sombre air of occupation.

He made his way towards the rue Royale, where the de Bouchet residence was situated. There were civilians about, and German soldiers, and he began to saunter. He noted the house, its handsome façade and its imposing door. He was tempted, in his feverish urgency, to damn caution and knock on that door, but the last thing he wanted was to fall into German hands himself. That would destroy whatever hope he had of locating Louise. In his self-disgust at the way he had let down his young comrade, it did not occur to him to wonder why his concern for her was so intense, why his emotions were so involved. If her house was under surveillance, he had to spot the watchers. He strolled up and down, eyeing everyone in the vicinity, for twenty minutes and more.

At a moment when he felt sure the German secret police were not in evidence, the door of the house opened and a woman came out. It was Madame Elizabeth Dupont, still in her mourning black. She carried a shopping basket, a sign these days of hope or optimism. The major watched her as she began to walk along the pavement. He also watched the movements of people. He let her proceed for quite some distance before he set out to catch her up, by which time he had a feeling there was no one on her tail.

When he arrived at her elbow and spoke to her, she recognized him at once, and they walked along together. He asked her if she had seen anything of Louise. No, she had not, and it was just as well that the Comtesse had kept out of the way, for the German police continued to make periodical calls and still watched the house at times. The major asked her all the same to keep a careful eye open for Louise, who had left the *Clinique*, apparently with the idea of trying to get to Petrograd. Madame Dupont was both worried and glad about that; worried because of the dangers, and glad because Petrograd was the best place for the Comtesse until the war was over.

'But wait, m'sieu. Is she by herself?'

'It seems so,' said the major, feeling a little savage that he had wasted valuable time.

'Why?' Madame Dupont was accusing. 'I thought, m'sieu, that you promised to take care of her.'

'I will take care of her. When I find her.' Wanting to stay in Brussels no longer, he added, 'I must go. Goodbye, madame.'

He went off, striding fast. Madame Dupont looked after him, sadness in her eyes.

On the tram back to Ixelles, the major was in deep, desperate thought, searching his mind, as Miss Cavell had searched hers, for something that would tell him which route Louise might have taken to the border. Overpelt? Yes. He had passed through it himself with Baucq and Quien, and Louise had mentioned it. She had also mentioned she had friends there. Overpelt it had to be. He must get there fast. His mind began to turn on details of the route.

'Your pass.'

He looked up. A German soldier had a hand extended. The major extracted the faked pass which gave him permission to travel on trams. The soldier examined it, looked hard at him, and handed it back. He moved on. The major's thoughts returned to Overpelt, to the journey in front of him, but something pulled him away from Overpelt. What was it? Something Louise had once said, something that had nothing to do with Overpelt? What was it? It was there, in his subconscious, but would not reveal itself.

Damn it, think. *Think*.

Not until he had left the tram and was walking to the *Clinique*, not until the potato fields came into sight, did the locked-in memory return to him of a dark and eventful evening, in which words had reached him through a thick curtain of pain. He did not enter the *Clinique*. He crossed the street and kept straight on, walking fast alongside the fields.

After all, it was only three kilometres from here. He could reach it in thirty minutes.

'My child,' said Eloise Herriot, 'I will come with you to the border. I can't let you begin such a journey on your own, especially in the dark.'

'No, you have done more than enough for me,' said Louise, 'you have given me so much kindness and understanding.'

Madame Herriot had been very kind indeed to her, from the moment Louise had arrived the previous morning. The girl eventually confessed that her English friend, her comrade, had gone on the escape route to Holland without her. Now she wished to get to Russia, to Petrograd, to her grandparents. Eloise Herriot soon realized why the girl was so unhappy. She talked to her, questioning the advisability of going alone to the border, when the Germans were so active and Louise was badly wanted by them. She had persuaded her to sleep on the matter for a night, but today Louise seemed just as set. Eloise Herriot no longer argued, only quietly insisted on accompanying her.

'I'm used to walking in the dark,' she said. And she was, for she served as a guide with Edith Cavell's escape organization.

'You go out at night to walk?' said Louise.

'I go to do what little I can for Belgium and our allies.'

'I see,' said Louise. 'Yes, I understand, madame. You are very brave.'

'It's something to do,' said Eloise Herriot. 'We'll leave here at dusk and walk through most of the night, if you like. In which case, you should try to get some sleep. And when you reach Holland, go to Amsterdam, to the Russian Embassy. They will tell you how best to get to Petrograd.'

'I feel I'm putting you to so much trouble—'

'I think we agreed that if you were in need, you should come to me.'

'I came because I knew I could talk to you.' Louise smiled brightly. 'And because I remembered how good you were to us that night. I am – I am sorry my English friend isn't here with me now, so that we could tell you together how much we owe you—'

'You'll meet again when the war is over.'

'No, I don't think so,' said Louise, and fixed her gaze on her hands, which were clasped in her lap. 'He would have left me a letter if he had thought we should meet again. He – oh, Madame Herriot, I did not think he'd do that – go without even a single word.'

'Perhaps he had to leave very suddenly, mam'selle. Now, will you try to get some sleep?'

'Yes. Thank you. I feel I should have left a note for Madame, that it was ungrateful of me not to let her know how much I appreciated all she did for me.'

'If you would like to write her a letter before we leave,' said Eloise Herriot, 'I will see she gets it.'

She went with Louise to the little bedroom she had given the girl for the night. It was bright and cheerful with chintzes. The afternoon sun, sailing out of the clouds, beamed warmly through the window. On the marble-topped washstand was a small enamel plate in which rested an old clay pipe. Louise had noticed it previously, and was curious about it.

'The pipe was your husband's, madame?' she asked.

'No.' Eloise Herriot smiled. 'I had an English soldier here once. He stayed a few days, until it was safe to get him away. He left his pipe. So it's still there, waiting for him.'

'He is going to come back for it?' asked Louise.

The faintest tint of colour showed on Eloise Herriot's face. 'I can speak only a few words of English, and he could speak only a few words of French,' she said, 'yet we had many conversations, and many laughs. So I hope he will come back for his pipe when the war is over. He said he would.'

'For his pipe?'

'He did not mention his pipe at the time.' Eloise Herriot smiled again. 'He had not yet left it behind. Mam'selle, I am not a woman who likes to live alone, but when the war is over, many of us will have to. So I sometimes pray my English soldier will survive. His name is Albert.'

'That is our King's name,' said Louise.

'Yes. Except that my funny soldier's name

is Albert Edward Lomax, and he used to be a blacksmith.'

'I shall pray for him too, madame.'

When Eloise Herriot left the bedroom, Louise stood by the window. The little village street did not look as it had on the night when the German cycle troops had invaded it. It was pretty in the sunshine, and there was not a German in sight, only a small girl and a man. The man was striding past the girl. He wore a dark blue jacket with brass buttons, grey trousers and a straw boater. His stride was long and easy—

Louise caught her breath. Her hand rushed to her throat, her eyes opened wide and became enormous. Joy brought hot, brimming tears. She ran from the room, flew down the narrow stairs and out of the front door. She ran into the path of the advancing major.

'Oh, *mon Commandant*!'

'Louise—'

'Oh, *mon Commandant*!'

'What's all this?' He tried to speak lightly. Louise was hugging him, clinging to him.

'Oh, I thought – they said – I thought – oh, you've come back – and you knew I was here—'

'I meant to come back, I only hoped you'd be here.' He did not want to dramatize. Louise Victoria was emotional enough. But the moment was extraordinarily sweet as her warm body pressed closer. 'Have a care, young lady. What kind of behaviour is this, with people looking on?'

Louise drew back, her face flushed. But she took hold of herself, for modesty's sake on the one hand, and, on the other, to deliver a reprimand.

'*Mon Commandant*,' she said, 'it is your behaviour which is regrettable, not mine. Despite all your promises, you went away without a word to me.'

'Yes, I know. It was only for a short while, but all the same I should have spoken to you. I went for a special reason I'll tell you about, and very early in the morning, long before you were up. However, will you forgive me, Louise Victoria, and come back to Ixelles and the school?'

'Yes, oh, yes,' said Louise in gladness, 'but first please come and say hello to Madame Herriot, who has been so kind to me again. Oh, and there's something else. When you finally get back to England, you must enquire of the British army about how to get in touch with a soldier called Albert Edward Lomax, who left his pipe in Madame Herriot's house. He must write to her.'

'About his pipe?' said the major, his gravity masking his delight in her.

'But don't you see, he left it behind to let her know he was definitely going to return. Therefore, he should write to her, and you must tell him to. I think it would please her immensely.'

'Whatever you say, Louise Victoria.'

As they went into the house, she said, 'Thank you, *mon Commandant*, thank you so much for knowing I was here, and for coming for me.'

They sat that evening in the *Clinique* garden. Louise had been reconciled with Madame, who had been only too glad to see her back. The sinking sun fired the gold of her hair and coloured her with its light as they spoke of Belgium's dire straits, with the British naval blockade and the Germans starving the people of everything but the bare necessities. They had to rely on the generosity of America for the provision of flour. Louise was sad for her country, but burning to help the Allies, in company with the major. He would help by returning to the Western Front to fight the Boche. She would help by going with him and finishing her training as a nurse. They could not stay much longer under Madame's roof. It was too risky for them, and too risky for Madame.

She confessed to him that although she was happy as a probationer, she did not feel settled. It was the Boche. Even when they remained unseen, she felt they were close and that they had eyes all over the place. Everyone knew they had descended on the *Clinique* a few days ago and searched it, and harassed Madame dreadfully. Then they just went away again.

'They've been here?' asked the major, startled.

'Oh, they say a number of them came,' said Louise, 'and that they searched every room in the *Clinique*, though they didn't disturb us. It was terribly lucky you were away, or they might have asked you questions and found out you weren't Philippe Rainier at all.'

The major was silent for a while, then said, 'Well, I'm not Philippe Rainier, not now. My new papers identify me as Henri Descamps, engineer, and uncle to Anna Marie Descamps.'

Louise sat up. 'I've never heard anything so silly,' she said. 'Such an absurdity coming on top of my recent travail, *mon Commandant*, is not something I can laugh at. Uncles are middle-aged, and mostly rather fat and jolly. They pat one on the head. I'm sure I've said before that anyone looking at you and me could see you couldn't possibly be my uncle, especially as I'm now past eighteen and going on for twenty—'

'Louise Victoria, are you sure the Germans came and searched every room, then just went away again?'

'That's what everyone says.'

'I missed it all?' The major was frowning.

'Yes, fortunately. *Mon Commandant*, we can be cousins, if you like.' Louise was not going to be manoeuvred into assuming a relationship that had no appeal to her at all. It might stick. 'Cousins would be much more suitable, don't you think?'

'Just as you like, chicken.' The major realized there had been trouble, after all, and of a particularly pointed kind. The Germans were obviously on to Edith. She had avoided telling him, perhaps because she thought he really would take steps to get her out of the place. Was it strength or weakness on his part to stand aside while she walked on a knife edge with almost impossible calm?

'Are you listening?' Louise was a little perturbed by his inattention.

'To what?' he said. But she could not be cross; the moment she saw him striding towards Madame Herriot's house, she had replaced him on his pedestal.

'I've been saying we should think about leaving. It isn't right to have Madame on such tenterhooks about us, and we aren't really safe here now, are we? When I get my diploma, perhaps in England, I could work in a hospital close to the Front—'

'You're set now on England, chicken?'

'Oh, England or France or Russia,' she said. 'We could simply let our feet carry us. We could leave it to them, wherever they take us.'

'Well, when we must we will,' he said cautiously.

'*Mon Commandant*,' said Louise, 'apart from

when you go off on journeys without telling me, we enjoy exceptional accord, don't you think?'

'Exceptional, Louise Victoria,' he said. But he was thinking about Edith Cavell and a closing net.

Chapter Fourteen

Henri Pinkhoff, motivated by professionalism and the acerbity of Lieutenant Bergan, was busily ferreting around. The raid on the Edith Cavell *Clinique* had been humiliatingly unproductive: no incriminating documents, and not one single flea-bitten soldier. Pinkhoff, not given to taking any step of importance unless he was sure of satisfactory results, experienced a period of savage disappointment. Then he took up the hunt with new determination. If he had not yet obtained any really conclusive evidence, he was piling up valuable information, including more names, such as those of Prince Reginald de Croy and his sister Princess Marie.

He and his colleagues were now keeping the *Clinique* under daily surveillance. They were also tailing suspects and following nurses. Pinkhoff pursued all leads with his own kind of diligence, which was noticeable to people who had reason to look over their shoulder. It lost him the chance of getting close to some suspects one day. He had fastened on to the tail of Prince Reginald de Croy when that gentleman visited Brussels to meet several associates in a café. Pinkhoff's inquisitive eyes and fixed interest from a nearby table were quickly noticed, and the prince and the other men left the café with a suddenness that outfoxed the German. Dispersing at speed, they gave him no chance to follow any of them.

He persisted with his leads, however. He made a thousand enquiries, but no arrests. It was agreed between him and Lieutenant Bergan that no one was to be brought in while there was still a chance that all would hang themselves. Bergan was after a multitude of suspects, and the evidence which would convict them.

In her capacity as Directress and Matron, Miss Cavell was responsible to the Council of Administration. She attended each monthly meeting held in the house of a council member. Her reports on the school and the *Clinique* were confined to what was official. Any comments on her unofficial activities were a matter for individual approval, disapproval, support or hand-washing. On the whole, the council turned a blind eye. The building of a new hospital at St Gilles was taking up most of their attention at the moment.

The institute at Ixelles had outgrown itself.

The new complex was a crystallization of all Miss Cavell's hopes and dreams. The plans had been laid down in 1912, and the building work had made such steady progress that it was now ready for administrative occupation.

That meant a great deal of welcome and diverting activity for the staff. Ixelles was an uncomfortable place now with its atmosphere of uneasy suspense, and it was a healthy relief to spend as much time as possible transferring all kinds of things to the new hospital at St Gilles, about a kilometre away. Only handcarts were available, but no one complained. Major Scott put on a cap and a green baize apron to join the activities. He helped to load the carts and to trundle them through the streets. He used a long, strong leather strap, looped around his shoulders with both ends fixed to the cart, thus taking the strain off his left arm. The arm improved apace with this kind of exercise. His rugged looks may have been distinctive to anyone interested in him, but Heilmann, whenever he had time, was confining his search to the city centre and never came out to Ixelles. Heilmann was looking for both the major and Louise. He had now tied them up with two people mentioned in a German army report: a girl, and a man who had assaulted a sergeant.

While moving operations occupied some of the servants and nurses, the enemy seemed to be lying dormant.

A feeling of alarm was reawakened in some, and delight in others, when Gaston Quien suddenly reappeared in August. Major Scott told him to go and lose himself. Miss Cavell told him the *Clinique* was under German surveillance, and she would rather he went elsewhere. Quien protested that he was a man who had no roof over his head.

Why had he come back? Miss Cavell put the question coldly.

Quien, smiling and self-satisfied, explained. The French military attaché at The Hague, having congratulated him on his escape, had discovered how much he knew of Brussels and German-occupied Belgium. He was persuaded to return and take on espionage work for France. And so here he was, an accredited agent for fair France, bound by his word to pass information to French military intelligence.

'What a fellow you are,' said the major, standing with Miss Cavell, 'you make all your gallant endeavours sound so easy of accomplishment.'

'It's merely a question, *mon Commandant*, of being reasonably elusive and using what little brains I have,' said the facile Frenchman.

One could not deny he seemed naturally equipped for espionage work, and the major had no doubt that within a week he might well become the closest friend of General von Bissing, Military Governor of occupied Belgium.

Nevertheless, Miss Cavell, not particularly impressed by any of Quien's talents, and under no illusion about the new havoc he would cause with his womanizing, allowed him to stay only one night. Quien departed in the morning with a smile and a shrug.

The information he had on the *Clinique* was of absorbing interest to Bergan and Pinkhoff. Gaston Quien was not one of France's greater heroes, but he could claim to be one of his country's better confidence men. When the war broke out he was serving a sentence for theft in St Quentin prison. By the time he was released, St Quentin was in the hands of the German army. Astutely reading how chaos and confusion could be used to advance his status and prospects, he took on the role of a French officer who had escaped during the battle of Charleroi. When he reached Bellignies, he was taken into hiding by Prince Reginald de Croy and subsequently given safe escort to Brussels. There he made his way to the Edith Cavell *Clinique*, as advised by the prince. He was well aware by then that an escape organization was operating, and that he was in a position to acquire detailed information about it. He knew how well the Germans paid for such information.

Bergan and Pinkhoff found in Quien an agent of considerable flair.

* * *

Princess Marie de Croy made an urgent call on Miss Cavell. It was some time before Miss Cavell, who was assisting in the theatre, could come down to her office. Princess Marie rose to her feet, her agitation obvious.

'My dear friend—'

'I wish you hadn't come,' said Miss Cavell, interrupting because of her concern for the princess, 'I am suspect, the whole place is.'

'So are we at Bellignies,' said Princess Marie in a rush of anxiety. The Germans, she said, had visited the de Croy chateau and searched it. Not once, but several times. Would it not be wise to cease all activities for the time being?

'They've been here too, the German secret police,' said Miss Cavell, pale and under strain, but showing none of the princess's agitation.

'They've been here? Then,' insisted Princess Marie, 'everything *must* stop.'

Her decisiveness was compulsive. Miss Cavell visibly relaxed, and a little sigh of relief escaped her.

'Wait,' she said a moment later, 'are there any more hidden men you know of?'

Reluctantly, the princess confessed there were – thirty. All in Cambrai, and all in need of help if they were to escape. But—

'Then we cannot stop,' said Miss Cavell with renewed resolution. They could not deny assistance to the fugitive soldiers. 'If only one of those men gets shot, it would be our fault. We must help them.'

It was Princess Marie who sighed then. But not with relief; with sadness. There was simply no way of persuading Miss Cavell to put herself first.

After Gaston Quien's reappearance and departure, Lieutenant Bergan decided to cast his net and land a fish or two. He had information in abundance now, and names. But no one had actually been caught in the act. What was needed was a confession or two. Information was helpful; confessions were evidence.

Philippe Baucq was to be brought in. It was certain that Baucq was not a small fish. Pinkhoff had him classed as a whale.

At ten thirty one evening, Louise Thuliez, a Frenchwoman and an escape guide, arrived at Baucq's house to talk to him about an assignment that seemed to have gone wrong. Her entry was noted by Pinkhoff, who was watching the house with two other detectives. He had orders to enter and search the place when he deemed the moment right. He showed the ghost of a smile when he saw Mademoiselle Thuliez. He had seen the lady before.

Inside the house, Baucq's family and two schoolboy friends were folding supplies of the current edition of *La Libre Belgique* for dispatch.

Pinkhoff, unaware of how much his luck was in, merely gave Mademoiselle Thuliez time to get comfortable. When Philippe Baucq opened the door a little later to let the family dog out, he was pushed back into the house by the three Germans, who rushed in. The noise alarmed the family and alerted Mademoiselle Thuliez. The family tossed bundles of *La Libre Belgique* out of windows, and Mademoiselle Thuliez did her best to hide her handbag. The searching Germans found it. She and Baucq were arrested, taken to the German police headquarters in the rue de la Loi and there interrogated. The two schoolboys were also taken into custody on suspicion of circulating the prohibited newspaper, *La Libre Belgique*.

Pinkhoff's written report to Lieutenant Bergan was both factual and dramatic:

During the watch kept over No. 49 Avenue de Roodebeek, we observed a person carrying a bulky package who was immediately admitted, and as it was to be supposed that this visit so late at night implied some equivocal object, when Baucq appeared in the street with his dog we followed him into the house and arrested him. Whereupon he set up loud cries, so as to be heard upstairs and in the neighbourhood, as the result of which large numbers of *La Libre Belgique* were thrown out of the upper windows. The following persons were found in the house in addition to Baucq and his wife: his two daughters and two nieces (all under sixteen), and a lady who pretended to be Mme Lejeune but confessed later that her name was Thuliez. (She was the same woman as we had observed entering the house.) A search revealed 4,000 copies of *La Libre Belgique* and other seditious literature, together with lists of addresses of a suspicious kind. Mlle Thuliez's bag contained a false identification certificate, and a notebook of addresses which can only be deciphered by means of a secret key. Constant Cayron and Philippe Bodart, schoolboys, were also in the house. Copies of *La Libre Belgique* were found on the former. The latter refused to make any statement. So, as both were suspected of circulating *La Libre Belgique*, they were both arrested and taken to the prison of St Gilles.

'What have we got out of them?' mused Lieutenant Bergan, his fingertips together.

'Not much,' admitted Pinkhoff.

'A hundred denials mean more than not much.'

'Denials were to be expected, *Herr Leutnant*.'

'They'll talk,' said Bergan.

'Eventually,' agreed Pinkhoff.

'Sooner than that, I hope. Now, is there someone who might be persuaded to talk immediately? The incomparable Fräulein Cavell, perhaps?'

'Not if her usual attitude is anything to go by,' said Pinkhoff.

'All the same,' said Bergan thoughtfully, 'I feel it's time I met her.'

'Today?'

'Not today,' said Bergan. 'The man Baucq is nervous, the woman Thuliez is frightened. In what condition, I wonder, is Fräulein Cavell, now that she knows of last night's arrests?'

'Hardly dancing,' said Pinkhoff.

'It might be profitable to allow her to worry herself sick for a couple of days. I'll meet her then. In the meantime, we'll interrogate our mute pair again.'

'Now?' said Pinkhoff.

'Late this evening. That's the best time, eh? Late this evening?'

'Not for suspects,' said Pinkhoff.

Miss Cavell did indeed know of the arrest of Baucq and Mademoiselle Thuliez. But she hid from her staff the pain she felt at the plight of her associates, and requested that no one should broadcast the news. Major Scott therefore remained ignorant of the development. Busy exercising his arm, he knew himself fit to reach and cross the border. It was his duty to, and he acknowledged himself a laggard. There was his regiment, his company – they were fighting. He was here, flexing an arm. But he simply found it impossible to leave without taking Edith Cavell with him, as well as Louise. While Louise was very willing, Edith Cavell, however, was not.

Visibly, she was thinner. The shadows were more marked, the grey eyes a little sad. He pressed her to go.

'With you?' she said. 'Ned, I couldn't consider it, you know that.'

'You could shut both eyes to it, Edith, and simply let it happen by leaving everything to me.'

She smiled. She could still look serene, still show him warmth. 'Ned, would you like to take tea with me in thirty minutes?'

'That's always a pleasure for me,' he said.

'And for me,' she said, faint colour tinting her cheeks.

So at four o'clock, her invariable time for this little custom, they took tea together, and they talked of things that had nothing to do with the worries that haunted her, or the concern that obsessed him and blinded him to the fact that a young Belgian comtesse was painfully and passionately in love with him.

They talked of Louise, of her bright promise and what she might make of life. Miss Cavell said that someone must give her back the love and companionship and protection that had cruelly been taken from her. Young comtesses were as much in need of these things as all other girls, although in a year or two she would no longer be a girl, but a beautiful woman. Did he realize that?

'I realize she needs protection from men like Quien,' said the major.

'Whether it's been wished on you or is the natural consequence of your feelings,' smiled Miss Cavell, 'yours is the responsibility. You must accept that, Ned, for her sake.'

They talked of the war, but only in the happy context of an Allied victory. They talked again of Norfolk, of its farms and its shimmering Broads, of the sun-washed beaches of golden sand in summer, and the ferocious crispness of the winters. Her descriptive gifts and her voice were part of the great charm she had for him, as was the light in her eyes when her reserve gave way to warmth. The time stretched. Eventually, she had to resume her work. He said goodbye to her for the moment.

'Take care, Edith.'

'I will. Thank you, Ned.'

'For what?'

'For caring, and for a very sweet and peaceful hour.'

He pressed her hand. They smiled at each other as he left. He did not know that that was the last time he would talk with her, the last time he would see her.

*　　　*　　　*

The following day, 4th August, three men arrived and asked to consult her. They claimed they were English, but she knew at once they were not. They asked her to help them, to take them in. She refused. They persisted, but she was adamant. She had no doubt that all three men were plants. They shrugged and went away. To pile Pelion on Ossa, a German officer called later, looked at her account books and found them wanting in entries for the last few months.

'Tell me,' he said curtly, 'have you received many letters from the War Office in London?'

It was a question that seemed to have little to do with her accounts.

'I have never received any letters from that source,' she said.

'Oh? Are you sure?' His look was one of undisguised sarcasm. 'I would have thought something of that nature could have been going on for months, occupying you so much as to give you no time to keep a good record of your financial affairs.'

He left Miss Cavell with her nerves shredded. For once her composure had cracked. But she recovered to face calmly what she knew was inevitable, now that they had Philippe Baucq, her closest associate. It had been inevitable from the beginning. Her great worry was not for herself, however, but for her staff. She could only pray that the Germans would be content to take her and leave her nurses and servants alone.

'It's time, I think,' said Lieutenant Bergan in his omnipotent way.

Baucq and Mademoiselle Thuliez were still denying everything, still refusing to talk. They had been encouraged to give names in order to make things easier for themselves, but they had said there were no names.

'Today?' asked Pinkhoff.

'Now,' said Bergan. He had finally given up waiting for people to hang themselves. So, confessions must be obtained. Beginning, if not with Baucq and Louise Thuliez, then with the one who mattered most and had most to confess.

Edith Cavell.

The date was 5th August, 1915.

Chapter Fifteen

Ixelles seemed very quiet as three members of the German secret police arrived at the *Clinique*. Pinkhoff had two colleagues with him. The quietness was shattered as they entered, for they literally burst in. They had come for Edith Cavell, and they did not intend to be hindered. Sister Wilkins and other nurses were thrust bruisingly aside and told not to move. Pinkhoff led the dramatic charge into Miss Cavell's office, rather as if a more civilized entrance might have given her time to grow wings and fly off through a window.

The waiting nurses, taut with anxiety, heard the Germans actually shouting at Madame. Her quiet replies were inaudible to them. Whether she had ever given serious thought to getting away is doubtful. She was not by nature disposed to run from anything. In her calm analysis of the situation she would have known, in any case, that she had left it too late to escape the vigilance of the Germans.

They brought her out of her office after a while. She was under arrest. They pushed her towards the front door. Pinkhoff, so painstaking and time-consuming in his investigation, now seemed in a great hurry. But she was as poised as she had ever been, and so impressive in her calmness that even Pinkhoff did not intercede when she stopped for a moment to speak to her distressed nurses.

'Don't be sad, *mes enfants*, everything will be all right. I'll come back soon.'

Pinkhoff, glancing at Sister Wilkins, made a gesture. She too was placed under arrest.

In custody, Edith Cavell walked for the last time from her beloved *Clinique*.

Major Scott, sitting in the garden, heard nothing of the Germans' arrival, nor did he hear their raised voices. The garden was too far from the scene of drama. He was reading, and while he read he flexed and reflexed his left arm.

The news of Madame's arrest flashed around the institute, but it did not reach the man in the garden until Louise came running.

'Oh, *mon Commandant*!' She dropped to her knees in front of him. She was crying.

'Great heavens, Louise Victoria, tears?'

'Oh, it's Madame – the Boche have taken her, arrested her. Why, *mon Commandant*, why?'

Oh, dear God, he thought, and his warm blood ran cold.

They both knew why.

At police headquarters, Sister Wilkins was again questioned at length about her involvement in the activities of the escape organization. Her replies were as vague as when she was previously interrogated. Lieutenant Bergan was polite but persistent with his questions, Pinkhoff clear and concise as the interpreter. Bergan followed a routine path at times, an unconventional one at others. He lost interest in the end. Sister Wilkins was of no real importance. By comparison with her matron, she was almost an insignificance. Bergan let her go, and she was allowed to return to the *Clinique*.

There the staff and nurses besieged her with anxious questions. Sister Wilkins felt hopefull that the Germans would be lenient with Miss Cavell, too, and so she assured everyone that Madame was not in serious trouble and would be released. By tomorrow, perhaps, or the day after.

The official German account of the arrests was brief:

On August 5th, 1915, in the afternoon, officers of the secret police, including the undersigned, presented themselves upon the order of the chief of the station, Lieutenant Bergan, at the Institute in the rue de la Culture, and there proceeded to a search in the course of which was discovered a letter from England which had been transmitted, in spite of a law forbidding it, through the agency of the American consul. Fräulein Cavell and her head assistant, Fräulein Wilkins, were arrested at four o'clock in the afternoon and brought to headquarters. After examination by Lieutenant Bergan, Fräulein Wilkins was released. Fräulein Cavell was detained.

It was signed by Detective Henri Pinkhoff.

A letter from Miss Cavell was brought by hand to the *Clinique* the following morning. In it she expressed neither fears nor worries. She was mainly concerned with making her detention a little more comfortable. She expected to be questioned eventually, she said, and meanwhile would like a few things. She would be grateful if someone could bring her a blanket, some towels, clean linen, utensils, a book, a toothbrush and some embroidery work. Nobody was to worry about her.

Everything she wanted was taken to her that same day.

Bergan kept Edith Cavell in detention for three days before interrogating her. He had met her, come face to face with her. Unlike Detective Heilmann, he had not allowed himself to be softened, but he was impressed by her bearing. He was wrong, however, in thinking her calmness a façade that hid a singular cunning. He had no idea that she was a woman motivated not by reprehensible adventurousness, but by a sense of Christian duty.

On 8th August she was brought before the man who had fashioned the net and taken his time to cast it. She was what she was, a woman of humanity and truth. He was a man of moods and subtleties. She looked pale but composed. He looked dark and intrigued. She was slender and graceful. He was full-jowled and fleshy. She spoke no German. He spoke only a very little French. She awaited the questions. He prepared himself to put them.

Bergan meant to exercise his mind, Pinkhoff his linguistic virtuosity. Bergan's facile changes of tone, mood and expression, together with Pinkhoff's gift for conveying the nuances of a question as well as its literal meaning, promised to confuse the prisoner unless she had superior talents. Bergan was prepared for a prolonged interrogation, but not an uninteresting one. A person of complicated mental processes, he was not to know Miss Cavell had no devious facets and was merely waiting to be convinced he had all the proof necessary to send her for trial.

The questions began, formal ones of an introductory nature.

'Your name is Edith Louisa Cavell?'

'Yes.'

'You are the Directress of the institute known as *L'Ecole d'Infirmières Diplômées*?'

'Yes.'

'You are of British nationality?'

'Yes.'

'Did you, as required by law, register yourself as an enemy alien?'

'No.'

'But it is true, you are British?'

'Yes.'

'You have British sympathies?'

'Naturally.'

The questions became more pertinent, and Bergan wore a changing mask of friendliness, reproof, encouragement and aggression. Miss Cavell, unimpressed, remained calm. Bergan could not help admiring her, though Pinkhoff's face took on darker hues.

Bergan paused. He introduced a psychological element. He had Philippe Baucq and Louise Thuliez brought in. They regarded Miss Cavell palely and silently. Baucq looked a little stricken.

Bergan's expression spoke for itself: there, Madame, there are two of your accomplices, and you can judge for yourself how much they have told us.

They had so far told the Germans nothing.

He saw Miss Cavell give her friends the briefest of sad smiles. With no great expectations that she would yield, he advised her, as Baucq and Mademoiselle Thuliez were taken out, that his department was now in possession of all the facts pertaining to her escape organization, and that if she wished to make things easier for her associates and everyone else involved, she could do so by a full confession.

Concisely, Pinkhoff interpreted. Miss Cavell listened carefully, but made no reply. In the few words of French he had at his command, and probably because these words came automatically from him during most interrogations, Bergan said, 'Say the truth, it is always better to say the truth.'

He did not know he was talking to a woman to whom truth was a Christian necessity. He followed with more questions. Then, abruptly interrupting himself, he again advised her that all facts were known, and accordingly she might as well confess. To do so, he repeated, would make things easier for all the others.

And again he said, 'Say the truth, it is always better to say the truth.'

Miss Cavell was convinced. She was without any lawyer to counsel and advise her, and because she was incapable of deviousness her-self, she supposed a man of strict professional code, like this German police officer, to be incapable of deceiving her. He had twice said he had all the facts. He had also said a confession would help everyone else. She believed him; it was not in her nature to imagine him a liar.

He asked her how long her escape organiza-tion had been operating. She answered him, and told the truth. For long moments Bergan could not believe what Pinkhoff was interpreting for him – it sounded like the prelude to a full confession. Was this possible? Was there to be no need of subtle darts and arrows? Had this composed English nurse really been broken down so soon?

But she had not been broken down. She had simply believed him.

She made her confession.

Bergan's subsequent comments, clipped to the trial documents, might have saddened Miss Cavell:

> All our suppositions based on the examination of the arrested persons were confirmed by the deposition of the woman Cavell. In order to accomplish this we made use of the trick of pretending that the information was already in the hands of the law.

Miss Cavell's statement was translated and set down in German. It was read back to her in French, an inadmissible practice in the eyes of any court of law. But she did not dispute it. She signed it. She had revealed everything. It did not make her at peace with herself, but it did unburden her. She had shouldered a mountain of difficulties, dangers and responsibilities. The mountain, at last, ceased to bear down on her.

She was held in solitary confinement in St

Gilles prison, while the police went to work rounding up people whose names appeared in her statement. Several of them, when questioned, fell into the same trap as she had, confessing their complicity as soon as Bergan said the facts were already in his possession, anyway. *Say the truth, it will help you and the others.* Not one suspect was allowed to have a lawyer present. Miss Cavell endured three such lonely examinations by Bergan. During each one, she answered all questions as truthfully as her memory would allow, in the belief she was making things easier for her associates.

It helped none of them. But it did help Lieutenant Bergan. In the end he was able to report that a grand total of thirty-five arrested suspects were to be brought to trial.

Not one of Edith Cavell's colleagues, friends or associates blamed her or reproached her for making so full a confession. To them she remained a woman who commanded their profound and unchanging admiration.

Miss Cavell endured a long and painful wait before the trial took place. The Governor of St Gilles, Monsieur Maron, was a Belgian, and did what he could to ease her lot. As expected, she earned the respect of the prison staff, although communication, even with her gaolers, was restricted to the minimum by German command. She was allowed to see no

286

one. Her nurses travelled to the prison day after day, waiting outside for hours in the desperate but vain hope of being allowed to visit her, or even to be given news of her. Her whole staff were in anguish for her. So was Louise. So was Major Scott.

He and Louise went frequently to the prison, the pair of them risking their own liberty in showing themselves so often in the streets. Like the nurses and everyone else, they too were refused admission. They wandered about in the vicinity of the prison. Louise was unhappy for Madame and uneasy for the major, who seemed so bitter about events that he abandoned caution.

Louise burst into reproach one day. 'It is too bad, yes, too bad!'

'What is?'

'Your behaviour. It's going to drive me crazy. Do you have to stare into the face of every German who passes us? What are you doing, are you challenging them to recognize you?'

The major, quite unconscious of having done this, said, 'I'm not aware I've been staring at anyone. There are people about, that's all I know.'

'Well, for your information, many of those people are Germans, and Germans have eyes just like everyone else. If some of them arrest you, what am I to do? Bite them all until they let you go?'

'Do nothing, Louise, except run like the devil.'

'Please, *mon Commandant*,' she begged, 'please be careful. It would be so unlike you to commit suicide.'

She was not only uneasy, she was very disturbed. He suffered moods of uncharacteristic bitterness. There were occasions when she thought him quite capable of attempting to storm the prison single-handed. Perhaps that was what he had in mind – an enterprise that would land him in the prison himself? What would he do then? Ask to be put in Madame's cell?

She prayed long and earnestly for Madame. She also prayed for Major Scott. Mostly she prayed for him to come to his senses. She knew now that Madame had run an extensive escape organization, using her *Clinique* to shelter cores of fugitive soldiers. It did not surprise Louise; she had suspected it for some time.

The major desperately decided to risk everything in an attempt to see Miss Cavell. He stole an item from the jacket of a visiting *Clinique* doctor. The doctor was in the theatre, and the major was restless and wandering. There was the hanging jacket, ready for plundering the instant the idea came. In the wallet was the doctor's identity certificate. The major took it, superimposed his own photograph, and declared to Louise the next day, when they were once more on their way to the prison,

288

that he had the means to present himself as Madame's doctor. He had the appropriate identity certificate and was carrying a purloined Gladstone bag.

'Madness!' gasped Louise.

'A little risky, perhaps. That's all.'

'*A little?*' Louise was pale with shock and fear at such craziness. 'Putting your head into the mouth of a hungry lion, that is only a little risky? You'll be suspected at once and arrested.'

'Don't worry—'

'*Don't worry?*' They were a short distance from the prison, and the greyness of the humid, cloudy day seemed to Louise to hold the portents of disaster. 'Of course I shall worry. I should be very odd if I didn't. *Mon Commandant*, if you do this thing, then I shall do it with you. We will go together. We shall say Madame needs a nurse as well as a doctor.'

'No, Louise.'

'Yes!'

'I think not,' said the major.

'Oh, what is it you're trying to do, be thrown into the prison yourself?'

He gave her some real attention then. Her eyes were a little fierce, a little glittering, her mouth unsteady.

'Louise Victoria,' he said as the prison loomed up, 'what good would that be for us – you on the outside, braving life, and me inside, behind bars?'

'Then please don't do it,' she whispered. 'We're all terribly unhappy about Madame, but you're far worse. Anyone would think you—' She stopped, averting her face.

'Wait for me,' said the major quietly.

He looked suitably grave as he presented himself at the iron door. The gaoler in charge of the keys showed little expression himself as he listened to the petition from a man who said he was a doctor. He had received a request from Miss Cavell to attend on her. They peered at each other through the grille. The impassive face of the gaoler disappeared and the grille closed. The major waited. The grille opened again a minute later. Another gaoler, a more important-looking one, surveyed him.

'You are, m'sieu?'

'Dr Henri Gebert.'

'Your identification, please.'

The major produced the document. It was silently inspected and handed back.

'I'm here to see Miss Cavell, who—'

'You mean you would like to see her,' said the gaoler. 'Wait, please.' The grille closed again. The major waited, every nerve stretched. It was some time before the grille reopened. A new face appeared, stern, sombre and yet not unsympathetic. It was Governor Maron himself.

'What is it you want, m'sieu?'

'To attend Miss Cavell.' The major spoke

confidently. 'I'm her doctor. I received a request from her.'

'M'sieu, even if you are a doctor, I don't know you,' said the Governor, 'and I'm sure you don't know me. However, we have now met, and I can tell you the prison has its own hospital and doctor, as you should know. Therefore, whoever you are, whatever you have in mind, please accept my advice and go on your way. Miss Cavell is not unwell. I can also tell you, if you're a friend of hers, that she is brave and uncomplaining. Take that with you for your comfort. Don't insist on being admitted, for that, good doctor, may lead you into trouble.'

The grille closed for the last time on the major. He walked away slowly and found Louise. She saw from his expression that he had not been successful. But he had not been arrested. She was thankful for that at least.

'We must go, *mon Commandant*,' she said.

'I know,' he said greyly, 'but I should like to have seen her.'

Miss Cavell was at last allowed to communicate with her staff, and Sister Wilkins was given permission to visit her on two occasions. The meetings took place in an interview room, and in the presence of a German guard. They were emotional meetings for Sister Wilkins, but Miss Cavell's calmness kept the tears at bay. She was almost wholly concerned with happenings at the institute. How was the school being run, how was the *Clinique* faring? Very little else was talked about. Miss Cavell seemed to regard the forthcoming trial as unimportant compared to affairs of the institute.

Four other nurses also received permission to visit her. It was an hour they were to cherish for many years, recalling with pride her fortitude and composure. Again she evinced little interest in herself. She wanted only to hear how they were getting on. They did not tell her that without her the school was falling apart, that the *Clinique* had lost its guiding light and inspiration. She asked after everyone. Yes, Major Scott was still there.

'Tell him I asked after him. Tell him he and every soldier are in my prayers. Tell him also that he must go.'

She asked them to see that her student nurses were looked after until she herself returned. Perhaps they would also be kind enough to send her some of her clothes. She would want them for her journey to Germany.

Germany?

Yes. Germany was where she would probably be interned or imprisoned after the trial.

But no one was to worry about her. The *Clinique* was far more important.

Chapter Sixteen

It was quiet again in Ixelles.

As far as the school was concerned, things were desultory. Madame had not yet been replaced and some students had left, upset by her arrest.

'Anna?'

Louise, sitting on her bed, looked up. It was Yvette, just back from a walk. Everyone was restless and went out whenever possible.

'Yes, Yvette?'

'Are you very sad about Madame?'

'Yes.' Louise felt a sense of doom at times. The school, the whole institute, was not the same without Madame, and never would be. Major Scott was talking of leaving. He could not put the staff at further risk, he said. If the Germans came again and found him, they would probably arrest every nurse in the place. And he had received a goodwill message from Madame which included her wish that he should go while he could. Yet he lingered still.

Louise had discovered him in Madame's office that morning, standing beside her desk and looking as if life had little to offer him except war and disillusionment. 'Aren't you sad too, Yvette?'

'Everyone is,' said Yvette, 'and so worried about what the Germans will do to Madame. I've been out walking; it's better than sitting and moping. I – oh, Anna, someone came up to me when I was out and asked if I knew you. She said her name was Elizabeth Dupont. She wouldn't actually come to the school. Just in case, she said. She has a message for you, an important one. Do you know her? She's rather plump—'

'Yes, I know her.' Louise, with the help of Miss Cavell, had smuggled a note to Elizabeth to tell her she had not left the school, after all. 'What did she say, what was the message?'

'She said she couldn't write it down. It was from your grandmama. She said you'd understand why she couldn't come here. She'd been waiting, hoping to see a nurse. She asked if it was possible for you to meet her, and if so to let her know somehow. She said there was a young boy she knew, and if she could get hold of him she'd try to send him here tomorrow for an answer.'

'Thank you, Yvette.'

'Anna, who is she? She's not going to make you do something dangerous, is she? Anna, do you really have Russian grandparents?'

'Yes, and it's nothing dangerous, Yvette.' Louise thanked her again, then made her way down to the basement and into the garden. Major Scott was there, walking about and apparently contemplating the troubles of the world. On the Western Front, the Allies and the Germans were locked in battle, in fierce trench warfare, and she knew he considered it time to rejoin his company.

'*Mon Commandant?*' She approached a little hesitantly. He gave her a smile. It quickened her, warmed her. She liked his smile, and the cheer it put into his blue eyes and on his face.

'What is it, young lady?'

'I'm going into the city, to my house. Elizabeth wishes to see me. She has a message for me. It must be important, for she has been out here and managed to speak to Yvette.'

'Should you risk going to your house?' he asked in concern.

'Oh, you care a little about me again?' she said.

'Have I been lacking, then?' he asked.

'You have been very far away from everyone except Madame,' she said.

He gazed at the rear windows of the *Clinique*, then took her hands and pressed them. 'You know, Louise Victoria,' he said, 'life has a very strange way of dealing with people, a very extreme way. It's never satisfied to offer us simple pleasures or simple worries. Head-spinning triumphs descend on us, or heart-breaking tragedies, or crushing blows.'

'Yes, I know,' she said, her eyes dark, her hands lingering in his.

'All the same,' he said, 'however indifferent we sometimes appear to be to friends and comrades, we remain constant. Those we love we shall always love, even if we do seem far away on occasions.'

'You care for me as your comrade?' she said.

'Always,' he said.

Louise thought that was something, but not enough, not now. 'Elizabeth's message, *mon Commandant*, was to do with my grandmama.'

'Which one?'

'Almost certainly my grandmama Victoria Petrovna in Petrograd. My other grandmama is fond of me, but she'd rather I'd been a boy. It's a Comte de Bouchet she would have preferred, because of the family name, not a Comtesse.'

The major smiled. 'I've a grandmother like that,' he said. 'I was a great disappointment to her. I've heard her say a hundred times, "Boys! I can't abide 'em, can't think why any woman can." Now, if you must go to see Elizabeth, I'll come with you.'

Her eyes shone. 'Oh, thank you,' she said, 'it's always better when we adventure together.'

'I hope so. But I shan't walk with you; I'll keep at a distance behind you, so that I can look out for you. When you go into the house, I'll stay outside. Please remember to do one particular thing, if you can. Adjust the lock on your front door so that it can be opened from the outside, will you do that?'

'Oh, yes,' she said, 'because when I am in your care, you have never failed me.'

The bustle of Brussels in the sunshine hid the suffering of its citizens. There seemed to be more Germans about than ever. The people viewed them in silent hostility. Everyone knew an English nurse had been arrested on a serious charge, but no one knew precisely what that charge was. There were rumours, that was all.

Louise, with the major a little way behind her, reached the family house in the rue Royale. Elizabeth opened the door, gasped to see her, then drew her quickly in. Louise was not in uniform, but Elizabeth was still fearful for her.

'Don't lock the door, Elizabeth,' said Louise, 'leave it so that it can be opened from outside.'

'Oh, to do such a thing as that, why? Oh, you should not have come, I'm sure they're still watching the house, that they still follow me at times. Child, we should not leave the door so that they can just walk in. And with Pierre out, visiting his mother—'

'Elizabeth, please do as I ask.'

Elizabeth complied, though with great reluctance, then went into one of the drawing rooms with Louise. The room had the atmosphere and appearance of an elegant salon. The decorative colours were delicate, the Louis XVI chairs and sofas so graceful that their lines were a flowing confluence of lightness. Louise felt pain, for here Mama had entertained friends and visitors so often, and the conversation had been renowned for its engaging feminine wit. Here, Papa had entered in dashing style to flatter all the ladies, to make his appearance for the sake of things, and as soon as Mama's eyes were off him, to make his escape to the music room.

'Elizabeth,' said Louise, looking around, 'you're keeping everything looking so beautiful.'

'What else is there for Pierre and me to do?' said Elizabeth. Tenderly, she added, 'It's your home, and one day you'll come back and live in it. It's always been a house for living in, yes, and it doesn't like being empty, without any of its family.'

'I know, Elizabeth, I know,' said Louise gently, 'but we had better be quick, in case of trouble. You've heard from Grandmama in Petrograd, is that what you wanted to see me about?'

'A man came,' said Elizabeth, 'a Swedish sea captain. He brought no letter. He said your grandmama, not wishing to write anything the Boche might see, asked him to tell you there's a coastal cargo ship, the *Christina*, which is to leave Rotterdam on October 15th. It keeps to coastal waters to avoid the blockade, and the captain will try to dock in Petrograd. The Boche won't touch it because Germany is trading as much as it can with Sweden. Oh, I hope I'm remembering all this properly – I think I am. He asked for nothing to be written down. The captain will take you to Petrograd, if he can, to be with your grandparents until the war is over. Oh, *ma chérie*, you must go. I'm frightened for you. It's said the Boche had good reason to arrest Nurse Cavell, and they may think they have just as good a reason to arrest you too.'

'I'll speak to my friend,' said Louise, 'and see what he says is best for me to do.'

'Your friend?' Elizabeth peered sharply.

'Yes, my English friend. Major Scott. You met him, and he said he saw you and spoke to you when I was thinking about going to Petrograd a little while ago.'

'He is still in Brussels? But what is he to do with your life and your decisions?' Elizabeth asked, with the disapproval of the privileged family retainer.

'Oh, fuss, fuss,' said Louise.

'You are thinking of marrying a man who looks like a boxer,' accused Elizabeth.

'He does not.' Louise coloured. She did not care to discuss the other point. 'Elizabeth, I must go now.' She went out into the hall.

Elizabeth followed, muttering a little. But she melted into emotion as they reached the door.

'Oh, it's so hard for you, sweet one,' she said.

'Elizabeth, I am eighteen and can look after myself,' said Louise, 'But thank you for being so good, for taking care of everything here.' She pulled the unlocked door open. 'I will—' She broke off, and stiffened. On the step stood a man in a black waterproof, smiling with satisfaction. Elizabeth stifled a cry. The man said nothing for the moment. He merely produced his badge, stepped through the open door and closed it.

Then he said, 'A word with you, mam'selle. Where can we talk?'

Elizabeth was petrified at the way he was surveying Louise, like a man quietly enjoying a long-awaited triumph. Louise, with a pride that hid her fear and dismay, walked through the hall and back into the salon. The man came on her heels. She turned and faced him. From the open door, Elizabeth looked on in despair.

'What is it you want with me?' asked Louise, and Elizabeth admired her quiet courage.

'Your name, mam'selle? And your reason for being here?' Detective Heilmann's French was good.

'*My* name? *My* reason?' Louise, scared from the pit of her stomach to her beating heart, fired her defiant words. 'How dare you? What is *your* name, that's more to the point? What is *your* reason for being here and accosting me? I'm a nurse—'

'You may be, you may be.' Heilmann felt entitled to a little pleasurable dalliance. Having an hour to spare, he had elected to spend it on watch in the rue Royale, and out of nowhere, after many months, the young Comtesse had appeared. He had given her a few moments before making his move. 'Yes, you may be a nurse. But you look more like a young lady my department is most interested in. Well, you may sit down while we wait for a colleague of mine to arrive, then we will question you together. That is the rule. I've sent someone to fetch him.'

'You may do as much sitting and waiting as you wish, if this lady will allow you to,' said Louise, gesturing at Elizabeth, 'but I must go. I have my duties to attend to.'

'I'm afraid, mam'selle, you must stay where you are,' said Heilmann, and again produced his badge as confirmation of his authority. At that moment, Major Scott quietly entered by the unlocked front door and made his appearance. He had watched Heilmann go into the house, and needed no time to read the situation.

There was a glint of regret in the major's eye as he said to Elizabeth, 'Trapped her, have you, madame?' and struck her a blow on the side of her neck. Elizabeth dropped like an emptied sack and lay senseless. Louise, incredulous, cried out. Heilmann swung the skirt of his coat back as the major swooped towards her. The German dragged at the pistol in his hidden holster. The major whipped round in his feinted advance on Louise, and struck Heilmann precisely as he had struck Elizabeth, but with greater force. It was done at lightning speed, and Louise, enormous-eyed, knew then that Major Scott, when the odds were stacked against him, could be a chillingly dangerous man. Heilmann crashed. He hit a chair first and then the floor, where he lay quite inert.

Elizabeth, not injured as badly as the German, stirred and moaned.

'Quick, Louise,' said the major to the bemused girl. He stooped over Elizabeth and pressed fingertips gently to her eyelids. They fluttered open, 'Elizabeth, tell the Boche you've never seen me before. Bad luck I had to hit you, but it was necessary, to keep you above suspicion. You understand?'

'Yes,' whispered Elizabeth painfully, 'but go – go – and take care of her.'

Louise bent low, kissed her and was then pulled violently from the room by the major.

'A back way?' he breathed.

'Only into the garden – and the gate there is always kept locked – Elizabeth says it's to keep the Boche from entering the rear of the house—'

'Front door, then – come on.'

'Yes. Oh, we must be quick. He spoke of a colleague coming.'

They went out quickly and walked fast, away from the German police headquarters in the rue de la Loi, towards the Palace, losing themselves among the conquerors and the conquered.

'Oh, poor Elizabeth,' said Louise breathlessly. She was at a high pitch of exultation, despite her pity for Elizabeth.

'It was necessary, don't you see, chicken? Otherwise they'd have taken her and bullied her with a thousand questions. Now she can claim, with our bruised German friend as her witness, that she knows even less about what happened to you, and to me, than he does.'

'But why did you accuse her of trapping me?'

'To give her, if she's clever enough to see it, and I think she is, the opportunity to tell the Germans she was willing to do her duty and that she let you into the house to persuade you to give yourself up.'

'Oh, you are very good at thinking for people,' said Louise. 'I was so confused myself – I couldn't believe it when I saw you hit Elizabeth.'

He hurried her on, saying, 'Well, I told you, more or less, that life is full of ups and downs and confusions, all of an extreme kind. Now, shall we risk a dash back to the *Clinique*?' They saw a tram stop. 'Yes, risk it we must, to pick up the things we need. Then we shall have to make our run for it. Brussels and Ixelles are too hot for us now.'

'Yes, I told the German I was a nurse,' said Louise, 'which will make them check all the hospitals again. But, *mon Commandant*, together we shall make a very good run for it, I think.'

They caught a tram. They were not able to talk as they wanted to, but Louise did not mind silence for a while. It gave her the chance to think about all that had happened so quickly, about Major Scott's protectiveness and how he aroused in her the kind of excitement and exhilaration that sent all fears flying. One moment she was in the hands of the German secret police; the next, she was free. Now they must make their longest run, she and her comrade. But they would be together, and she did not mind anything as long as they remained together.

As soon as they had alighted from the tram at Ixelles, she told him of the message Elizabeth had received from her grandmama in Russia, through a Swedish sea captain.

'That's fate, then, isn't it?' said the major. He was sombre now. She knew why: in leaving the *Clinique* for good, he would also be leaving Madame for good. But they would not forget her. They would pray for her acquittal. 'You shall go, Louise Victoria. We'll make for Rotterdam when we reach Holland, and there I'll see you aboard this ship, the *Christina*. We've time enough to get there, and more.'

'You will see me aboard?' said Louise, as if he had suggested he would escort her to the top of a high cliff to watch her throw herself off it.

'I have to find my way back to England, and you must join your grandparents in Petrograd.'

'Must? *Must?*'

'Yes, for your own sweet sake,' said the major. He was striding fast, Louise swinging along beside him, her eyes hot and mutinous.

'You are mistaken,' she said.

'It's the best thing,' he said, wondering how he was going to endure not knowing what was happening to Edith Cavell. 'The Boche seem to want you as much as they wanted Madame. They've taken her. We can't let them take you too. We must get you on that ship to Petrograd.'

'I won't go,' said Louise.

He did not seriously want to see her go, but she was entitled at her age to the joys of life, to the excitements of Petrograd and the love her grandparents would give her. He himself was committed to return to the war. He could only hope with every fibre of his being that he would come to hear of Edith Cavell's release.

'Louise Victoria, you must see—'

'I will not be put aboard a ship,' she said

proudly. 'I am not something to be exported, like a crate of Delft china.'

'Of course you aren't,' he said. 'You're very precious, you know that.'

'So, to some people, is Delft china,' said Louise. '*Mon Commandant*, does it appeal to you, this idea of putting me on a ship to Russia while you go off to England?'

'I thought it was your grandmother's idea,' he said, but he was well aware it had very little appeal. He knew it would be the hardest thing in the world to say goodbye to Louise Victoria, just as it was going to be the bitterest thing to leave Brussels while Edith Cavell was still in prison. But when the day came for him to rejoin his regiment, the goodbye to Louise would have to be said, and unless she was with her grandparents, she would be alone again. 'But no, shipping you off to Russia doesn't appeal to me at all. However—'

'Then we should go to Russia together,' she said, 'and from there to England.'

Because of his feelings, he capitulated.

'Well, wherever our feet take us, aboard ship or over land,' he said, 'we'll go together, my child.'

'I'm eighteen now,' said Louise, as they approached the institute, 'and will soon be twenty-one.'

'Well, you're still not quite an old lady,' said the sombre major.

He had collected the few things of his own he needed. He had said goodbye to the nurses, to whom he owed so much. They were still in terrible anxiety over Madame. Nurse Duval took only a second to shed tears as he kissed her goodbye. All he could offer any of the staff was something that was obvious to all of them – his own deep and abiding affection for Edith Cavell.

He was in her office now, waiting for Louise to come down. Outside, Ixelles was in its new phase of quietness. Here, in her office, it seemed even quieter. So did the sitting room. He had a sense of deep foreboding. She had gone, and no one knew if she would ever come back. There was no one who could take her place, for most of her staff. There was probably no one quite like her; no one with her warm love of humanity or her serenity.

Here he could take his own personal leave of her. Everything was just as she had left it, in perfect order. The quietness itself was a reflection of her tranquillity. The sitting room, so much the haven of a woman of peace, looked ready to receive her.

'*You don't mind taking tea with me, Major Scott?*'

He shook his head at his imaginings, but it was, after all, just four o'clock. And he felt her presence, as if neither the strongest prison nor what lay beyond it could divorce her from the place she loved. There was a small photograph of her and her dog in a frame on the mantelshelf. Deliberately, he took it down and extracted the photograph. Almost he felt her shake her head; almost he saw her smile.

Whatever happened, she would not be easy to forget. But then, he had no desire to forget.

He heard footsteps as he re-entered the office. The quick footsteps of the young. Louise came in, her face flushed with urgency, her eyes bright with hope for the future. Yes, she was young. And unspoiled.

'The days of our youth, Ned, remain our days of innocence.'

He said his silent farewell to her as he left with Louise.

Chapter Seventeen

It was a long trek and a hazardous one, with German troop movements and manoeuvres compelling them to retrace their steps or to find new paths all too often. The weather was governed by the variability of uncertain autumn. Sometimes it was cold, grey and wet; sometimes the wind rose, and the trees were blown out of shape, and the leaves fell in brittle noisiness; sometimes the sun shone, and the autumn greens emerged deeply lush, and deciduous leaves blazed red and gold.

They travelled lanes and fields, farm tracks and village byways. Here and there they were taken aboard canal barges. The bargemen asked no questions, and Louise and the major left the vessels whenever there was a lock ahead. German guards were posted at most locks. They made detours at these points, and were either taken aboard again or continued on foot. They were not too badly off for food. The nurses had given them as much as they could from the larder, and this they eked out sparingly to avoid looking for village shops except when absolutely necessary.

They walked together, the major a compulsive strider and Louise matching his pace with her swinging, supple grace. They were always able to talk, except when they were lying hidden from marching Germans and silence was a necessity. They had Miss Cavell on their minds, but they talked about their own lives. The major told Louise about his years in the British army, and especially the first battle of Ypres. It fascinated but appalled her.

She knew he thought often of Madame. But she did not complain, nor did she drag him out of his thoughts, for there were hours and hours when they were close to each other in sympathy and endeavour.

They went cautiously into a village one day, and there in a shop they were sold some milk and, of all things, a little cheese, which they snapped up gladly. The woman who served them was talkative.

It was from her they learned that an English nurse called Edith Cavell had been tried for treason before a German court in Brussels.

Treason?

That was what she had heard, the woman said.

Brussels was now nearer black despair than ever before. No one smiled, and the people only hoped on because hope they must. Then a deed was done that threw a black and monstrous shadow, not only over us, but over the whole world.

Brand Whitlock, American Minister in Brussels, October 1915.

Thirty-five prisoners were brought to trial on Thursday 7th October, including the aristocratic Princess Marie de Croy. Her brother, Prince Reginald, escaped arrest.

The trial took place in the Senate of the National Palace, the home of the Belgian Parliament. It was an impressive setting, favoured by Stober, the military prosecutor, and imparted an atmosphere of splendour, even grandeur, to the proceedings. Stober had been specially picked for his role. He was a man of haughty correctness, a prosecutor of clinical eloquence, and an advocate of stern justice. Mercy he left to others. He was faultlessly German, wearing a monocle and dressing with a touch of elegance. His bible was the German military code, and he did not like people who broke it or who questioned its infallibility.

Surrounded by German guards, the seated prisoners awaited the opening of the session. A tribunal of five military judges presided. The galleries were packed with German officers, who had arrived in large numbers to witness the trial, and they gave the impression of being at a circus.

Stober got to his feet. He looked at Miss Cavell. She was not in uniform. She had elected to come to court in a blue coat, blue skirt, white muslin blouse and feathered hat. She felt that to be tried in her nurse's uniform would be a slur on the nobility of her profession.

She returned the prosecutor's glance without emotion. This, she knew, was the man who would decide her fate; not the judges. His was the voice which would carry the day.

Stober read the charges in German. They all had a similarity. They all suggested, in one way or another, that every prisoner had rendered assistance to fugitive Allied soldiers which enabled many of them to escape and rejoin the Allied armies. This endangered the German cause. At the end of the reading, all the accused, except Miss Cavell, were removed from the Senate. They would be brought back, one by one, to face Stober. Meanwhile, Miss Cavell was to have the privilege of being the first to be tried – a clear indication that the prosecution considered she had been the originator and the brain of the organization.

Brand Whitlock, the American Minister in Brussels, had been energetic and determined in his desire to provide a lawyer for her. He had secured the services of Maître Sadi Kirschen, an advocate of compassion and skill. But Sadi Kirschen had not been allowed anywhere near his client. He had never seen her until she entered the Senate that morning. Now he could only sit and listen as Stober began to question her.

Stober may have felt the same curious urge as Lieutenant Bergan to exercise subtlety in his examination of this English nurse. But there was no need, any more than there had been with Bergan. She had made her confessions; she had signed each statement. She was not here to deny what she had admitted, only to do what she had done with Bergan: answer all questions as truthfully as she could.

Stober began casually: 'Your name is Edith Louisa Cavell?'

'Yes.'

'You are Matron of the *Clinique* which bears your name?'

'I am Matron and Directress of *L'Ecole d'Infirmières Diplômées*, Ixelles.'

'Quite so. You are a British citizen?'

'I am.'

'An enemy alien?'

'I am English.'

'Dear me. English. You did not register as an enemy alien, as required by law. Was that because, being English, you considered yourself above the law?'

'I did not register, that is all.'

Stober stared hawkishly at her. He lost his casualness. 'It is not all. It is far from being all. It is only the beginning.' Stober was determined to prove her a highly dangerous woman. Miss Cavell, with her responses, was demonstrating she was certainly an exceptional one. 'You are charged,' continued Stober, 'with conspiring with other persons to help Allied soldiers escape. You are charged thereby with endangering the soldiers of Germany. What is your answer to this?'

'I considered it my right to do my patriotic duty.'

'Right? Duty?'

'As you would have considered it yours in reversed circumstances.'

'The law in this country is German law. It gives no citizens or enemy aliens the right to commit acts tantamount to treason. Do you realize, by the admissions you have made and signed, that you have confessed to treason?'

'I was asked questions. I answered them truthfully.' Miss Cavell seemed quite composed.

Her lawyer, Sadi Kirschen, became spellbound by the way she conducted herself in the face of further prosecution questions that dripped with sour sweetness, contempt and sarcasm. If she had suffered a natural nervousness at first, it had soon given way to a calm renunciation of anything but the truth, even though at times truth managed a cool avoidance of further incrimination of herself or others. No matter how Stober put his questions, Miss Cavell remained in complete control of her emotions, and her answers were models of quiet economy. She chose to say nothing not already set down in her statements which might have worsened things for her associates. She accepted her own guilt and was resigned to conviction and sentence, and Stober was therefore attacking a woman who had already bowed her head. He became crisply brief during the final stages.

'You have lodged French and British soldiers?'

'Yes.'

'You have helped Frenchmen and Belgians of military age?'

'Yes.'

'You have furnished them with the means of reaching the frontier?'

'Yes.'

'You have taken them into your institute and given them money?'

'Yes.'

Stober expressed acidulous disgust, as if such frankness and honesty were not merely too good to be true, but were as reprehensible as her acts.

'Who was the chief of your organization?'

'We had no chief.'

'Was it yourself?'

'We had no chief.'

'Was it the Prince de Croy?'

'No. He was only concerned with sending us men.'

'Why have you committed these acts of which you are accused?'

'Because, in the beginning, I was confronted by two English soldiers who were in danger of their lives.'

'Quite untrue,' said Stober coldly, 'they were in no danger under German military law.'

Since an official warning had been published by the German commander in the Mons district to the effect that any fugitive Allied soldiers who did not give themselves up within ten days would be shot, Miss Cavell restated her belief that the original two British soldiers were in danger.

'How many men have you helped to get to the frontier?'

'About two hundred.'

'Two hundred?' Stober's cutting edge was sharpened by sarcasm and disbelief.

'Not all British,' said Miss Cavell in the unruffled way that gave such credibility to all her words. 'French and Belgian too.'

'French and Belgian?' asked one of the judges. 'That makes a serious difference.'

'Haven't you been foolish in helping the English?' asked another. 'They are an ungrateful people.'

Miss Cavell embarked on a cool contradiction. 'No, they are not,' she said.

'How do you know?'

'Because some of them have written from England to thank me.'

Stober let it rest at that.

There were no more questions.

She stepped down.

She showed no anxiety as to the outcome, only a pale acceptance of what was to be. She had come a long and tiring way to these crossroads. There was only one route for her now, that which led to certain conviction and sentence. She had thought the sentence might be prison for the duration of the war, but having looked into the cold eyes of the prosecutor, she knew she had to prepare herself for the ultimate.

From the next prisoner, Louise Thuliez, Stober tried to extract an admission that she and all the others obeyed the head of the organization. Namely, the woman Edith Cavell. Mademoiselle Thuliez stated quite firmly that there were neither heads nor subordinates. There were only people, each of whom did what she or he could for the whole.

'Why did you do these things?' asked Stober curtly.

'Because I'm a Frenchwoman,' replied Louise Thuliez, one of many guides who had landed in the net. Eloise Herriot, a woman quick to recognize options, had slipped away the moment she heard of Miss Cavell's arrest.

One by one, each of the accused came face to face with the prosecutor. He questioned Baucq and others at length. He gave short shrift to those of minor account. He dealt with all thirty-five prisoners in that single day's sitting, even though a number were arraigned on charges carrying the death penalty.

Lieutenant Bergan was called as a prosecution witness after the last of the prisoners had stepped down. He excelled himself in that he was bland of mien but accusing of voice. He said, among other things, 'I am now of the opinion that this was a highly organized affair. All the accused deliberately helped in bringing back to the ranks of the Allies, particularly for Joffre's recent offensive, soldiers and as many other men of military age as possible. The woman Cavell managed the headquarters of the whole thing in Brussels.'

He also said that the interrogation of all the accused men had been incontestably fair and correct.

And it had been, apart from denying the help of lawyers to the accused, reading German-written statements back to them in French, and exercising a liberal amount of professional licence.

*   *   *

'*Treason!*' said the major as he and Louise left the shop. He was appalled.

'It can't be true,' said Louise, 'she was exaggerating. People do.'

'Oh, my God,' he said. He stopped and turned.

'No, *mon Commandant*,' said Louise, 'we can't go back. Madame would not want us to.'

He came slowly about and walked on with her. 'Louise, do you realize how serious a charge of treason is in wartime?'

'Yes. We must pray for her. She will face up to whatever happens. So must we. Oh, *mon Commandant*, don't you think I feel for her too? But we must go on. That is what she would want. I know – I know your feelings for her. I love her too. And I think you and I – I think we have a little place in her heart.'

'It's beginning to rain,' said the major in an odd, matter-of-fact way, 'we must find shelter.'

They found it in a barn just outside the village. They had been sleeping rough on their journey, and barns were more often than not their nightly habitat. They sat and talked of Madame.

Eventually Louise, unable to hold the question back, said, 'You would, perhaps, have wished to marry her?'

He looked startled. Then he smiled, faintly. 'She has gone past the marrying stage. She did so when she became wholly committed to nursing.'

'Even so, *mon Commandant*, you would have liked to marry her?'

'I never thought of it,' he said. 'I only know I should have liked to save her from herself, to have been a caring and affectionate friend. No, I shouldn't have asked her to marry me, Louise.'

In the dim shadow of the barn, Louise took a deep breath and put her hand on his. 'Be of good cheer, *mon Commandant*,' she said softly, quoting the kind of words he used himself, 'they will only send her to prison.'

'Yes, we must pray for that, Louise Victoria.'

They resumed their journey when the rain had stopped, heading towards Overpelt, which they hoped to reach the next day. They had a week before it was necessary to present themselves to the captain of the *Christina*, in Rotterdam. A week was time enough, providing they were not held up, and providing the border crossing did not involve them in prolonged manoeuvring.

They risked going through a town called Demer to save time. They passed a German area command post in the Hotel de Ville. The people were as silent in the face of the German occupation as they were in Brussels. Going up a short street towards the west exit of the town, a woman came round the corner ahead of them.

She was attractive, with a good figure, and had a gliding walk that carried her fast over the cobbles. She glanced at them as she passed. Her eyes flickered and darted, but she went on, even faster.

'*Mon Commandant*, that was Madame Herriot!' Louise turned.

'Wait, Louise, wait. Walk on. She would have stopped, had it been safe. Someone's after her. Walk on.'

They reached the corner. The major cast a look back and saw the whisk of Eloise Herriot's coat as she turned left. He and Louise turned right, into the long street that led out of the town. Four men almost collided with them. Two men in plain clothes and two German soldiers. Pushed aside, Louise and the major staggered a little. One of the men in plain clothes checked his stride.

'You there,' he said in French to the major.

'M'sieu?' said the major, and Louise saw the little glint in his eyes that told her that if anyone was in danger of being poleaxed, it was not her comrade. She knew too what he wanted her to do. She strolled casually on, though her heart was beating fast.

'The woman in the brown coat and hat,' said the man. His colleague and the German soldiers had turned into the short street. 'You saw her?'

'Yes,' said the major, 'a man notices an attract-ive woman.'

'Did you see her turn at the end of the street? Left or right?'

'She went into a house,' said the major. He thought, or he seemed to think. 'Last but one on the right. Are you her husband, m'sieu?'

Louise, waiting now at a little distance, heard him ask the question, and a little spasm of delight pierced her apprehension.

The man did not reply. He turned, darted and shot round the corner into the street. The friendly nature of his informant had completely convinced him.

The major rejoined Louise. 'Walk fast, chicken,' he said. 'Once they find I've led them up the garden path, they'll be cross with us. Turn right at the next street. We may just catch up with our good friend Madame Herriot, who is making them run around in circles.'

'They want her, I expect,' said Louise, 'because she too helped Allied soldiers. You remember Albert Edward Lomax, of whom she became very fond?'

'I remember you mentioned him. Faster, Louise.'

They turned right at the next corner. When they reached the street into which Eloise Herriot had turned, she was there, standing just inside the entrance of a narrow, arched alleyway. At the end of the alleyway was a gate leading into a yard behind the shops. The major led Louise across. He walked past Eloise Herriot, through the alleyway and up to the railed gate. It was rusty and locked. He lifted it on its hinges, forced it sideways and freed the lock. When he turned, Louise was standing with Madame Herriot. The major gestured them to enter the yard. As he fixed the gate into its lock, the rusty catch quivered.

They were out of sight when two men in plain clothes went by ten minutes later with the German soldiers. The yard was quiet. They stood against the rear wall of the shops, hidden from eyes at back windows. They did not speak, but Eloise Herriot turned warm eyes on her friends. Louise smiled at her, and the Belgian woman pressed her hand.

They waited until the October afternoon became dark before emerging from their safe retreat. Quietly, they traversed the street and left the town. The black countryside loomed up, offering them silent security.

'Thank you,' said Eloise Herriot then, 'it's good in all situations to be with friends. In some situations, it's a blessing. The Boche were so close to me, then *voilà*! – they were not there at all. Why was that?'

'We sent them off to search a house,' said the major.

Louise, with a little laugh, said, 'My English friend, Madame Herriot, has a way of thinking for everyone. Oh, I don't mean that is a rather superior fault in him – except, of course, it would never do to have him think he's too clever.'

'We are all very clever,' smiled Eloise Herriot. 'We have to be. In Belgium today, fools walk early into their graves.'

'The courageous walk precipices,' said the major. 'Eloise, do you intend to cross the frontier? If so, will you come with us?'

'No, I will stay,' she said. 'I will stay and fight them. I will fight them for Belgium and my husband. And for Madame, for Edith Cavell. I've been hiding with friends in Malines. A few days ago I had to leave. They are thorough and painstaking, the Boche, when they're trying to find someone they want. Now I'm on a wandering way to Turnhout, where I also have friends. You two are going to Holland?'

'Yes,' said Louise.

'Good. You have heard about Edith Cavell and all the others?'

The major winced and said, 'Yes, that the trial is on.'

'Today,' said Eloise Herriot, 'the German prosecutor has been summing up. My friends, we must wish Edith Cavell well with all our hearts, and everyone on trial with her. And here I must leave you.'

They stopped at silent, night-shrouded cross-roads. Eloise was to turn left, the major and Louise to go straight on.

'Madame Herriot, oh, it has been so good to have known you,' said Louise.

'It's been a great privilege,' said the major.

'We are friends, aren't we?' Eloise Herriot's teeth glimmered between her warm lips as she smiled. 'You will remember about my amusing English soldier, Albert? He will be back in the trenches by now, sucking a new pipe, and perhaps even in the trenches he will still be making jokes.'

'I'll look out for him,' said the major. 'Eloise, will you be all right?'

Eloise Herriot looked down the dark, winding road that she was to walk alone.

'That is only Belgium at night,' she said, 'and I am not afraid, if that is what you mean. Or if you mean I shall be alone, it will not be quite like that. I shall think of Liège and the guns and my husband, and of my English soldier who made me laugh so much.' She smiled again. 'M'sieu – mam'selle – you find it strange for the widow of a soldier to have both her husband and another soldier on her mind? But both men belong to my life. You understand?'

'Without question,' said the major.

'After the war,' said Louise, 'I shall want to know if Albert came back for his pipe.'

'Goodbye, *chérie*.' Eloise Herriot kissed Louise, and Louise held her tightly for a moment. 'Goodbye, *mon Commandant*.'

The major kissed her warmly on the lips.

She, liking the soldiers of war, responded just as warmly.

She walked down the dark road, a gliding shadow. They watched her. She was a soldier herself, in her way, enduring and unafraid.

The major and Louise went on until they were tired.

Late each afternoon, when dusk was smothering the land with creeping grey, and farmers and labourers were at last leaving the fields and thinking of supper, the major and Louise had sneaked into barns or outhouses and there searched for precious hay and the warmest corners in which to sleep. Today, darkness had claimed them before they could find a barn. But they had their cats' eyes and their sharpened instincts, and they crossed black fields and found their shelter.

Usually the major, a hardened soldier, slept well in any of the primitive beds he made for himself. Tonight, thoughts of Edith and the trial kept him awake for a long while.

When the trial was resumed on the second day, Stober took the stage and occupied it for over two hours. In detail he catalogued the activities and crimes of the accused. Clinically, he defined the leading roles played by Edith Cavell and her chief collaborators, making it quite clear that the tribunal was not to believe there were neither heads nor subordinates.

The prisoners had to sit through it all without, for the most part, understanding a word of it. Stober spoke only in German, and there was no interpretation offered. Towards the end, he drew the tribunal's attention to the fact that many of the accused had, by their acts, been guilty of treason. Treason of almost any kind, under the German military code, was punishable by death. His constant repetition of the word *Todestrafe*, meaning death penalty, began to penetrate the general incomprehension, and to fill some of the accused with alarm.

When Stober had finished his lengthy performance, the official interpreter, for the benefit of the accused, translated into French the sentences the prosecutor had asked for. Among those for whom he wanted the death penalty were Edith Cavell and Philippe Baucq. Miss Cavell took the shock as calmly as she had taken so much else.

Counsel for the defence were now allowed to speak. Since they had been permitted no access to their clients, or even been notified of what the charges were, they were compelled to exercise whatever defensive ingenuity they were capable of. Miss Cavell's lawyer, Sadi Kirschen, made an impressive and eloquent effort on her behalf. He spoke of her devotion to duty as a nurse, her care of the sick and her undoubted desire to serve the cause of humanity. He pleaded, logically, that it was impossible for so compassionate a woman to refuse help to the men who needed it – the fugitive soldiers of the Allies. Whatever the prosecution maintained, the fact was that Miss Cavell, like all her collaborators, thought these men were in danger of being shot.

The prosecution, he said, had declared her to be guilty of treason. It was necessary in law, he pointed out, for the prosecution to prove whether any of the men she helped actually did enrol again for military duty before she could be convicted of this offence. Especially if it entailed the death penalty. Respectfully, he did not think the tribunal had the moral right to execute a nurse, particularly one who had nursed German soldiers. What would be more appropriate, in the event of her being convicted at all, was a sentence that would put her out of the way until the war was over.

Other lawyers made out what cases they could on behalf of the rest of the accused, and at the conclusion of their submissions the trial was over. But before the session was officially declared closed, Princess Marie de Croy came to her feet and asked if she might address the tribunal. Permission was given, and the Senate fell quiet as she began to speak. She was a woman of physical frailty but the same spiritual strength as Miss Cavell, and she made her address clearly and courageously.

'Everyone must be prepared to take the full responsibility for their acts, and I want to bear full responsibility for mine. It has been said that Edith Cavell was at the head of a conspiracy, that she organized the escape of the British and the recruitment of French and Belgians. It is not true. She was forced into it by my brother and me. It was we who at the beginning sheltered and hid these men. When she told us she could not lodge any more men, that her institute would be endangered if we sent more to her, we still took her others, and so did our confederates. It was under the pressure of circumstances that Edith Cavell had done that of which she is now accused. Therefore, it is not on her, but on us, my brother and me, that the greater part of the responsibility for these acts lies.

'For myself, and I repeat, I am ready to take the consequences of this.'

It was not precisely true that she and her brother forced Miss Cavell into her escape work. Miss Cavell, entirely of her own accord, had begun the work when she admitted Colonel Bodger and Sergeant Meachin. But Princess Marie de Croy had come courageously to her feet to do what she could for the English nurse she so admired.

The trial was finally over. In only two days, thirty-five men and women had been arraigned and prosecuted on charges ranging from the comparatively light to the treasonable. The death penalty had been demanded for eight of them; long terms of imprisonment for the rest.

With her friends, Miss Cavell walked quietly from the Senate. They were taken back to St Gilles prison. There they awaited the verdicts and the sentences.

Chapter Eighteen

Louise, young and healthy though she was, had not found sleeping rough as easy as the major. She had gone down into the corner of a barn each night in a state of promising tiredness, but cold and discomfort woke her, and it was difficult then to recapture sleep.

She could not sleep at all that night.

The major awoke. The barn was dark, the night cold, the amount of straw meagre. He saw Louise faintly outlined. She was sitting up, her back against the wall. Warm from sleep, he contemplated her.

'Louise?'

'Oh, it's a hard floor, *mon Commandant*,' she said, 'and a cold one.'

'And you're cold too, are you?'

'Yes.'

He was in the dreamy state of a man who had slept, and who could go off again as long as anxieties did not return to plague him.

Well-being should be shared, especially with a comrade.

'Come close, then,' he murmured.

She hesitated. Even in wartime and even though the world was fifteen years into the twentieth century, she could not forget propriety. Then she moved close to him. She lay beside him. They were touching. She could not help her shyness, or her confusion or the rise of suffusing colour. But as he put his arms around her she exhaled a sigh of bliss, because the comfort and warmth were immediate. They lay on their sides, very close and very warm. Cold retreated altogether as her curving body breathed against his.

'Oh, *mon Commandant*,' she whispered, her face burning against his shoulder.

Dreamily he remembered the ditch, and the confusion of a very young girl.

'You're quite safe, Louise Victoria, so have no worries,' he murmured, and out of his well-being came the vague thought that he sounded impossibly smug.

'Oh, I have no worries, none at all,' she said muffledly.

He awoke fully then, the drowsy sense of protectiveness slipping away. It was unlikely to return, for in its place was a wide-awake physical awareness of her. She might have been cold before but she was not cold now. Her warmth was incandescent, her closeness a temptation and a danger, her garment-smothered body alive with vibrations.

'I think—' He was about to say he was beginning to have worries of his own. Instead, for safety's sake, he relaxed his embrace. Louise moved. She turned her face up to his. He could not help himself any more than she could. They kissed. Her taut, vibrating body uncoiled and she clung in breathless response. The kiss, lingering and communicating, ran into her blood, and her blood coursed so fast that her heart beat like a pounding, whirring clock. She felt an incredibly feverish desire to cast off her clothes, and a shameless desire to be touched. Not here, not there, but everywhere. Her body burned and her lips moved against his, telegraphing a word fifty times and more.

Yes, yes, *yes*.

The major experienced again a sensation of extraordinary sweetness. It had happened once before, on the day when she had run into his arms outside the house of Eloise Herriot. The sensation transmitted its message. The warm, shapely body of Louise Victoria was rich in its promise of exquisite pleasure, and could make him forget for brief but enchanting moments the foreboding that was beginning to haunt him. Was that what the temptation of her body represented – an antidote? Or did he simply want Louise? The thought forced on him the stark necessity of protecting her, not using her or robbing her.

Again he relaxed his embrace and released her. 'There,' he said with careful lightness, 'are you warm enough to go to sleep now?'

She sighed, and curled up, their bodies no longer in contact.

'Oh, yes,' she murmured. She had a little smile on her face. 'Thank you, *mon Commandant*.'

Thank you? Didn't she realize what she had aroused in him? Probably not. Louise Victoria in her innocence was a singular and precious young lady.

But she was not as safe with him as he had thought.

Louise's little smile came from the fact that she knew it too. It gave her a feeling of delicious pleasure. Knowledge drew aside the curtain of inexperience and innocence. It sent her into contented sleep close to him, though not in his arms. In his arms, neither of them would have slept. The major did lie awake for a short while, remembering how he had once told Edith he was not always the gentleman.

He had achieved something by being one that night.

Chapter Nineteen

They reached the little town of Overpelt the next afternoon. Their journey on the whole had been one of careful detours, on the basis that it was healthier to take time than risks. The exception had been Demer, a tempting short cut which had proved almost fatal. Overpelt, which could not be avoided, presented even greater risks. It was only a short distance from the border, and a garrison of German troops was stationed there.

Louise and the major strolled casually down a street with shops on one side, houses on the other. For all their air of unconcern, each was tinglingly aware that they might be stopped and questioned. The major's papers identified him as Albert Descamps, an engineer. Louise was his young cousin, Anna Marie Descamps. Their reason for being there was to visit friends. Louise was in a blue coat, blue jacket and skirt, and a white blouse. On her head was a pull-on woollen hat that kept most of her bright hair hidden. The major wore his blue jacket and grey trousers, and a soft blue cap with a peak, something the nurses had found for him in place of the boater. They both looked respectably bourgeoise. Their few belongings were carried by the major in an old canvas valise.

'When I was here with that French fellow, Quien,' he said, 'there was a café in the next street, where we were handed over to a guide who had contacts with the men who work the canal boats and barges. We might perhaps try that café.'

'For once,' said Louise, 'you aren't thinking very well. People who have been helping Allied soldiers have probably all been arrested or have gone into hiding.'

That made them think of Madame again, and the trial.

'You're right,' said the major, 'but we'll try the café, all the same. We can look at the customers' faces and make a guess about who might be able to take us on a barge or a boat.'

It was their intention to reach the canal that marked the border between Belgium and Holland, and to make a water crossing. They were not going to chance any well-guarded bridge.

Louise smiled. Life was newly precious today, despite the German soldiers and all the other worries of war, because the major had discovered at last that she was not a girl but a woman. And because she had discovered, much to her delight, that there was every prospect of her being able to wind him around her little finger, as Mama had with Papa. Well, perhaps that was not so much a discovery as an immensely pleasant feeling.

She said, 'I don't think we should look too hard at people or make guesses. It would be terrible, when we're so close to the border, for guesses to turn into mistakes. So many brave people were arrested with Madame, and it has probably made everyone very cautious and careful, don't you think?'

'I agree,' he said soberly.

'Also, it might not be necessary to ask help of someone we don't know. Do you remember, I told you I had friends here? It's a family whom my parents knew. They're bound to be living here still. It will be better, won't it, to ask help of them?'

'Much better, Louise Victoria.' He felt very tender towards her. 'Where do your friends live?'

'In a house about half a kilometre on the north side of Overpelt. *Mon Commandant*, you go to the café while I go to my friends. They have a boat.'

'Should you go by yourself?'

'Well, you see,' she said, 'they're very correct people, and extremely proper and respectable. They'll be sympathetic towards me, because of friendship, but it's just possible they may be a little nervous and reluctant if you appear too. See, I will arrange to use their boat tonight, then come back after I've discussed this with them. We will use the boat together without their knowing about you. Isn't it right, that what they won't know of they won't worry about?'

'You're sure, are you, that this is the best way?' He knew he would worry about her, but she seemed very confident.

'Oh, yes.' She was eager to make a contribution of her own. And she knew her friends, although kind, would be very hesitant about taking risks for an Allied soldier. They would not deny help to her, but they would not want to be involved with Major Scott. She only needed to know about the boat, to get their permission to use it. 'You go to the café,' she assured him.

They were walking slowly. On the other side of the street two German soldiers, rifles slung, had turned from a shop to gaze with interest and enquiry at them. A little farther on, at the corner of the street, stood two more.

'All right, I'll wait in the café,' said the major, keeping his fingers crossed for her now that they had got this far.

'I should be back in an hour,' said Louise. 'If you have to run, please try to leave a message with the proprietor.'

'I will.'

'I should not recover if you forgot about me again.'

'I cherish you too much to make the mistake again, little Belgian nightingale,' he murmured. As they approached the corner he said a casual, cheerful goodbye to her. He crossed the street towards the two Germans, passing them as he turned right into the next street. Louise gave him a wave and a smile as she kept straight on, heading north out of the town. The Germans, ignoring the major, had their eyes on Louise, as she proceeded at a lazy stroll. She gave them a wave too. They smiled across the street at her.

The major realized that in Edith Cavell he had found a woman of remarkable character, and in Louise a girl of bright courage. It had by no means been an arid six months. However useless he had been to his country during that time, he would not have exchanged those months for any others. He would have asked for only one day to be different – the day of Edith's arrest.

Louise Victoria. She was on his mind as he walked to the café. A girl beginning to acquire some of Edith's coolness.

Except that she wasn't a girl. Not any longer.

The thirty-five prisoners were all in St Gilles, awaiting the tribunal's verdicts and sentences. In her cell, Edith Cavell reflected on what was to be. And she was sure what it would be for her. The judges would give Stober what he had demanded – her head – because Stober had shown she was guilty and because she was English.

She wrote what she was certain would be her last communication to her nurses. The letter became an account of the work she had enjoyed so much among them and with them. It was also a declaration of her abiding interest in the *Clinique*, in its accomplishments of the past and in the brightness of its future. And it was a revelation of her feelings towards everyone there. She asked them to keep faith with God, and to understand she was sorry if at times she had been too severe. She wished happiness to them all.

'I have loved you all much more than you have ever thought.'

That was how she finished the letter that was to be her farewell to them.

The major checked the time and confirmed it with the beetle-browed café proprietor, who pointed to the clock on the wall above the major's head. The clock face was yellow with age, but its tick was as steady as the healthiest heartbeat. It showed the time to be a few minutes to four. Louise had left him at a quarter to two. She would be back in an hour, she had said. Two and a quarter hours had passed. For the last hour he had been restless with anxiety. Several times he had gone outside to look around.

He got up. He spoke to the proprietor, telling him he was expecting a young lady and describing her. The proprietor, aware of his accented French, gave him a speculative look, turned a careless eye on two German customers drinking cognac, listened to further words from the major and then nodded.

'I understand, m'sieu. I'll ask her to wait for you. Good luck.'

The door had opened to Louise nearly two hours before, though she had had to ring twice. Jean appeared. He was the son of the family, a young man who had made darkly ruminative eyes at her. She had last seen him two years previously, when he and his parents called on her parents in Brussels. She had thought then how introspective he seemed. He talked little, except to her. He cut a rather dramatic figure, preferring to stand rather than sit, his back against a wall, his arms folded and his eyes following her. Mama said Jean was a little repressed, the only son of parents who were too proud of him and too possessive with him. Wishing to have him perfect, they chose his friends for him, and so he had few friends, even at the age of twenty-two.

She wondered why he had had to open the door himself, and not a servant. She also wondered at his look, which made her think of an artist. He was very pale, with blue stubble of beard, thin, ascetically handsome, and seemed hungry, and suffering from self-neglect and overwork. His eyes were dark hollows. For a moment or two he stared at her, then his smile came – a flash of welcome in his starved face.

'Louise! How wonderful. Come in, come in.'

She went in. He closed the door. The huge hall looked dusty. There were even cobwebs.

'Jean—'

'Oh, Louise, how good to see you.' His smile flashed again. 'There's no one, no one. This is marvellous.' He was brittle, excited. He took her hands and kissed her on both cheeks. His lips were moist.

'No one?' said Louise, puzzled.

'My parents.' He sighed. 'Imprisoned, Louise. Imprisoned. For hiding soldiers.'

'Hiding soldiers?' Her surprise was sharp.

'There, you too find it unbelievable. And it is. Who would have thought them capable of such a thing? And they were such a trouble, those men. But Father said the time had come to be good Belgians, not respectable ones. The Boche came three months ago and arrested them.'

'Both your parents?' Louise could not imagine his precise, fussy mother and father taking any reckless role upon themselves.

'Both of them, would you believe it?'

342

'I'm sorry, Jean,' she said, and felt she could like his uninspiring parents better now.

'Seven years they were given,' said Jean, locking his hands together and pulling on them. 'Think of it, think how good they were, how they looked after me so well. Who would ever have thought them capable of sheltering enemy soldiers?'

'Not enemy soldiers,' said Louise gently. She felt sympathy for his obvious wretchedness.

'They were such kind parents, so caring. Ah, Louise, aren't you pretty? Even in that funny hat? Come, come in here.'

He led her into a drawing room. Once it had been elegant, with not an ornament or cushion ever out of place. Now it was cluttered with books, papers, piles of brown-tinted photographs, dirty cups and saucers, and even a plate still greasy from a meal. And the grease was green with film.

'Oh, Jean,' said Louise, aghast at the dirt and neglect, 'what has happened to everything? What are your servants doing?'

'There's no one,' repeated Jean, and gestured with his hands in contempt of beings who had deserted their responsibilities. 'The servants went. They were afraid.'

'What of?'

'Oh, the Boche.' He swept papers off a chair so that Louise might sit, but she shook her head. 'The Boche took Mother and Father away. The servants – the pigs – were afraid they might be taken too. So there's no one, Louise, and see how untidy everything is. But it isn't so bad now that you've come. How glad I am to see you, and how you've grown. Louise, you're beautiful, like a bright flame in this old house.'

She felt she preferred his introspective silences to his nervous, staccato rushes of speech. His emaciated look and his unshaven chin made him seem older than twenty-four. Her feelings towards him had never been much more than lukewarm, and although she was sorry for him now, she deplored his weakness. The dirt and neglect gave off the faint odour of decay.

'Jean, I can't stay,' she said. 'Listen, I need help. The Boche are after me—'

'The Boche?' he said, and his eyes darted and flickered, as if he suspected German soldiers were about to appear and lay their hands on her. 'Louise, have you too been a good Belgian? My mother and father, would you believe they could bring so much trouble on themselves?'

'The Boche did not arrest you?' she said.

He laughed with a quick nervousness. 'No. I'm here, as you can see. They were content to take my parents.'

'That's something, isn't it, then, that they didn't take you? Jean, you have a boat and access to the little canal.' She explained how she could use the boat to get to Holland across the main canal. Could she have it? She did not mention Major Scott; reason and instinct told her not to. Jean had neither resilience nor courage. He was suffering from the imprisonment of his parents, and she did not think he felt too kindly towards the fugitive Allied soldiers. His parents had ordered his life for him and fussily kept him remote from the imperfections of the world. In doing so, they had given him no chance to develop self-reliance. The beautiful house stood now as a neglected, wasting symbol of his helplessness. The fact that the servants had deserted him was a disgraceful thing, for she had never heard that his parents had treated any of them badly, but no young man should wallow in self-pity to this extent. He would not want to know about Major Scott.

'Do you see, Jean?' she said. 'I must get to Holland, or eventually the Boche will find me. I helped Allied soldiers too. Do you still have the boat? I can handle it myself and arrange with the Dutch to see it gets back to you.'

His deep-socketed eyes took in her health and loveliness. She stood in this room of decay like life's brightest image. She alone was clean and wholesome.

'How beautiful you are, Louise,' he said. 'Why have you never written?'

That was a ridiculous question. They had never been close. His parents had been friends of her father, that was all, and the families had visited each other, but not frequently. Sometimes she had shown sympathy to Jean because he did not seem able to enjoy life, but never had she felt any desire to correspond with him. She could think of Major Scott, her vigorous and quick-striking comrade, and be swept by sweet excitement, warm longing, imaginative hopes and even fierce jealousy. She could look at Jean and only feel pity and distaste.

'Jean,' she said, 'it is you who should have written to me to tell me about your parents.'

He had not asked about her own parents, and she was relieved. She did not want to talk to him about Mama and Papa in this unhappy place. She wanted to leave. But there was the boat.

'I wanted to write,' said Jean, 'but you were always so discouraging. Think how close we could have become if you had stopped looking into your mirror sometimes and looked at me. But no, it was always some mirror or other, to find out whether you were still pretty or not.'

'Oh, that's not true,' said Louise, who knew it wasn't.

Jean's laugh was a little high-pitched. 'No, I was only joking, Louise. You never needed any mirror. It will be different here now that you've come.'

'Jean, I've only come—'

'You can't think of going again.'

'I must,' she said, 'I told you why.'

His eyes shifted, darted. 'You can stay here,'

he said, 'I'll hide you. No one comes here now. The Boche used to, but yesterday they stopped. Yes, stay here, Louise.'

She shuddered at the thought.

'I can't,' she said, 'it would be too dangerous for both of us. You'd be sent to prison, like your parents.'

'There's no one here, no one,' he said again.

No, thought Louise, no one would want to stay in a house inhabited by a man who was only half a man. 'Jean, the boat, will you let me have it?'

He smiled, his eyes wistful in his thin face. 'The Germans took it, weeks ago,' he said.

Her heart sank. She had so wanted to go back to Major Scott and tell him they were as good as on the last step to freedom. She wanted him to know they were indispensable to each other.

'I'm sorry,' she said, 'I must go, then.'

'Wait,' said Jean, and his smile was teasing. 'It's not as bad as that, Louise. I can prove the Boche haven't left us with nothing. Come upstairs and I'll show you where you can lay your eyes and hands on another boat.'

'Oh, thank you,' said Louise.

She climbed the wide staircase with him. Its carpet seemed to be thickly cloudy with dust. He took her into his parents' bedroom. She thought the Germans must have come for his mother and father at dawn, for the bedclothes were in the rumpled disorder of an enforced rising. They appeared not to have been touched since.

'Come to the window and look,' said Jean.

She went to the window, long and high and leaded. She saw the view of the estate in the cloudy light, the sweep of spreading green still wet from overnight rain. The little jetty where the boat was usually moored was not visible from here. She glimpsed the streak of dull grey that was the water of the inlet which led to the little canal, and the little canal led to the main canal, which was fed by the Meuse.

'What am I to look for?' she asked, then felt the wrench that pinned her arms behind her, and the binding imprisonment of a silk stocking around her wrists, all accomplished so violently and swiftly that it was done before she could react. She screamed.

'There's no one, no one,' said Jean in a voice pitched on a high note of excitement. 'You must stay here, Louise, and be the most beautiful thing in the house.'

She jerked frantically and broke away, her hands and wrists working frenziedly to loosen the silk shackle. Jean smiled, his eyes feverishly bright with triumph. Louise screamed again. He swooped. Swiftly and easily he lifted her. He was thin and starved, but he tossed her like a doll on to the bed. Louise kicked, and again she screamed. With another stocking, he gagged her. Horrified, terrified, she stared up at him, her eyes huge, her teeth biting on the stifling silk.

'It's not to hurt you,' he said, his breath

rushing, 'but to make sure you stay. You shouldn't have talked of going. That was unkind, wasn't it, when you saw how much I needed you? Oh, Louise, when I opened the door and saw you, I thought that life was being good to me at last. You were like a sweet gift from God, standing there and smiling at me. My mother and father, they are only poor, miserable people, making so much trouble because of the men they brought here. Don't look so frightened. I shall be good to you, and kind. You wouldn't stay if I untied you, would you? Oh, I shall untie you sometimes, out of goodness and kindness, and when you finally realize how necessary you are to me, you'll freely stay, won't you? Then there'll be no need to tie you at all.'

He sat on the edge of the bed, his paleness touched with spots of colour, and out of his mouth, starved of talk, came floods of words. He poured into her ears his feelings for her, his history of want that had begun when he saw her just after her fifteenth birthday, a want she had sadly ignored. His parents had discouraged him, telling him he must not think in that way about a girl so young she was still a child. But then, his parents had discouraged him in everything he really cared about.

And Louise, in sick despair, knew why his parents had kept such a careful eye on him.

He was mad, quite mad.

Chapter Twenty

The major was now worried out of his wits over Louise. Where was she? Where was the house? Again and again he had retraced his steps on the narrow road that led north out of Overpelt. He was in flat countryside, and had found only a square-fronted stone mansion standing far back from the road on the right. The place had an almost ghostly quietness to it, and not a light showed at any of its windows in the gloom of the failing October afternoon. But because it was the only residence he could see, he investigated, going up the long drive and over the forecourt to the wide front door. The quietness spoke of emptiness. However, he rang the bell, loudly and insistently. It was not answered.

He went back to the road, traversing it for a full kilometre, although Louise had said the house was only half that distance out of the town. He explored up and down. Not a house, not a habitation of any kind. He convinced himself he was on the wrong road, retraced his steps again, and looked for another north exit from Overpelt. There was no other.

He re-entered the town. Two men passed him on the corner where he and Louise had parted with airy cheerfulness. They slipped by him like shadows, their coat collars turned up. He hurried to the café. Louise was not there, nor had the proprietor seen anything of her. The major spoke to him about a house he could not find. The proprietor's beetle brows drew together. Well, what man could find any house in that location? There were none. There was only the canal, if one walked far enough, and then one came up against German troops and barbed wire. Just outside Overpelt there was the chateau of the Rommes family, that was all. Except that the family was not resident there now, not to speak of. The major, desperate, wanted to know why his young cousin should mention a house that didn't exist.

The proprietor, weighing him up, said, 'Permit me, m'sieu, to recommend care. Myself, I exercise great care. Have you been here before?'

'Yes, a few months ago.'

'Ah, I thought, m'sieu, I'd seen you in here on a previous occasion.'

'I've a distinguishing mark or two,' said the major, touching the slightly dented bridge of his nose. His fears for Louise were beginning to crucify him, and his flippancy had a savage edge.

The proprietor asked, 'Is it the Boche who worry you, m'sieu?'

'Not as much as my missing young cousin does.' The major paid for the cognac he had just swallowed. Outside, the evening was dark, the sky full of rolling black clouds. The moon shone silvery for a second or two as it found a gap, then its light was smothered again. The need for action churned at the major's nerves, and the need to be here if Louise arrived tore at him.

'Why do you recommend care?' he asked.

'Because, m'sieu,' murmured the proprietor, 'she could only have meant the chateau, and that is an unhappy place.'

Oh, great God, of course. What, thought the major, had happened to his brain? Had it stopped functioning except in relation to that trial?

Louise Victoria, Comtesse de Bouchet. Of course. A house, she had said, a house in which friends lived. Friends of the de Bouchet family *might* live in a village house. But they were more likely to live in a chateau, whether it showed lights on a gloomy afternoon or not. People conserved fuel of every kind in every way in Belgium. But the unanswered door-bell?

He turned to go, then a thought held him

back. 'You said there was no family to speak of at the chateau now?' he asked.

'Only the son, Jean,' said the proprietor, keeping to a murmur. 'There are no complaints about him. He's as good a German as a German himself. For the sake of German law and order, m'sieu, and to keep the peace here, he is said to have informed on his parents, who were sheltering French and British soldiers. So they took his parents away and put them in prison for seven years. Unfortunately, m'sieu, such is the way some people misunderstand those who seek to keep the peace with the Boche, the young man Jean was deserted by all his servants. Every one, m'sieu. There's ingratitude for you.'

'And there's a young man lucky not to have been cut up into small pieces,' said the major. 'But he's still at the chateau, is he?'

'That is so, m'sieu. If she has gone there, your young cousin, then hurry.'

'Why?'

'Who can tell, m'sieu, in these days?'

The major left, walking fast. He passed two German soldiers. They looked at him but they did not stop him.

The banking clouds kept the night dark. Two men approached the Rommes chateau as silently as ghosts. A moment later the bell pealed inside the hall.

Jean, startled, shot to his feet. In the light of the bedside lamp, which he had lit only a few minutes ago, Louise's face showed white and tortured. Pain darkened her eyes, for cramp was seizing her still-bound wrists. Twice he had removed the gag from her mouth to ease her choked breathing. Once he had kissed her. His wet, voracious lips had made her shudder and think the gag infinitely preferable. He had talked and talked, going round in feverish circles of complaint about her indifference and complaint about his parents, and in such a frighteningly unbalanced way that she knew her life was in danger. There was not another soul in this huge, cold place. She prayed and prayed for the major to come. He would. He *must*. But in growing despair, she knew Jean would be cunning.

If the peal of the bell startled Jean, it rang for her like a message of hope. Would he answer it? He had not answered the previous ring.

It pealed again. Swiftly, he put out the light. She saw his face the second before the room plunged into darkness. His pallor was clammy, as wet as a man in fever. She prayed with every fibre of her being. The gag stifled her. He opened the bedroom door and stood listening. He heard the shouted command that came through the mail slot and boomed through the hall.

354

'Open up! Open up!' The language was German.

'Ah, the Boche,' he said calmly. 'Stay there, pretty Louise. I shan't betray you to them.' He went out, closing the door quietly behind him. He turned the key and put it in his jacket pocket. He went down to admit his callers as the bell pealed a third time. He had nothing to fear from the Boche. They had given him protection for his help and loyalty up until yesterday.

'Open up!' The command boomed gutturally again.

He opened one of the double doors. They confronted him from beneath their caps and between their turned-up coat collars. The moon sailed free and beamed light into the hall. He stared, then tried to slam the door shut, but they were in, and they were at him like wolves. He screamed as knives flashed. The blades turned red, and heavy, drifting clouds obscured the momentary beam of light.

In the darkness they looked down at him. He lay on his back, quite still. They crossed themselves, silently asking for dispensation. Then they left. Upstairs, in the blackness of a locked bedroom, lay a frantic girl, her wrists bound and her mouth gagged. She had heard the screams. And all was terrifying silence now.

There was no one, no one at all, in the great old chateau. Except Louise and a young

·man who stared up out of dead eyes at a dark ceiling.

The major, about to break into a run as he reached the outskirts of the town, saw a German patrol and ducked inside a hedge path leading to the door of a house. He flung himself down and waited. His left arm ached. The solid sound of booted feet thumped in his ears without pause. The Germans tramped steadily up and steadily by. He was on his feet and away a minute later, striding fast along the narrow road. In a while he began to run, his desperation worsened by new fears. He knew there could only be one reason why Louise had not returned: because she could not.

He ran, pounding the road, sick with himself for not realizing earlier that it had to be the chateau.

Two men heard him. They left the road, and the darkness of a field swallowed them. Aware of neither of them, he passed them, pounding on, the canvas valise bumping against his ribs.

He went up the long drive with plane trees on either side. He lengthened his running stride. The great square front of the chateau loomed up darker than the night itself. Not a light showed. He reached the doors. One was open. Interior blackness yawned, and he thought he could smell death before he saw it. It was there, just inside the hall – an inert shape and a pale, glimmering oval. The oval was the face of death.

His blood froze. He stepped over the body and the spacious hall echoed to his footsteps. He stopped and listened. The place was as silent as a huge tomb. No one, the café proprietor had said, lived here now, except the son of the family.

That corpse was the son. Someone had come for him, someone who had decided in the end that the honour of Belgium had been stained beyond forgiveness.

Or had it been Louise? Had it been his bright and beautiful Louise who, fighting for her life, had struck down the informer? His every limb turned icy.

'*Louise! Louise!*' The eerie silence was rent apart by his shouting voice. He ran at doors, flinging them open and calling her name.

Upstairs, her frozen body jerked into life. She rolled off the bed and thumped to the floor, then staggered up. She turned her back on the locked door and pounded on it with the heel of her shoe.

He heard her and charged up the dark staircase. He made for the door that was vibrating from kicks. It was locked. He rattled the handle, calling her name. The vibrations stopped. He heard a muffled, choking gurgle. He put his shoulder to the door. It was solid oak. The key? *God, the key?* The corpse. That was where it had to be, on the corpse. He ran down the stairs. He dug into the pockets of the jacket, which was as limp as the body itself. The pale, dead face leered up at him and blood stained his searching hands. He found the key and surged back up the staircase.

Louise, gagged and in excruciating pain from cramped wrists, opened her eyes as the major materialized. Tears of luminous brilliance started. He released the gag and untied her bonds. She cried out at a new pain, the pain of resurgent blood, then flung her arms around him and wept on his chest.

'Oh, my sweet and beautiful girl,' he said, his relief intense.

'You – oh, thank you, thank you,' she gasped, her joy and gratitude no less emotional than his relief. She held on to him until her shivers subsided, and she spilled out her story, reaching the moment when the bell rang and Jean didn't answer it.

'My God, what a fool I was,' breathed the major. 'I was there at the door, ringing the bell, but when it wasn't answered, I left. I wasn't thinking. I had my mind on a house, not a chateau, and the place seemed so empty.'

She was willing to forgive him anything, even that error of judgement. She told him how the bell had pealed again later, and how Jean had calmly said, 'Ah, the Boche.'

'Yes, for the Boche probably paid him

protective calls. He betrayed his parents to them. But someone beat the Boche to it this evening. He's dead.'

'Dead? Oh, that's awful, dreadful.' Louise shuddered. 'I heard his screams. But he was mad, crazy, saying how much his parents had denied him all the good things of life. I was terrified – oh, *mon Commandant*, you came back for me – thank you, thank you.' Headily demonstrative in her gratitude, she kissed him.

'We must go,' he said, quite aware now of the exact nature of his feelings for her. 'If the Boche come, we'll really be in trouble. What about the boat?'

'He said the Boche had taken it.' Louise cast off her shudders, and the major gave her a squeeze. 'He said they took it weeks ago.'

'He strikes me as the kind of lunatic who might have said anything, poor devil.' The major felt his brain was working again. 'Do you know the way to the mooring?'

'Oh, yes.'

'Then shall we investigate? Shall we see whether he was lying? Yes, come on.'

Louise, who would willingly have attempted to walk on water with him, needed no encouragement to put the horror of the chateau behind her. In the pervading darkness that was like a shroud for the dead, they made their way down the staircase to the hall. A few shudders came back to her as they stepped over the body that lay close to the open door. Then they ran around the chateau to the gardens and grounds. Louise led the way, the sickness she felt at the fate of Jean swamped by a surging sea of warm bliss and love. The darkness of night was a friend, as it had been at other times to her and the major. Their eyes picked their course over thick, unmown grass as they cut through the middle of the estate towards the inlet. The dull glimmer of water was just ahead. They reached it, and the outline of a boat peered at them as they stepped on to the jetty. It was a splendid craft.

The mast lay on the jetty alongside the boat, and the sail was stowed.

'Where does this inlet lead to?' asked the major.

She told him: to the little canal, and the little canal ran into the wide main canal. They must turn left when they reached the little canal, and then bear left into the mainstream which, with a canal on the Dutch side, flowed into the Meuse canal that divided Holland and Belgium. They could ground the boat on Dutch soil.

'It sounds too easy,' said the major.

'If we are very quiet,' said Louise, 'and if it stays dark, perhaps at least it won't be too difficult. There's a moon tonight. Did you know?'

'Yes, I did. It's shown itself once or twice. Pray that it stays covered up from now on.'

He thought about fitting the mast and hoisting the sail, but decided against it. Too visible. He must use the oars. They boarded carefully and cast off. They became quiet then, as quiet as the cloud-muffled sky, except for the soft wash of water running over slow, steady oars. The major's left arm ached, but it stood up to its work without any other complaint. Louise at the tiller watched their course, her body warm and life a great, glowing revival within her.

They made uninterrupted progress to the little canal, where they caught the tide in their favour. The major stopped rowing and let the flow of water carry them. Louise, competent with the rudder, kept her eyes straining ahead, watching the dark, rippling surface of the canal. Her heart jumped as she saw the sweep of a German searchlight in the distance. They both knew they would soon enter the stretch where they would be courting the danger of discovery. German activity along the Belgian side of the canals was even more concentrated at night than by day.

The major moved and sat beside Louise. She responded by edging close to him, the tiller between them, their hands sharing it and establishing comforting contact. It was cold out on the water, but she thought how warm his hand was, how warm a man he himself was, not a frightening and clammy half-man. The boat glided on without a sound, its course governed by tide and rudder. They held their breath as they bore left to converge on the mainstream. They were running parallel now with the Dutch canal, separated from them by a tongue of flat land on their right. The tongue bristled darkly with miniature bastions of German lookout posts. They felt eyes must be on them, despite their noiseless progress, and they waited for a hostile light to snap on and uncover them. They steered close to the bank on their left, keeping as far from the lookout posts as they could. The tongue of land remained dark and silent, dividing them from the Dutch stream, and no lights flashed.

But ahead the sweep of the beam was constant, covering the entry of all craft into the main canal, the border waters. In a few minutes the tide would carry them into the hazard of searching light.

'Louise Victoria.' The major's voice was a whisper.

'I know it's going to be dangerous,' she whispered back.

'Yes. So I want you to know something you must never forget.'

'Yes?'

'I love you, little Belgian nightingale.'

Her hand closed convulsively over his on the tiller. 'Then I am not afraid, *mon Commandant*, only very happy in a way you cannot imagine.'

The tongue of land ended, dipping into the water, and the twin canals, Dutch and Belgian, merged to become a wide, flowing flood.

'Louise—'

'We are together, *mon Commandant*, and no one will ever love you as much as I do.'

They were silent again then, but closer in courage and spirit than they had ever been, as they wondered how to run under the light. It ranged and swept, casting brilliance over dark waters. The major's firm hand kept their craft hugging the Belgian bank, and Louise heard slithering sounds as the boat scraped mud and grass. Apprehension took its hold on her. Only a few moments more, and then as the light ran back they must make their dash across. The major had one oar out on the starboard side as the light bathed the canal. It moved above them and swept on. Together they began to take the boat across. The light swept back and caught them in a searing, white-hot incandescence, or so it felt to Louise.

'*Achtung! Achtung!*'

The loud German voice smote their ears. It was followed by a shouted command to stop, a command that was like the bark of a watchdog of doom. The tide rushed at them, propelling them, and the light became a great, steady, revealing flame. The canal was so wide. They went on. They had to, they were in midstream.

The German voice was louder. It was joined

by others. In the middle of the fast-flowing tide of water, the earth of Holland seemed so far still. A *rat-a-tat* of fire cracked the night open. The major, using the oar to keep the boat steady on its angled course, while Louise gripped the tiller, felt his every nerve was under siege. The Germans were using a machine gun. He flung Louise down as bullets whistled and whined. Another beam blazed on, and a huge circle of intensified light covered the boat and held it. It swung crazily as bullets riddled it from bow to stern. The major rocked, steering desperately, as the tide, the boat and the bullets were all at calamitous odds with each other. Louise, thinking him hit as he lurched on the seat, leapt upwards into the great circle of light. Forty yards behind them the Germans were running a boat into the water. The machine-gunner carefully sighted.

Louise was beside the major again. Together they grabbed the tiller. The boat swung back on course, and Holland came nearer. The Dutch frontier guards were out, staring at the drama.

'*Get down!*' The major's voice rushed at Louise.

The machine gun cracked fire. Louise jerked. The major watched in stunned horror. Her eyes opened wide, the light swamped her in brilliance, and she sighed, slumped and fell forward. He saw the wetness of blood on her back, her rich blood, her life's blood.

Unbearable rage and grief seized him, and as he plunged in an effort to reach her, he too was swamped by light. A running fusillade of bullets smashed into his left arm, the arm that had kept him so long at the Edith Cavell *Clinique*. The kick of the bullets literally staggered him, and he knew a split second of numbness before violent pain savaged him. The light burned his eyes and his brain. He pitched forward, struck his head on the stowage compartment, and fell face down across the still form of Louise Victoria.

The boat whirled, rushed and careered for a hundred crazy yards, outlined by the inescapable searchlights, before thumping against the Dutch bank. The Dutch guards came running.

They got them both out. The major was unconscious, Louise hanging limply.

The heavy, drifting clouds separated, and the moon bathed them in its own light.

Chapter Twenty-one

On Monday morning 11th October, three days after the trial, the German Prosecutor, Stober, arrived at St Gilles prison in company with German officers. The thirty-five prisoners assembled in the hall listened as he read out the verdicts and sentences. He looked elegant and cheerful, and sounded very much as if he were reading out a list of awards and honours.

Five of the accused were condemned to death, including Edith Cavell and Philippe Baucq. Princess Marie de Croy was sentenced to ten years' hard labour. Eight of the accused were acquitted. The rest were also given sentences of hard labour, some for as much as fifteen years.

Philippe Baucq was in despair. Miss Cavell seemed quite unmoved. *Appeal*, cried her friends.

'No,' said Miss Cavell quietly, 'I am English. An appeal is useless. They want my life.'

She was right. General von Sauberzweig, the

newly appointed Governor of Brussels, issued the following order the same day.

Brussels, October 11, 1915

(1)
I consider that the interests of the State demand that the death sentence of Philippe Baucq and Edith Cavell be carried out immediately and hereby order this.

(2)
I adjourn the execution of the death sentences on the other prisoners until such time as a decision has been reached concerning the appeals for clemency now pending.

von Sauberzweig

Pastor le Seur, Lutheran chaplain of the prison, was faced with the ordeal of informing Miss Cavell that her execution would be at dawn the next day. He led her quietly into a small room after Stober had departed.

She, intuitively perhaps, said, 'How much time will they give me?'

He could not make the moment any better for her by being vague or dissimilating, so very gently he said, 'Only until tomorrow morning.'

For the first time the serenity of resignation wavered. Her face flushed and her mouth trembled. Her clear eyes clouded. He offered her his services as a churchman. She, however, not being a Lutheran, had to refuse.

She was quite composed again. Pastor le Seur, distressed in the face of her courageous acceptance of death, begged her to forget he was German and to let him do all he could for her. 'Can I not show you some kindness?' he asked.

Miss Cavell asked him if he could possibly let her mother in England know what had happened. Pastor le Seur gave her his promise, and kept it. Affected by her bearing, and by what he knew was a spiritual necessity to her – to receive the Sacrament from an Anglican priest – he broke the strictest of rules. He asked her if he might bring to her the Anglican chaplain in Brussels, the Reverend Stirling Gahan. Miss Cavell accepted the offer with intense gratitude.

Pastor le Seur also offered to meet her not at the place of execution, two miles outside Brussels, but to come to her cell and accompany her all the way.

For that too she was deeply grateful.

On her return to her cell she sat down to write her last letters. She had already written to her nurses. Now she wrote to Sister Wilkins. Amazingly, she was still more concerned with the affairs of the *Clinique* than with herself, and she gave Sister Wilkins details of one or two little things which needed to be straightened out in respect of the accounts. She ended briefly but affectionately, *'My love to you all. I am not afraid, but quite happy.'*

She also wrote to her mother in England, and to other people, but these letters never left the hands of the German authorities.

In her prayerbook, Miss Cavell noted down with characteristic candour the fateful dates of her destiny.

Arrested 5th Aug. 1915.
Imprisoned at St Gilles 7th Aug. 1915.
Court-martialled 7th October 1915.
Condemned to death in the Salles des
Députés on 8th Oct., with four others.
Died at 7 a.m. on October 12th, 1915.

At nine thirty in the evening, Pastor le Seur brought the Reverend Stirling Gahan to her cell. The Anglican chaplain, who knew her, found her neither distressed nor agitated. She received him with quiet pleasure and relief. And when they had spoken together, and she had assured him she was spiritually at peace, she said, 'Life has been so full that I have had no rest and no quiet. Now I have. And I have been kindly treated here. I expected my sentence and believe it was just.' She looked gently resolute as she added, 'I have seen death so often that it is not fearful or strange to me. This I would say, standing as I do in view of God and Eternity. I know that patriotism is not enough. One must love all people and hate none.'

She received the Sacrament. When the blessing had been said, he repeated the line, 'Hold Thou Thy cross before my closing eyes.'

With him she took up the next words: 'Shine through the gloom and point me to the skies.'

They spoke every line of the hymn together until they reached its finish: 'Swift to its close ebbs out life's little day.'

She was content and at peace then. Her last words to him as they said goodbye at her cell door were, 'We shall meet again.'

And she smiled.

Several of Miss Cavell's nurses, having received the news that she was to be executed in the morning, arrived during the evening at the American Legation. Sister Wilkins begged desperately for something to be done.

Brand Whitlock, the American Minister, ill in bed with influenza, was incredulous when the nurses' message was brought to him. No announcement of the pending execution had been received by his legation. He was certain, however, that no authority anywhere would condemn a woman one day and actually carry out the sentence first thing the next, unless the Germans intended to get it over with before telling the world. He called the Secretary of the Legation, Hugh Gibson, to his room. They agreed that in this instance they could not take a conventional stay of execution for granted.

Mrs Brand Whitlock was doing her best to comfort and reassure Miss Cavell's nurses, who were close to utter desperation. One of them was beside herself in her grief.

Brand Whitlock told Hugh Gibson to act. Gibson, together with the Marquis de Villalobar, the Spanish Minister, and Maître de Leval, lawyer to the American Legation, hurried off to see Baron von der Lancken, head of the German political department in Brussels. It was necessary to get him out of the theatre. A lengthy wrangle ensued, but eventually the baron was persuaded to call on the city's Military Governor, General von Sauberzweig. Only he could make the decision to commute the death sentence, or at least postpone it.

General von Sauberzweig, suffering from an almost fanatical hatred of the English, angrily refused to do either. The sentence would stand; the execution would proceed. When advised of this by Baron von der Lancken, Hugh Gibson and the Marquis de Villalobar refused to accept that it could possibly be final. They argued for hours with the baron, demanding that he appeal to the German Emperor. The baron insisted he was unable to.

It was early morning before Gibson and the

marquis returned to the American Legation. They had spent most of the night fighting for Miss Cavell. Greyly, they told the waiting nurses of their failure.

Not long after, the nurses walked slowly out of the legation.

They were weeping.

Perhaps, since she loved to look back and talk about the days in Norfolk when she was blissfully young and happy, it was those days Edith Cavell thought about before she closed her eyes for the last night of her life. Perhaps in her reflections on the sweetness of simply being young, she found her final moments of tranquillity.

Perhaps she remembered the days when duty had not yet taken its uncompromising hold on her, the days when life was full of untarnishable dreams. In those days she had been sentimental enough to write romantic verses in the copybooks of the children to whom she had been a young and understanding governess. There was one little poem she would have remembered:

Storms may gather, Oh love, my love,
But here shall thy shelter be,
And in my arms, my dear, my dear,
The sun shall come back to thee.

The winter of age, Oh love, my love,
For us no shade shall bring,
In those eyes divine, my dear, my dear,
For me 'twill always be spring.

And perhaps she thought of Major Scott and all the other soldiers she had known and cared for.

Before dawn had broken on Tuesday 12th October, Pastor le Seur was at the door of her cell. Miss Cavell came out, immaculate in look and dress and carriage. She was back in her uniform, which symbolized her love of nursing and her service to life and people. She had the serenity of a woman content to go to her Maker.

A friend in his compassion, Pastor le Seur escorted her down the long prison corridor. She did not make one faltering step. Silently and almost reverently, the Belgian Governor and the gaolers bowed to her as she passed.

Philippe Baucq was also brought out. Pastor le Seur and Miss Cavell rode in one motor car, Baucq and a Catholic priest in another.

Outside the prison were Sister Wilkins and the nurses. They had never been far from her in love and spirit. They had come to catch their last glimpse of her, and to bid her a silent, anguished farewell. It was 6 a.m. when the cars emerged from the prison and Edith Cavell's devoted staff caught their last sight of her. They saw her, in the first car, in her cape, her Matron's blue dress and her white cap. Slender, she sat straight-backed and incredibly composed. She appeared; she was glimpsed; she was gone.

Tears flooded the eyes of the nurses.

At the place of execution, a rifle range outside the city, a German company of two hundred and fifty men awaited the arrival of the condemned. Immediately the cars pulled up, Miss Cavell and Philippe Baucq obeyed the request to step down. They had time for a last glance and last smile at each other, Baucq with his head high, she in spiritual peace. The sentences were read to them in German and French. Pastor le Seur spoke the Grace of the Anglican Church to her. She touched his hand. He caught her final quiet words.

'. . . and I believe my soul is safe and am glad to die for my country.'

She was tied lightly to one pole, Baucq to another. She was still calm, still composed, but as a German soldier blindfolded her, he saw her clear grey eyes fill with tears. They seemed like the tears of a woman to whom life had given so much and to whom death was a bitter-sweet sadness.

Edith Cavell and her loyal associate, Philippe Baucq, died instantly under the dawn volley of shots.

Chapter Twenty-two

Louise opened her eyes. A face, grave, enquiring and full of professional interest, seemed to be floating above her. A neat, iron-grey beard pointed the chin. The beard grew hazy and the face wavered. A little smile flickered on her pale mouth.

She slipped away again.

The Dutch doctors and nurses were still fighting for her. Four bullets had been taken out of her ribs and back. She had been unconscious for two weeks. The major, haggard and racked by the news of Edith Cavell's execution, had been allowed to leave his bed two days before. Out of the worst of his physical pain, he had seen Louise four times in those two days, and to his tormented eyes she was plainly slipping farther and farther away.

Today, for the first time, she had opened her own eyes.

She had closed them again, but there was hope now. She had been drained of strength and blood. But if she had opened her eyes once, that was something to take hold of. And the flicker of a smile probably meant she had been dreaming.

Dreaming could be interpreted as a very hopeful sign.

A few days later she was still comatose for the most part, but she had opened her eyes several times. They let Major Scott see her again. She seemed very peaceful, her breathing quite even.

'What are her real chances?' asked the major. 'I'd like to know.'

'Her chances?' The Dutch doctor expressed surprise, even reproach. 'It isn't a question of her chances now, simply how long her recovery will take.'

'You're absolutely sure?' The major was living on a tightrope; he had almost lost faith. What more could life at its cruellest demand of this girl?

'I am confident,' said the doctor. 'Look at you. You are recovering well. And she, I am positive, is as strong in her spirit as you are. She has contributed more than we have to her recovery.'

'Recovery?' The major, gazing down at the pale, sleeping face of his brave and beautiful Louise, was bitter and caustic. 'You can say that when in over two weeks all she's done is open her eyes a few times?'

'You are suffering for her,' said the doctor.

'We are watching her. My friend, do you hear her? Do you hear the way she breathes? Here is a young lady who does not wish to die and has fought every moment of crisis.' The doctor's French was impressive and explicit. 'Have you studied the effects of the subconscious on an inanimate mind? In my opinion, Comtesse de Bouchet's mind is linked only at the moment with her subconscious determination to live. Her instinct to stay alive is because life means so much to her, and her natural health and strength are an additional help. In cases like hers, other people might not last twenty-four hours or even survive the operation.'

'Doctor, are you in the realms of medical wishful thinking?'

The doctor smiled. 'I am in the realms of great hope, my friend. Do you realize there were four bullets in her back, running at an angle from her left shoulder to her lower right rib, that one entered so close to her heart as to inflict what you might call a frictional bruise, and another lodged close to her spine? Do you realize that before she reached us she had lost half her blood? Now look at her, healthily asleep.'

'Healthily?'

'I think so. Consider the damage done by the bullets, the excessive shock suffered by the system, the extensive nature of the operation, and yet here, after two weeks and a few days, she is not only still alive but drawing the kind of breath that to me means she has fought her fight and won.'

But the major, sceptical in his bitterness, thought how pale she looked, how bloodless. Even her bright hair had lost its lustre.

'You can say that?' he said. 'You can say she has won?'

'We shall see, we shall see,' said the doctor. 'But you should not lack faith, Major Scott.'

What the major was lacking was belief in the impartiality of Providence. Providence, it seemed to him, laid far harsher hands on the good than the undeserving.

'No one has earned a greater right to life and happiness than she has,' he said.

'I know that, my friend,' said the doctor. 'I hope, in the end, you will both have won.'

Two days later, Louise was awake and dreamily aware of herself, though not how she came to be here, or who she was. She spoke for the first time, weakly and huskily. A French-speaking nurse bent over her, warmly glad that so sweet a girl was going to get better.

'My dear?'

'What has happened to me?'

'Nothing too terrible. You are better now.'

'Who am I?'

The nurse felt a little sad worry about that, and said, 'Just rest while I fetch the doctor.'

She went quickly to find the doctor and report that the patient had finally come to. Louise lay in vague, dreamy curiosity about herself. Something *had* happened. She did not seem to have any arms or legs.

She was asleep again when the nurse returned with a highly interested doctor.

The major was beside her bed later. He looked down at her. Magically, there was the tiniest hint of colour in her cheeks. The nurse put a finger to her lips. He sat down on the bedside chair. Louise lay in a little room of her own. There were vases of flowers, sent by Dutch well-wishers and Belgian exiles. Her right hand lay on the blanket. He gently took it. Her fingers were warm. She opened her eyes. She smiled a faraway smile, then slipped away once more. But her fingers stirred in his.

She awoke in the night. She felt thirsty, she even felt hungry, but she did not call anyone. She lay there in warmth, her eyes open. She picked out the tiny glow of the night lamp. Her mind searched for a thought she had had sometime. How silly, of course she had arms and legs. She could feel them. They were alive. She was alive.

She remembered then.

'Nurse! Nurse?'

The night nurse arrived in a warm, comforting

379

rush to lean over her. Everyone in Holland knew the story of the young Comtesse de Bouchet, how she had helped Allied soldiers, defied the Germans and been shot while escaping them. The Dutch had heard too of the execution of Edith Cavell, and waves of emotion were sweeping the country.

'What is it?' whispered the nurse.

Louise was trying to sit up, her mouth working. '*Mon Commandant, mon Commandant!*' she cried.

The nurse smiled. So, here was a blessed gift from God, the return of her memory.

'Hush,' she murmured, 'you will make yourself ill.'

From out of the weeks of her subconscious fight, from out of the reviving memories of life and endeavour, from the character given to her by her parents, came the response that was Louise Victoria's alone: 'I am already ill.'

It was said quite clearly, and with such a perceptible little touch of imperiousness that the nurse hugged it to herself as a recountable gem.

'I know, Comtesse, but—'

Louise, returning to agitation, cried, 'Where is he?'

'Comtesse, it's the middle of the night.'

'Where is he? What has happened to him? Oh, please tell me.'

'Oh, is that what you are worried about?'

smiled the nurse. 'He's here, in a men's ward. This is Roermond Hospital.'

'He's hurt? Oh, he's not badly hurt, is he?' Louise's voice was a struggle against weakness, against a dread made worse by weakness. 'Please?'

The nurse hesitated, then said softly, 'No, not at all. He's been to see you many times.'

Louise lay back. She sighed. 'Thank you,' she whispered.

'He'll come to see you in the morning, I'm sure.'

'Yes.' It was the faintest murmur from Louise. 'Yes. We are always together. Even in hospitals.'

Yes, the major was informed, she was awake and very much better. She wished to see him. He could visit at ten thirty this morning.

The major arrived at the door of the room precisely two minutes early. He smiled at the day nurse as she let him in. He was experiencing a revival of faith.

'For five minutes only, please,' whispered the nurse.

'Thank you,' said the major. Her glance begged him not to excite the patient. He nodded and she left them to each other. He came to the bedside, his dressing gown loose over his shoulders, his arms inside it. A nurse had dressed Louise's hair and lightly tinted her cheeks and lips with rouge. Her eyes were shining as she looked up at him. He was not sure, in his surge of emotion, exactly what to say to her. Then he smiled and said, 'Dear Louise.' He bent and kissed her. For all her weakness, she did not want a light kiss, a peck, and her lips clung to his. His right hand emerged from the loose dressing gown and pressed hers.

'Oh, I'm so glad, so glad,' she breathed.

'Louise, although neither of us came off very well—'

'But we did, we are both alive and still together,' she said, her smile a caress. 'Oh, it was a brave run we made, and see, we are free now to fight the Boche in other ways. You were shot too?'

'Yes. But it's nothing. I'm afraid, however, that we've missed the *Christina*.'

That signified neither calamity nor disaster to Louise. She was dreamy as she murmured, '*Mon Commandant?*'

'Well, sweet girl?' he said. She had only to ask and he would do whatever she wished. She was yet to know he was free of his most critical commitment.

'As much as we can,' she said, 'we must always be together. Don't you think so?'

He smiled. She was alive. He felt there could have been no greater compensation.

'Are you saying, Louise Victoria, that if I asked you to marry me, you'd say yes?'

'I am saying,' said Louise, her hair bright and her eyes warm, 'that I would never let you marry anyone else.'

He sat down on the chair and took her hand. 'Then I formally propose,' he said.

'Yes?' said Louise, and waited.

'Oh, I see,' said the major. He coughed. 'Louise Victoria, will you do me the honour of becoming my wife instead of my niece or cousin?'

Louise smiled. 'Oh, yes,' she said, 'yes a hundred times.'

He kissed her again and said, 'Louise, you're the dearest girl.'

'Thank you, *mon Commandant*, but I'm not a girl, I am well on my way to being quite mature, and have been since I told you there was something else I'd much rather be than even a nurse.' Life danced in her eyes as she smiled and added, 'I think, *mon Commandant*, considering how close we were in that ditch, you should have proposed to me then.'

'It would have been the gentlemanly thing to do, I suppose,' he said.

'Oh, yes.' She was wholly taken up with her dreams of the future, but she would ask about Edith Cavell, about Madame, when she was more alert, he thought. 'We shall have a long time together before you have to go back to the war?'

'Yes, a very long time,' he assured her. He

did not open up the dressing gown to show her his left forearm had been amputated. He did not want to distress her today, about his arm or about Edith Cavell, when she had come back to life more precious than ever. He knew, when she was quite better, when she was fully recovered, that his handicap would not worry Louise Victoria at all. His more active army career was finished. He supposed he and she might still do something together to help the Allies, for she was so set on that. The army might offer him an administrative post, or work on war recruitment. He would accept anything that was offered. Louise would be with him.

'*She is your responsibility, Ned, you must realize that.*' Louise Victoria was more than his responsibility. She was his young, unconquerable love and his bright future. They would enter that future together, with their memories of the incomparable Madame and her haunting serenity.

He felt they would have her blessing.